THE HOUSE AT 3 O'CLOCK

Broadsheet replica printed for selling of slaves in years following th
Civil War

Vigilante cartoon distributed after Civil War for terrorism tactics
Louisiana and Tennessee, (courtesy, *Walter Sloane Histor-
Archives and Regional Society*, New Orleans.).

THE HOUSE
AT 3 O'CLOCK

Volume One
in the series

SLAVES WITHOUT MASTERS

by

RUPERT GILCHRIST

SOUVENIR PRESS

Photoset and Printed in Great Britain by
Photobooks (Bristol) Limited,
Barton Manor, St Philips, Bristol

CONTENTS

AUTHOR'S NOTE

General Robert E. Lee's surrender to General Ulysses S. Grant at Appomattox Court House in 1865 concluded the American Civil War, emancipated four million negroes from slavery, and devastated the South. The economy was left in shambles. Cities and the countryside smoldered from battle. Southern pride had been drastically shaken. Diehard Confederates formed regional vigilante groups called the 'Knights of the Camellia', 'Ku Klux Klan', 'Liberty Lodge', and set about to squelch constitutional rights being extended to Negroes. One of the most atrocious – and closely kept – secrets was the movement during the Reconstruction years to resume the trafficking of Black slaves. Support for this criminal plot was given by recently freed slaves themselves, desperate behavior influenced by lack of work, food, shelter: *Freedom meant no more to many Black people than being slaves without masters.*

R.G.

PART ONE

THE DREAM

Chapter One

A WHITE CAMELLIA

Gemma Rickers paused on a dirt knoll to shade her eyes
against the midday sun and appraise the land spreading
in front of her, neglected fields, dark woodlands, vine-
tangled swamps – a dream in the Louisiana wilderness for
which she had abandoned a small, tidy home on Dumbarton
Avenue in Philadelphia, Pennsylvania.

The dream to move to Louisiana belonged to Gemma's
husband, Warren Rickers, a tall man with skin the color of a
coffee bean, who stood proudly alongside her on the dusty
country road.

'Beautiful, ain't it, honey?' Warren fanned his face with a
wide-brimmed straw hat.

Gemma did not reply. She pushed a twist of hair back into
the red calico bandana knotted around her head. She dabbed
at her cocoa brown cheek. She felt the grit of the road
between the tips of her forefinger and thumb.

Warren resettled the hat back on his wiry black hair and
lifted the heavy suitcases he had been carrying for the last
five miles from Palmetto Landing.

'We won't see nothing good from here. Let's keep going.
Let's try reaching the Dasher place by nightfall. The Dashers
are supposed to direct us to our land.'

Gemma and Warren Rickers, loaded with leather suitcases and canvas backpacks and knotted bundles and bulging
carpetbags, resumed walking in the midday sun; Gemma
tried not to lag, not to stop too often and switch heavy
suitcases from hand to hand, not to let the cord of the canvas
backpack cut into her shoulder, not to complain about
leaving civilization for a tucked away corner of . . . 'Why do I
feel like some damned Black fool marching straight into
hell?'

Warren, descended from the sinewy plainsmen of far-away, long ago Africa, looked with growing interest at the Louisiana landscape as he continued plodding through the yellow dust in ankle-high leather boots.

He nodded at the charred skeleton of a burned house.

'I wonder if Yankee soldiers put a torch to that old place in the war.'

Gemma remained silent, kept trudging. Her mind had been wandering five states to the north of Louisiana. She had been thinking about the white clapboard house she had left on Dumbarton Avenue in Philadelphia, about the coolness of her kitchen where flies buzzed behind the parchment windowshades on hot afternoons, about Mr Signoricci's blue and white ice wagon and the old dappled mare greeted by the children on the street with as much excitement as a three ring circus would get, about the White ladies in the Methodist Church Auxiliary Club inviting her to bake peach pies for the Union Soldiers Uniform Raffle.

She asked, 'You sure people down here know the Civil War's over, Mister Fast Walker?'

Warren laughed, slowed his pace, answered, 'You got nothing to worry about, Miss Honey Wife. This may be backhill country but folks arond here are more pleased than city folks to have the war over and ended.'

'War leaves a country poor,' Gemma grumbled as she still lagged behind Warren, 'and this looks like it could be mighty poor country.'

'Longchamp Parish never was rich. Not like parishes down around New Orleans. Not even when my Daddy lived here.'

Warren paused in the middle of the country road, gulping fresh air, expanding his chest, again waiting for Gemma to catch up with him.

'Parish,' he explained, 'that's what folks down here in Louisiana call their counties. Parishes. Goes back to old Napoleon times. When the Frenchies ruled here. Before President Tommy Jefferson made that Louisiana Purchase from the Frenchies to buy this land for the U.S. of A. Fact is,

12

this neck of the woods got its parish charter around the time the Chatgrove family freed my Daddy. Daddy told me how old Mrs Chatgrove complained –'

Warren looked at his young wife; he was surprised to see her sitting on a suitcase in the middle of the road, pressing her eyes shut as if she had suddenly become sick.

*   *   *

'Tender gal, you all right?'

Gemma nodded but did not open her eyes.

'You wrinkling your face. You got . . . pain?'

Gemma shook her head. 'Something you said.'

'What'd I say?'

'Freed, Warren. You talked about the Chatgrove family freeing your Daddy. Freeing. Liberating. Made me think about us – you and me – moving bag and baggage down here some place we wouldn't dared stepped foot in three, four years ago. Not before, not during the war.'

'But war's changed things, Gemma, gal. President Lincoln and Civil War changed a whole lot of things in the South. Slavery's over. The Confederacy's back in the Union. We Black folks are all free.'

'You and me, Warren, we were born free. We grew up free. Nothing freed us. No President Lincoln. No war. No banners and trumpets and big speeches. But the fact still holds – we wouldn't have dreamt of moving here three, four years ago.'

'How many times I got to tell you –'

'Spare me lectures, Warren. Please. I'm spent. My feet hurt. My head aches. I feel so dirty somebody's got to shake me out on the back porch like a dust mop to get me halfway clean. You asked me why I was squinching my eyes shut. I told you. So let's get walking again.'

Gemma moved to stand.

Warren stopped her; he stood in front of the suitcase and ordered in a stern voice, 'Look at me, Gemma Mae Rickers.'

'I'm looking,' she wearily answered.

'Tell me once and for all, you worried about us coming here?'

13

'Course I'm worried.' She frowned at him. 'I said all along I'm worried. What you planning now? To turn around and go home? Some plan!'

Warren argued, 'Lots of Blacks living up North still say their home's down here in the South.'

Gemma and Warren were both in their mid-twenties; Gemma was keener in mind, more cunning than her tall, broad-shouldered husband; she occasionally felt protective of him, his ideas, his dreams. She knew how much he had planned on this move to Louisiana; she knew he had hated working in Philadelphia, loathed being the only Black man clerking in Dewitt's Hardware Emporium, having White people treat him as if he were some oddity, although politely and respectfully, but still a peculiarity, as if a colored face were a lapse in Mother Nature's plan. Warren had been looking upon this move to Louisiana as a chance to go unnoticed, to live like human beings, a man, a woman, a husband, a wife, a family which could build, sew, harvest, multiply and prosper, do everything the Bible urged the Lord's children to do.

Gemma knew all these things but, nonetheless, she did not want to sit on a suitcase in the middle of a country road in the scorching heat and argue about dreams, politics, the Emancipation Proclamation.

She gathered her long cotton skirt and moved to stand. 'We can just hope for the best, Mister.'

Warren continued to block her way. 'No. I want to settle this once and for all. Now understand this. No Black man could inherit property from no White folks if he didn't have same rights as White folks.'

'Newspapers, Warren', Gemma said, trying to keep her voice calm. 'Northern newspapers say we got equal rights. But what White folks down here in the South choose to do and say and give us Black people is a completely different kettle of fish.'

Warren patted the chest pocket of his blue serge suit jacket. 'I'm not talking about newspapers! I'm talking about legal proof! Legal courtroom. Legal Philadelphia lawyer. Legal paper proof I got right here in my pocket. Documented and stamped papers saying, *Mrs Emmaline Chatgrove wills her land, Candlewick Plantation in Longchamp Parish, Louisiana, to Warren Otis Rickers, first son and only heir of Mr Longrow Rickers, in event all Chatgrove issue, son or daughter, dies or is killed by natural or unnatural causes.* That's proof, Gemma. That's proof to stand up in any court of law, North or South. And I got that legal, bonafide paper right here in the pocket of my fifteen dollar Fairweather suit!'

Gemma rose wearily from the suitcase. She shook out her long skirt.

She said, 'Then let's get going because we don't want to keep no welcoming committee waiting for us when we claim this land you inherited, do we, nigger?'

Warren gaped at his small but statuesque wife. 'What you call me, gal? What name you just call me?'

Gemma and Warren Rickers regularly called one another nicknames – terms of endearment, occasionally coy names, funny names, silly names, playful names frequently understood only by each other – but they never used the slang words, *nigger, coon,* any derogatory name for a Black person.

Warren angrily insisted, 'What name now you call me?'

'Nigger! I called you nigger! And don't get so het up about it. This probably won't be the last time you're going to be called nigger . . . coon boy . . . jigaboo . . . jungle bunny . . . because, Mister Chocolate Drop, you've come back – *home!*'

*　　　*　　　*

Gemma and Warren Rickers trudged seven more miles on the dusty country road north-west from Palmetto Landing until Warren suspected they could not reach the next small town – Bossburg, Louisiana – before nightfall. He found a secluded spot located away from the parish road, a level site tucked between two gulleys with a surrounding protection of poplar and pine trees.

Warren immediately began pegging a canvas into the ground to prevent dirt, pine needles or chunks of dried moss from becoming mixed with the few belongings they chose to unpack from their baggage.

Gemma heard a creek tinkling nearby in the woods; she shed her clothes, welcoming the cool air on her naked body, shivering with delight as she stuck one toe, a foot, then both feet into the creek rushing over the bed of brown, grey, and white speckled rocks.

The creek water soothed Gemma's nerves as it relaxed her body; she stepped refreshed onto the bank and hummed a song to herself as she patted her short hair dry; she wrapped a fringed shawl around her hips and, knotting the shawl over her breasts, she tip-toed over prickly branches and pine cones to the camp which Warren had made. She happily began slicing thick pieces of smoked ham and chunks of brown bread for their supper.

Warren dropped his own dusty clothes into a heap and stepped carefully across the carpeting of pine needles for a dip in the creek; he emerged tingling from the water and, after drying himself with a small towel, he decided to sneak back through the mossy trees and surprise Gemma.

Gemma, busying herself with the preparations of their light supper, saw Warren from the corner of her eye creeping through the forest but did not acknowledge him.

Warren, raising his arms like a pantomime ghoul, lifted one bare leg, then the other, as he moved playfully, in full nakedness, toward Gemma.

Gemma also felt playful; she continued to ignore Warren and instead sang a Gospel song:

Carriage of gold coming to get me,
Carriage of gold coming to get mine;
Carriage of gold coming to get all God's children,
We're going to Heaven and shine . . .

Pausing, Gemma waved a large butcher's knife in the air and said, as if speaking to herself, 'I sure hope there's no goblins hiding in this big forest. No, sirree. I sure hopes there's no goblins or big, greasy, old bull snakes around here. But if I see a big, greasy, old bull snake I'm going to grab him and I'm going to hack him right in . . . two!'

16

Gemma spun around on her haunches; she grabbed Warren's penis hanging at eye level; she used one hand to grip its brown foreskin and, holding the penis as if it were a long piece of sausage, she raised her butcher's knife higher in the air to cut it in two.

Warren, shrieking, lowered both hands to his crotch.

Gemma's laughter filled the forest as she released him from her grasp.

Warren reached for a flannel sheet; he grumbled, 'Miss Gospel Singer, you're one mean gal.'

Gemma, chuckling, returned to her work. 'You worried about your pecker, Mister Big One, you better move on up that dusty road.'

'Woman, what's this mountain air doing to you?'

'You keep parading that big thing of yours around here, Mister Goblin Man, and you're going to find out.'

Still chuckling, Gemma shook her head and said, 'Yum, yum, yum. I can hardly wait for dessert time. Get me some of that Louisiana pudding roll.'

Yes, the evening, the creek, the promise of supper outside in a balmy forest was fine, relaxing, a moment definitely earned.

*   *   *

Warren, wrapped in the flannel sheet, worked alongside Gemma on the canvas, helping make the final preparations for supper; they agreed not to light a bonfire to boil coffee and risk having the smoke attract the attention of passersby on the parish road. Stars slowly began to appear in the sky, making a twinkling chandelier for Gemma and Warren as they ate the small meal and quenched their thirst with a jar of creek water.

A large moon soon hung in the sky; Gemma and Warren snuggled closer together on the canvas, satisfied from their meal, comfortable in each other's arms, romantic on their first night alone in the Louisiana wilderness.

Warren lowered his eyes from the sky and kissed Gemma on her temple; he ran his forefinger through the long yellow

17

fringe dangling from the silk shawl knotted over her breasts and complimented, 'This here shawl looks a heck of a lot better on you than it did on that player piano.'

'Don't mention my piano,' she sniffed. 'I'm still upset about having to sell it to Dorothy Bliss.'

'Dorothy Bliss paid us a good price for that player piano, sugar gal. A dang good price. And you never know when that money's going to come in –'

Gemma interrupted. 'Stop talking about Dorothy Bliss and my piano. Just stop. Some things money can't replace.'

Warren reached under the shawl and squeezed Gemma's breasts; he leaned forward and pressed his lips against her ear; his penis crept with excitement down his inner thigh into an erection.

He whispered as his fingers squeezed, 'I didn't mean to upset you, lady lovely. I was just complimenting you, saying how good you look in your new gown.'

Warren began nibbling Gemma's ear; he tongued his way down her neck; Gemma turned, twisted, stretched her neck like a lap cat being petted, luxuriating under attention, gentle fondlings, appreciative strokes.

He said, 'I'm just braving up to discovering what this dangerous mountain air does to you.'

'Hmmm.'

Gemma lay back in Warren's arms; she locked her hands around his neck as he shed the flannel sheet from his own body.

Warren gently, lovingly, lowered Gemma down onto the canvas, plunging his tongue into her mouth; he soon lay upon her nakedness. Gemma's legs wrapped around Warren's darker brown thighs, the pink soles of her feet resting on the back of his calves. Warren's erect penis glistened like a shaft of black marble connecting their bodies as it began to slide into, pull out, slide deeper into the expanding wetness between Gemma's thighs.

'Tonight, Warren,' Gemma whispered as she felt the plunges deepening inside her womanhood. 'Please, let's make one tonight . . .'

'Tonight, honey?'

18

'Tonight, Warren. Please, tonight.'

Gemma and Warren had both shared a dream since their wedding night, a wish to conceive a child in their love-making, but, so far, they only pursued their dream as a fantasy, doing no more than speaking about their hopes as they made love, adding to their excitement, their devotion to one another.

Warren whispered, 'Sure, we make one tonight . . . we'll make our own baby right here tonight, dumpling . . .'

'Make your baby in me, Mister Husband Man . . . Make your beautiful child in me tonight . . . Put your seed in me . . . I want your seed, your baby in me . . .'

Warren quickened his drives; he enjoyed Gemma's contracting, expanding, accommodating vagina; he basked in her plea, her desire for his working, pounding, driving penis to explode, to plant an infant in her womb; he listened to her begging; he felt a virile strength increasing in him.

'Plant your seed,' Gemma repeated as she increased the movements of her hips, heatened the clutch of her vagina onto his penis.

Warren drove harder; he withdrew his penis to its crown; he enjoyed the sensation of Gemma's pressing lips; he dipped back into her warmth, sinking the crown of his penis in and out, in and out; he gently tweaked her nipples which sat like berries on her breasts; he listened to her groans, gasps, pleas, as he continued teasing the outer limits of her womanhood with prodding and poking and probing; he dipped deeper into her, smiling as he heard her gasp, feeling her wetness surrounding his masculine hardness.

Gemma thrashed beneath his pumping body; she thrust her groin upwards, working for his deeper drives, pulls, plunges, the fullest sensation of his penis, she chewed his chin as he deepened the dips of his penis into her; she surrendered her body to him, reaching new fulfillment, until . . .

Warren suddenly, without warning, removed his penis from Gemma's grip and splashed an arc of white seed across the wiry mound of her pubic hair, over the flatness of her stomach neatly tucked with a small navel, up the curve of one

19

breast still sensitive from his persistent manipulations, all the way up to the tip of her thin brown shoulder.

Gemma and Warren clung to each other; their dark bodies heaved with deep breaths.

The stars twinkled brightly in the sky; Gemma's and Warren's gasping finally lessened; but, still, they did not move.

Gemma, clinging tightly onto Warren's naked body, wondered how long they would have to indulge in fantasies, dreams, not only about begetting a child but also wishful thoughts concerning their entire life. How long would they have to continue making believe they were ordinary, normal people? Were they fools to think they could really make a home here in Louisiana? Or in any of the Southern states which little more than five years ago – in 1861 – had seceded from the Union on account of the South's demand to own Negro slaves?

*   *   *

The night riders, garbed in hooded white robes which glowed in the moonlight, reined their horses in a circle around the man. The man wore no white hood nor robe, a condemned man who sat bareback on a roan in front of the oak tree down in the gulley.

The first hooded rider emerged from the circle and threw the noose of a rope around the condemned man's neck; the hooded rider tossed the other end of the rope around the sturdy branch of the oak.

The condemned man began to whine, beg, plead for the group of hooded horsemen to have pity on him, to spare his life.

'I didn't mean no harm. I wasn't hiding in no camptown. Honest. Believe me.'

The men sat motionless on their horses, the peaks of their white hoods static in the moonlight.

'Please don't kill me,' the man cried. 'Don't hang me like some criminal. I ain't done nothing. I got a wife. Kids. Old folks to support. I ain't even from around these parts.'

His pleas went unheeded.

'I ain't broke no law. Honest. I was just passing by that camptown. Looking for food.'

Gemma and Warren could hear the condemned man's pathetic voice but they did not understand what his words meant; they lay on their stomachs on the knoll above the gulley where they had been cradling one another after lovemaking when the hooded riders had unexpectedly galloped out of the night and into the gulley below them.

Gemma, pressed tightly against Warren's naked body, whispered, 'Who are they?'

'Shhh . . .'

Another hooded horseman emerged from the circle; he danced his horse forward and stuck a small white object into the condemned man's shirt pocket.

'What'd he do there?' whispered Gemma.

Warren squeezed Gemma and shook his head.

The horseman danced his animal back into the circle; the next hooded rider emerged from the group; he raised a leather riding crop above his shoulder and slapped the condemned man's horse on the rump.

The horse whinnied, bolted forward: the condemned man slipped over the back of the horse.

The hooded riders sat in a motionless circle around the tree watching the man bounce up and down on the end of the rope, flailing his arms in death jerks, kicking his legs like a wooden puppet, dripping a puddle of urine from his trousers.

The hooded men waited until they were satisfied that the rope had choked the condemned man to death and then they galloped away into the forest, leaving him dangling from the tree, the death rope creaking in the night.

*　　　　*　　　　*

Gemma and Warren remained hidden in the darkness of the knoll long after the hooded men had ridden out from the gulley; they at last stood from their secret position, hurriedly dressed themselves, looking around them, listening for the

21

riders before they descended the clay incline to the gulley.

'You thinking the same thing I'm thinking, woman?'

'I'm thinking a whole lot of things.'

'About cutting him down and burying him?'

'That's one thought I'm having . . .'

Gemma listened to the night but heard no galloping, no distant horse hooves pounding the earth.

She looked overhead at the twinkling stars which only a short time ago had seemed so magical, romantic, even welcoming to her.

She asked, 'Think they'll come back?'

'Been some time now since they rode out of here.'

'You don't think they'd sneak back, do you? Sneak back here on foot? Sneak back to see if relatives or friends might try to cut him down?'

Warren looked again at the man hanging from the tree; the man's face was contorted into a dark, gruesome death mask but Warren could plainly see that the man was White, someone dressed like a poor dirt farmer or unprosperous small town merchant.

'We can't leave no man go unburied,' Warren said. 'Even if he is White.'

'Color's got nothing to do with burying,' Gemma agreed.

'We got to bury him, stranger or not, White or Black.'

Warren had removed the head of a shovel from the handle before leaving Philadelphia and had included it with the few tools he had chosen to bring to the new home in Louisiana; the sound of the shovel head cut into the night's stillness as Gemma searched through their belongings for the King James Bible she had packed; Warren buried the body; Gemma read over the grave from Corinthians. They both stood side by side in the bright moonlight at the foot of the heaped dirt now covered with pine boughs.

Gemma held the dog-eared Bible. 'I wonder who he was. What he did to those men. Why they wore those white peaked hoods and long robes.'

Warren lifted the flower – a wilting white camellia – he had removed from the dead man's shirt pocket.

He sniffed at the camellia. 'Why did they bother sticking

this flower in his pocket before killing him? What's this flower supposed to mean?'

'Maybe a sign,' Gemma said. 'Some mark or signature for them.'

Warren tossed the camellia onto the grave. 'Pretty flower. But I sure don't want to see no more of them.'

'They grow on trees down here in the South, Warren. Trees full of them. Great big camellia trees.'

'I still don't fancy seeing none. Not after tonight.'

Gemma and Warren slowly climbed the slope from the grave.

Chapter Two

THE PEOPLE OF LONGCHAMP PARISH

A powerful new sun beyond a faraway horizon bleached the
the early morning sky from indigo to periwinkle to
robin's egg blue, but it did not begin throwing spears of
morning light through the forest until Gemma and Warren
had been walking for two hours. They had packed their
belongings after burying the hanged man and evacuated the
mossy knoll with its nearby creek; they tried to find another
comfortable spot for sleeping but the lynching had unnerved
them; they listened for horse hooves in the darkness; they
discussed in whispers what a 'camptown' might be and the
reasons why hooded horsemen would hang somebody; they
decided that the hooded riders must have been a vigilante
group of White men who were executing a criminal from
their community; Warren assured Gemma that the Civil
War had probably left many Southern towns and rural
communities without organized justice, that many citizens
probably had to take justice into their own hands during
these times.

Warren and Gemma tried to convince themselves of these
facts to calm their nerves, to keep from questioning their
decision to move South, to keep themselves from thinking
that vigilante action could also become racial and aimed
against the more than four million recently liberated Negro
slaves.

Gemma and Warren kept pressing deeper and deeper into
Longchamp Parish, determined to find the land they had
inherited from a White family, but keeping to the trees as
they moved, skirting the thick bushes lining the parish road,
only emerging from the protection of dark shadows a short
time after daybreak when they saw a curve-shouldered
White farmer straddling a scrawny mule on the road. They
learned from the farmer that they were only over the hill

from the Dasher place, the farm where they hoped to find directions to their land.

*   *   *

Warren spotted a thin ribbon of smoke curling into the morning sky. 'That must be the Dasher place there.'

Gemma, loaded with suitcases, followed Warren from the parish road and trekked wearily down a dirt track running across a weed field toward a squat log cabin sitting in a garbage-strewn yard.

'Hello!' Warren shouted at the cabin, then lowered his hands from his mouth and waited for an answer.

A yellow bitch dog raised her head from the front porch; the dog gruffed weakly at Warren, chewed at ticks burrowed between the rows of pink nipples lining her sagging belly, then lowered her head back down to her mangy front paws.

Warren cupped his hands around his mouth again and called, 'Anybody home?'

The yellow dog did not budge at the second call.

Gemma looked at the smoke rising from the fieldstone chimney. 'They wouldn't still be sleeping. The fire wouldn't be lit.'

Warren tried a third time. 'Anybody here?'

A voice asked behind him, 'Trying to wake up the dead, stranger?'

Gemma and Warren turned at the sound of the voice; they saw two Black women standing by the corner of a rickety shed.

Warren doffed his straw hat and cheerfully greeted, 'Good morning, ladies. We're looking for the Dasher place. This it?'

The first Negress, an old shrivelled woman with a mop of snow white hair, removed a clay pipe from her toothless mouth.

'The *what* place?'

'The Dasher place,' Warren said in a louder voice and then forced himself to smile. 'They around here this morning? Mr and Mrs Dasher?'

25

'Shout loud enough, stranger, and you might see them both climb right out of their graves.'

'They're . . . dead?'

'Dead and buried over two years ago. Gnat fever got them both. The few field slaves they had run off before Freedom came. Damned fools, those field slaves. Should have stuck around like us house helpers.'

The old white-haired crone sucked in her clay pipe and studied the baggage heaped between Warren's and Gemma's dusty feet. She said to the taller, younger Negress lingering behind her, 'First nigger carpetbaggers we've seen, ain't it?'

Gemma and Warren were familiar with the term 'carpetbagger' which people were applying to Northerners moving South, Yankees said to be able to pack all their worldly possessions into one carpetbag, adventurers and opportunists eager to profit from the rebuilding of the South.

'We're no carpetbaggers,' Warren quickly protested. 'We're landowners. Fact is, we understood we could find directions to our land from the Dasher folks. I'm sorry to hear about their passing away. The Lord rest their souls. But maybe you ladies can help us on our way. We're looking for the place once owned by the Chatgrove family.'

'Chatgrove?' The old woman's small shoe button eyes studied Gemma and Warren.

'Yes, Mam,' Warren answered, 'the place that once used to be called Candlewick Plantation. My Daddy worked there way back for the Chatgrove family. His name was Longrow Rickers. The Chatgroves freed my Daddy way before the Civil War. He and Ma moved North. That's where I was born and raised – Pennsylvania.'

The crone turned to the tall young woman still lingering behind her.

She said, 'Niggers living at three o'clock now.'

Warren was tired from little sleep last night; he also was becoming both perturbed and confused by the old woman's rude ways.

'Honey,' he said to Gemma. 'Maybe you better try talking to these two gals.'

26

'Itching to do just that.' Gemma stepped forward, eager to try to glean some information from the two women.

*   *   *

'We're Black, Mam. Negro same as you and your young friend. But we ain't 'niggers' like you called us. Where we come from, Mam, 'nigger' means rude and ornery folks, people who most often don't own a bar of soap, can't say 'please' and 'thank-you' and are never civil to strangers.'

Gemma was not a large person but she readjusted her weight on the other foot with the authority of a Titan and continued. 'We're people, Mam. That's what we are. People. Hard-working, clean-living, ordinary people. We also got names. This man here is my husband. Warren Rickers. I'm called Gemma. Gemma Mae Rickers.'

The old crone chewed on her pipe, finally saying, 'Gemma Mae, you be a feisty wench, ain't you, gal?'

'I can get feisty as the next person, yes, Mam, I can. But I don't like showing feisty ways less I have to. Now, I told you our names. Why don't you tell us yours?'

'Broody Hen.' The old crone put the pipe back between her gums and chewed on the stem.

'Broody . . . Hen?'

The crone nodded. 'I be midwife hereabouts. I also tell time. Miss Coralee Dasher, she learned me the face of a clock right after she bought me off a string of slaves passing through these parts. Telling time, that got to be my job same as cooking and midwifing. Birthing suckers and ringing the dinner bell every day for them damned fool field niggers to come in for their grub. I never lost a mother. I never lost a sucker. And no nigger hereabouts never went without his grub. Right doodie, I know the face of the clock good enough to use for a map to this very day.'

The words made little sense to Gemma. She wondered if the old woman might be more crazy than rude, that she might be a backhill woman slightly touched by years of isolation.

'What is your friend's name?' Gemma asked.

27

'This here be Spanker.' Broody Hen nodded at the young woman.

'Spanker?'

'Big Spanker we call her. Always was a big girl. Bucks come sneaking around here after dark to have Big Spanker paddle their bottoms with the cup of her hand. Bucks get a taste for a dab of good spanking, you know. Getting their bottoms warmed with the cup of a hand and their peckers diddled while you're doing it. They likes it best when you cups your hand, too, and makes a real loud sound they can hear to Kingdom Come. Bucks like it that way, don't they, Spanker?'

The younger Negress – tall, light-skinned, with black hair that fell softly around a large face, a statuesque woman whose large breasts and round hips strained against her cotton dress – nodded her head and grinned widely at Gemma and Warren.

Broody Hen proceeded, 'Right, doodie, they do. But not many bucks drop around to get their bottoms spanked these days. Most folks taken to the roads. Left the slave quarters and taken to the road.'

'We're on the road, too,' Gemma said. 'Like my husband told you, we're looking for our new house. We're anxious to get on our way. We were wondering if you could direct us there. The place was once owned by the Chatgrove family. Do you know where it is?'

'Three o'clock.'

'Three o'clock?'

'Yep.'

'I don't understand.'

'Sun comes up there.' Broody Hen pointed the stem of her clay pipe toward the East where the sun was lighting the sky. 'That's Palmetto Landing. Five o'clock in the morning I call it. Then comes Moss Humps. Seven o'clock. The Crowforks Road runs to nine o'clock. Twelve noon be down that way, toward the town of Bossburg. One and two o'clock be High Hill and Belrose. Lone Oaks be half-past one. Then Candle-wick Plantation – the old Chatgrove place you're jawing about – it's the house at three o'clock.'

28

Warren whispered, 'What's she saying?'

'Shhh. I think I know. But I'm not sure yet.'

Gemma asked the old crone, 'So we go East?'

'Go toward the sun, follow the road past noon, straight out to three o'clock. But you won't get there, not before Bossburg, because Bossburg is twelve o'clock noon.'

'Bossburg,' Gemma repeated, struggling to make sense of the old woman's directions. 'That's the name of the town over there – Bossburg?'

'Yep. Noon. You won't miss it. Noon's dusty and tired and you'll be hungry around about noon, too. But don't expect to find nothing there unless you crave bed bugs and stray dogs.'

'How exactly will we know when we reach three o'clock?'

'Keep your eyes to the sky.'

'On the sun?'

'You could, if you don't mind scorching your eyeballs. I'd say best to keep your eyes on the sky to look for a scabby old wooden candlestick hanging from the crossbeam of a gate.'

'A wooden candlestick?' Gemma asked. 'Like a signpost? The name of the plantation? Candlewick?'

'Used to be Candlewick.'

'And that'll be . . . three o'clock?'

'Right doodie.'

Warren whispered, 'You're beginning to sound crazy as her.'

Gemma, ignoring Warren, reached for her suitcase and carpetbags. She called, 'Thank-you very much indeed for the help, Miss Broody Hen. You too, Miss Spanker. Hope to see both you ladies again some time. Maybe next time we can help you.'

'What about him?' Broody Hen called. 'Your buck there?'

'His name is Warren.'

'He got juice in his pecker, your Warren? Nice, hot jissum? Lots of spunk for you? Able to give you suckers like a good husband should?'

'Best husband a gal could ask for,' Gemma called over her shoulder.

'Then you'll be seeing me and Big Spanker again,' Broody shouted. 'I be midwife hereabouts. Big Spanker's my helper

29

since her kin run off to Alabama chasing rainbows. I be the best midwife in the parish. I never lost a mother in birthing. I never lost a sucker. There ain't no niggers to come running no more from the fields when I ring the dinner bell. But I ain't forgot nothing. I still can make a map read like the face of a clock.'

Gemma quickened her pace on the path which led across the weed field toward the parish road; it was Warren's turn now to catch up with her; he called, 'You planning to tell me what that was all about?'

'She's the local midwife.'

'Yeah, I heard that part. But what's this one, two, three o'clock business?'

'She sees the land round here like the face of a clock.'

'A clock?'

'That's right. To her all of Longchamp Parish is a clock. Every town or farm is a different hour.'

'Crazy as a loon,' Warren mumbled.

'You and me, we're going to three o'clock.'

Looking back over his shoulder to the cabin, Warren said, 'You too, crazy as a loon –'

Warren stopped. He saw a young White girl walking across the back field toward the cabin.

The girl was bare-footed, wore a faded cotton shift, and a long, raggedy white net wedding veil trailed behind her in the morning air.

A big white dog trotted alongside the girl who walked with her hands dangling loosely from her wrists, swinging back and forth as she hurried through the weeds.

'Lookee there!' Warren said to Gemma. 'That White girl. What's she doing? Where she going all dressed up like that?'

'Some place in a mighty big hurry.'

Warren and Gemma lingered to look at the girl in the soiled wedding veil and the large white dog trotting alongside her through the weeds.

*   *   *

The girl, ignoring Gemma and Warren standing in the

field in front of the cabin, talked to the dog as if it were a person, someone who could understand words.

'You go back to that Lulubelle wench, Hiram, and you'll be the cause of my breakdown. The total, utter cause of my breakdown of nerves. I took enough. I give enough. I give and take all is humanly possible. Understand, Hiram? Understand what I'm saying?'

Gemma and Warren guessed that the girl could be no more than fifteen, sixteen years old; the wedding veil flowed behind her as she stepped through the field on what appeared to be a very important errand.

The girl suddenly stopped; she stared at the cabin's front porch, she bent down and picked up a small rock from the field; she threw the rock at the yellow bitch dog laying with her head on her front paws.

The yellow bitch dog sniffed, then settled her head back down to the porch.

'Lulubelle!' the girl in the wedding veil angrily shrieked. 'Lulubelle! You high yellow slut! I told you to get off my land! Get off my land and never come back here! Never show your face here again.'

The old Negress midwife shouted, 'Miss Francey! Miss Francey Dasher, mam! Tame yourself, Missy. Lulubelle didn't mean no harm against you.'

'No harm? No harm, my foot! Lulubelle came back to this land to take away my man! To take Hiram here away from me. That high yellow bitch knows there's not enough marriageable White men left in Longchamp Parish to shake a stick at! Lulubelle's come back to spite me! And I'll whip her! I'll whip her within an inch of her life!'

The White girl, Miss Francey Dasher, turned to the white male dog beside her and, smacking it on its side, she scolded, 'Men! Let a man have his way and he goes running right back to that Lulubelle! Just because she can give you suckers! Oh, you men!'

'Miss Francey?' called the old Negress. 'What you been doing with that dirty old dog down in the berry patch, Miss Francey Dasher? Dirty old dog! Dirty old dog!'

'Mind your own business, you crazy old darkie,' shrilled

the girl named Francey Dasher. 'This is a family matter, an argument among White people! Not niggers! Not niggers like you and Spanker! I won't have you questioning me on no matter, you crazy old nigger lady and your crazy big friend. If I'm going to marry Hiram that's my business!'

Francey Dasher stuck out her tongue at both the Black women.

Warren, taking Gemma by the arm, said, 'Come on, honey. I think we better keep moving.'

Gemma watched the girl again pound the dog; she shook her head, saying, 'That poor girl, Warren. She must be the last of the Dasher family. The folks meant to direct us to our land.'

Warren said, 'I don't think we're supposed to be seeing or hearing none of what's happening here. Let's keep moving.'

Gemma picked up her suitcase. 'No wonder the old midwife said the Dashers were all dead and buried. No wonder – if the only living Dasher thinks she's going to marry a . . . dog!'

'Gemma, I said this is none of our concern.'

Gemma and Warren proceeded across the weed field to the parish road; they did not look back over their shoulders; Warren pushed forward, asking, 'You remember how she said to find the old Chatgrove place?'

'Follow those clock face directions.'

'Let's just hope the rest of the parish is not quite so strange and nutsy.'

'What we just saw back there wasn't nutsy, Warren. Broody Hen, maybe. Big Spanker, maybe. But that Francey Dasher girl, she should be in a hospital or some special home, some kind –'

Gemma stopped; she sighed, 'War, war. What strange things fighting and killing does to people's minds.'

'I said it once and I'll say it again – let's just hope the rest of the parish people are not so strange and nutsy.'

*　　　　*　　　　*

The town of Bossburg in Longchamp Parish, Louisiana

was little more than a cluster of small greyboard buildings facing a single dirt street, a small settlement which had not changed from the sleepy years before the Civil War, nor during the four year conflict which had changed the rest of the South.

Gemma and Warren walked slowly down the dirt street looking for some sign of life but saw no activity in the small town, no people strolling along the rickety boardwalks, no proprietors peering out the dirty windows of the few stores lining the street.

Gemma and Warren's arrival in Bossburg was observed, though, from an upstairs window in Fowley's General Store, the only two storey building in town.

'Rosie, come here and look at these niggers down on the street. She's the kind of coon gal I've been talking about getting.'

A barrel-chested White man with a shock of sandy hair stepped back from the upstairs window for a White woman to look at Gemma and Warren passing along the dusty street below them.

'Never seen them before,' murmured the woman and stepped away from the window.

'Course you never seen them. They're just passing through town.'

The barrel-chested man smiled, then laughed, saying, 'Just two more freed niggers looking for that 'forty acres and a mule' those Republicans are promising them. Poor dumb bastards. They're going to get . . . shit!'

'But don't you get no ideas about that wench, Junior Dehasset. World's changed. You can't grab every wench you wants and drags her behind some cow barn for horseplay. Slave days is over.'

'Slave days? Cow barn? What shit you talking, Rosie? I was thinking about us - you and me - playing diddly with that little coon gal in the comfort of this very room. I was talking about that pretty little piece of coon poontang joining us in that big iron bed we got set up for you here.'

The White woman - named Rose Starett - struggled to control the hatred she felt for the burly man; she tried to sound flippant, carefree, as she replied, 'Junior Dehasset, you get too spoiled on those visits to New Orleans. You didn't set me up in one of those fancy French bordellos like you visit in New Orleans. This is just a one room cathouse where you screw on a corncob mattress and piss out of the window if the wind's right.'

'I got my taste for two girls in bed in no place other than this nation's fine capital city, Rosie, old gal. I sampled two girls at one time when I went up visiting Washington.'

'Visiting your Pa?'

'None other.'

'Don't tell me, Junior Dehasset, that your Pa indulged in filth when he's away from Longchamp Parish for those Senate meetings in Washington?'

Junior Dehasset laughed at the idea of his father being a philanderer; he sank down onto the crumpled sheets hanging from the iron bed and said, 'My Pa's too much of a saint to screw with two gals in bed. Too much of a saint even to visit a whorehouse. I went snooping around Washington when I got lonesome. Ordinary sight-seeing didn't satisfy me. I must be one of the horniest guys in this whole wide world.'

He beckoned for Rose to come toward him, ordering, 'Squat down on your haunches, woman, and suck my dick.'

Rose Starett was tired; she wanted nothing more than to relax in a bath, to have a nap; she complained, 'You rode me all night, Junior Dehasset.'

'I was horny when I got here. I'm horny again.'

'You've been horny quite a bit lately, Junior Dehasset. But I ain't seen much money coming out of your pocket.'

'Money?' Junior eyed the pale woman with blonde hair hanging in unkempt shanks around her face; he rubbed his hands across his hirsute chest and asked, 'What you saying, Rosie?'

Rose could not return Junior's commanding stare; she shrugged, turned her head, murmuring, 'Nothing much, Junior. I'm just saying I ain't seen a heck of a lot of money lately. A working gal like me's got to have money coming in on a regular basis if she's going –'

'A working gal!' Junior Dehasset threw back his head and

laughed. 'I'll tell you what a working gal like you needs. A working gal like you needs a place to work, that's what! But if I tell my good friend, Sheriff Laird, that Rose Starett is a hazard to the morals of our community, and if I tell Kit Fowley that Rose Starett's presence above the general store keeps away potential cash customers, then you know what would happen?'

Junior Dehasset knew better than anyone that Rose Starett had been duped into becoming a prostitute after her husband had been killed in the first years of the Civil War; Rose had abandoned her small farm and moved into this one room above Fowley's General Store at Junior's suggestion; she remained living – and working – here by the grace of Junior Dehasset and the few other local White men who ran the day to day life in Longchamp Parish.

'Now that's my good girl,' Junior praised as he watched Rose sink to the board floor between his bare legs. 'Go on . . . take my dick in your mouth.'

Rose's red knees rested on the dingy white sheets spilling off the rumpled bed; she moved to lift the limp penis in her slim hand.

Junior observed her like an instructor; he ordered, 'Now I want you to suck that dick nice and easy, you hear?'

Rose nodded, took the limp penis into her mouth and began to chew on it as she listened to Junior's words; she knew from experience that Junior liked to talk himself into hardness, that he spoke more for his own benefit than for hers, that he often spoke as if he were a snake charmer charming his penis into an erection; Rose also knew that Junior liked to believe, to pretend that his penis was bigger than its actual size; Junior had a smaller than average penis – an organ with a head barely larger than an acorn – but he liked to speak as if he were hung like a stallion.

Junior's voice was no more than a murmur; he said, 'I want you to love that dick for me . . . I want you to really work your mouth on that dick . . . that's my girl. Take it deep in your throat . . . take that old head deep in your throat . . . don't be afraid of that dick . . . don't be afraid of choking on it. Swallow that dick right down your throat. That's right,

you treat that big dick nice for your man . . . treat that
dick special for your man and maybe he'll tell you about a
secret soon that makes his dick go hard like a piece of
iron . . .'

Secrets. Rose Starett did not want to hear any more of
Junior Dehasset's secrets, stories which sexually aroused
him. Rose only wanted to be free of Junior and his friends.

Junior's small penis grew harder, protruded stiffly into
Rose's mouth; she coughed on a pubic hair.

Pulling back, Rose grabbed alongside her for the bed sheet
on the floor to wipe her mouth. But she grabbed only a small
piece of sheeting fabric which had been lying under the
bed.

Junior saw the fabric which Rose had lifted accidentally
from the floor and he snatched it from her hand.

'Give that here. That's just an old rag of mine.'

Rose Starett did not argue. But she was certain the piece of
sheeting was no old rag. She was certain she had seen a
peaked hood into which two holes had been cut for eyes,
some kind of strange mask which Junior Dehasset had
accidentally dropped from his saddle bag when he had
arrived late last night.

*　　　*　　　*

Gemma and Warren had been confused by Broody Hen
and Big Spanker, depressed by Miss Francey Dasher and her
white dog, Mr Hiram, and disappointed with the ramshackle
appearance of the town of Bossburg, Louisiana. But their
hearts sank when they saw the sudden dirtscape surrounding
them beyond Bossburg. They wondered if the land they had
inherited might lay in this dull part of the country where the
woodlands were scrub pine and the buzz of flies in the dust
replaced birds singing in treetops. But they continued
dragging their baggage through the heat, climbing a steep
grade and finally saw a green horizon spread before them, a
vista of oak trees, an expanse of evergreen hills graduating
into taller hills, valleys veined with poplars growing along
creek beds.

Gemma praised a landscape for the first time in her life; she set down her bags in the road and said, 'Now there's a sight for sore eyes.'

'It sure is, gal, it sure is.'

'We've been travelling quite a spell since that ugly little town. Let's just hope our place is somewheres near here.'

'Let's just hope,' Warren said, then laughed. 'Wasn't that an ugly little town?'

'Bossburg? Ugliest little town I've ever seen!'

They both laughed, their agreement over the town's unattractiveness somehow restoring their cheerfulness and a modicum of energy; they lifted their bags again to head down the hill.

Warren reached the bottom of the hill before Gemma; he called, 'Where did that old woman say our place was?'

'Past noon . . . three o'clock.'

'No! Apart from that business.'

'She said to look for an old wooden candlestick hanging from a gatepost.'

The air became sharper at the bottom of the hill; the smell of fresh earth was tinged with jasmine and honeysuckle; a forest of bushy evergreens lined one side of the road; vine-covered oaks crowded the other side.

Warren, his heart beating with renewed excitement, hurried down the road.

Gemma shouted, 'Where you going?'

'I'm hoping, Coffee Cup! I'm hoping our place is around here.'

Gemma was buoyant again; she called, 'Don't look now, Moses, but you just passed The Promised Land!'

Warren stopped; he glanced back over his shoulder; he saw Gemma standing in the road, pointing at a wooden gatepost obscured by vines.

'You find it? The old candlestick marker?'

'There's something suspicious hanging from that cross-beam up there. Something cut to look like a . . .'

'. . . candlestick? For Candlewick Plantation?'

Before Gemma answered, Warren dropped his suitcases, carpetbags and satchels; he grabbed Gemma's hand;

37

together, they ran down a driveway choked with weeds, pine
seedlings, and vines trailing over fallen logs.

*   *   *

'It's not Dumbarton Avenue. That's for sure.'

Warren, looking at the slope-roofed shingle house set at
the end of the driveway, shook his head and agreed, 'Nope.
And it's a lot smaller than I'd expected. Smaller and I'd
thought there'd be white pillars . . . great big white pillars all
the way across the front.'

'I can live without pillars.' Gemma shaded her eyes to
study the house against the sunlight; she gauged, 'Two floors
and probably attic rooms under that shake roof.'

A chorus of crows, caw, caw, cawed behind him in the
shadowy forest.

'The fields must be near,' Warren said, glancing at a row
of tumbled down outbuildings.

'Probably quite a bit of land. But more than likely grown
over, gone to seed.'

'It's hardly no plantation, sugar gal. We knew from the
lawyers there wasn't going to be as much land as there used
to be. It's more like a farm.'

'Nothing matter with a farm, Warren. Not a good farm.'

'Be honest, Coffee Cup.'

'Honest?'

'Do you hate it? Do you want to turn around right now
and go back home?'

'Want the truth, Warren? The real truth?'

'The real truth.'

'It's not much more than a rabbit hutch, is it?'

'No, I guess not.' Warren kicked at a clod of dirt, trying
not to become despondent.

'Raccoons and skunks and chipmunks have probably made
their home here since old lady Chatgrove died. Pigs probably
took over from there.'

'You're being honest.'

Gemma had started and was not stopping, not altering her
opinion. 'The fields are probably worse than the house. A

38

man would probably be lucky if he could get even a kitchen garden started this year.'

'Don't spare me nothing.'

'You asked me.'

'Yeah . . .' Warren ground the toe of his boot over the dirt clod, kept his head lowered, fighting depression, hoping the feeling he felt behind his eyes was not tears.

'You asked me, Warren, so I'm telling you. The place is a mess. And you know something else?'

'Do I want to hear it?'

'I hope so, lover man, because I don't remember ever being so excited in my life.'

Warren thought he had misheard, misunderstood.

'You like it? You mean it?'

'The most excited I ever remember being.' She added, 'That is, except maybe when I first met you, Warren Otis Rickers.'

'You mean it?'

'Cross my heart, big love.'

Warren, grabbing Gemma in his arms, twirled her around and around in the driveway, repeating, 'Coffee Cup, Coffee Cup, Coffee Cup, I love you, I love you, I love you.'

Gemma's laughter rang through the treetops.

*   *   *

The two young Negresses, their chocolate brown nipples pierced with small golden rings, peered out through the cracks of the dilapidated tool shed as they heard the sound of strange voices; the two girls' mouths still tasted from the sweetness of one another's vaginas; they clung onto each other's slim waists as they knelt on the dirt floor and watched the handsome Black man spinning his small woman around and around in front of the old Chatgrove house.

'Who they?' whispered one girl.

The other answered, 'Two crazy darkies.'

'Do you thinks we safe here?'

'I thinks we better get dressed and makes a run for it when we can. The White Pedlar Man likes us making love but we

39

don't know about the two darkie strangers, how they think of two gals loving their own little pussies so much.'

The second girl, still romantic from their love-making in the tool shed, asked, 'You really loves my pussy like I loves that sweet pussy of yours?'

'I loves your little pussy like I loves my own little pussy.'

The second girl sat flat on the dirt floor, bent forward and lowered her head over her naked body like a nimble gymnast. She tongued the lips of her own vagina; she raised her head, kissed the other Negress firmly on the lips, sharing the taste of her vagina; she then clutched her girlfriend by one hand and grabbed their cotton shifts with the other; they waited for a chance to escape and then, quickly, together, the two young Negresses with their chocolate brown nipples pierced with small golden rings slipped out from the dilapidated tool shed and scampered through the woods. They were going back to the plantation where they lived in the backhills of Longchamp Parish.

Chapter Three

THE RECONSTRUCTION

'Hello, I'm your neighbor. I'm Sabrine Dehasset. I live with my family down the road at Belrose Plantation.'

Gemma stared blankly at the pretty young White woman standing in the doorway of the makeshift kitchen.

Little more than a week had passed since Gemma and Warren had arrived in Longchamp Parish; they had immediately sat down by sputtering candlelight on their first night at the old Chatgrove place and made a rough plan of work to be done to transform the derelict house, the barn, a few out-buildings and fertile sections of fields into a home, a small working farm.

Warren took charge of the outside chores while Gemma concentrated on everything inside – eating, sleeping, washing, day to day living – which concerned their domestic life.

Four years of total abandonment had taken a sad toll on the land and many major changes had to be made; food once had been prepared in a kitchen built apart from the main house; slaves had carried the food from the kitchen and kept it warm in a serving-room before taking it into the dining-room; Gemma still struggled to make the chimney draw correctly on the iron stove in the serving-room so she could use it as her cookstove and transform the serving-room into her kitchen adjoining the dining-room. She had already scrubbed down a pine table and Warren had begun to mend straight back chairs so they would not have to keep sitting on nail kegs.

'Do you mind if I come in?' asked the young woman standing in the doorway.

'Excuse my manners!' Gemma reached for a rag to wipe the soot from her hands and face. 'You surprised me. We've been here almost a week but haven't met one of our neighbors.'

41

'You must be Mrs Rickers.'

Gemma was surprised anyone knew her name. 'You've met Warren?'

'No. But I knew Mrs Chatgrove had willed this land to a young family named Rickers from Pennsylvania. To the son of someone whom the Chatgroves had long ago freed and helped move North.'

'You knew the Chatgrove family?'

'I was betrothed to marry Alfred Chatgrove.'

Gemma remembered Warren mentioning the name. 'Alfred Chatgrove. He was the son who got killed in the war?'

'Yes. At Bull Run. The first victory for the South in the war. But sad for us here in Longchamp Parish.'

'I'm sorry.'

The young lady smiled, 'You've no need to apologize. I'm over Alfred's death. It happened five years ago.'

Gemma hurried to produce the one straight back chair on which Warren had mended the cane seat. 'Please forgive my bad manners, Miss . . .'

'Dehasset. Sabrine Dehasset.'

'Please come in, Miss Dehasset, and let me fix a pot of coffee. I've got some applesauce cake I managed to bake in that old kitchen out back. Let me cut a few pieces.'

'No, no, please, Mrs Rickers, I'm intruding on your work. I can see you're having trouble with the stove. You'd have to start a fire to boil coffee.'

'I've got to light this danged stove anyway if Warren's – that's my husband – if he's going to get any hot food for supper tonight. I'm tired of cooking everything in that fireplace out there in the old kitchen. I never was much good swinging big iron pots back and forth on those fire brackets.'

'You've got no time to fuss over me, Mrs Rickers. Please. Go about your business. I just wanted to stop by. To introduce myself. I heard you'd moved in here.'

'How did you hear we were here?'

Sabrine Dehasset laughed. 'Oh, very little happens in Longchamp Parish that people don't hear. Especially when two Black people . . .'

42

Suddenly realizing what she was saying, Sabrine Dehasset blushed and lowered her head.

But Gemma finished the sentence for her. 'Especially when two Black people move into a house that used to belong to a respectable White family, right?'

Sabrine Dehasset raised her head; she held Gemma's eyes and said, 'I will accept your offer of hospitality, Mrs Rickers. Not coffee. Just a glass of cool water – and maybe a slice of that applesauce cake.'

Gemma pushed the one good chair toward the table. 'Be my guest, my very first guest, Miss –'

'Dehasset. Sabrine Dehasset.'

*   *   *

Sabrine Dehasset gave Gemma a brief sketch of Longchamp Parish, the rural neighborhood and the few villages lying within a fifty mile vicinity, as well as a short history of the land which Warren and Gemma had inherited from the Chatgrove family.

She stopped to break off another morsel of moist apple cake and complimented Gemma on it; Gemma explained how she had found small red apples in an orchard and baked them as a test for the flour, spices, pans, bowls, she had either brought from Philadelphia or found in creaky kitchen drawers.

'Much better than I could bake at home, Mrs Rickers.'

Sabrine Dehasset then continued with the land's history.

'I probably know Candlewick Plantation better than anybody left in Longchamp Parish and probably even as well as I know Belrose – that's my family's home.

'Charles Ely Chatgrove pioneered this land when Indians still lived in the hills. He made the wilderness bloom with cotton fields, fruit orchards, the plumpest vegetable garden for miles around. When Charles Ely Chatgrove died he left his holdings to his only son, William Ely Chatgrove, who preferred books to the soil, but prospered nevertheless. He married Emmaline Pasteur, the daughter of a distinguished old Creole family from New Orleans. They had one son,

43

Alfred. My mother's maiden name is Bonheur, another Creole family. The Creoles are descendants of original French settlers and consider themselves to be the aristocrats of the South. It was always understood that Alfred Chatgrove and I would become betrothed and married.

'William Chatgrove died in '57. Yes, I think that was the year. Then Alfred went off to war as a captain of his own regiment. I used to come here, to Candlewick, every day to visit his mother, the dear thing being left alone. Most of the slaves had run off. Then Alfred was killed. Mrs Chatgrove passed away the following fall. I still kept making my daily visits here. I suppose the walks over the hill from Belrose gave some order to my otherwise dreary days. Gave me something to think about during those horrible last years of the war.'

Gemma offered, 'Maybe coming back here was your way of keeping in touch with the memory of your beau.'

Sabrine nodded. 'I considered that fact. Of course. But to be perfectly honest, Mrs Rickers, that's why I stopped coming here. I decided it was no good for me to dwell on death. I had mourned Alfred's death. He was gone. I had mourned Mrs Chatgrove's death. She was gone. I decided I had mourned quite enough and that it was doing nobody any good, least of all . . . me!'

'Does it bother you to find strangers living in this house you knew so well?'

Sabrine hesitated. 'You see, Mrs Rickers, I was meant to live here. To be mistress of Candlewick.'

Gemma bit her lip. 'Of course.'

'So, naturally, it did bother me when I heard somebody finally had moved in here, that strangers had come to claim what was left of a plantation meant to have been my home.'

'Did it trouble you that these 'strangers' were Black people, Miss Dehasset?'

'Mrs Rickers, let me try to explain how difficult it is for many White people in the South to adjust to the new ways forced upon us by the North. It surprises many Southerners to see Black people having the same privileges as we do.

44

Owning land. Being promised the vote. Told they will receive education in public schools. Mrs Rickers, do not forget that little more than eighteen months ago White people had legally been masters to four million Black slaves and if somebody had said that slavery was actually going to be abolished, that four million slaves were going to be set free to roam the hills and villages, the entire South would have laughed in their face.'

'But there were free Negroes in the South before the Civil War, Miss Dehasset. Warren's father was one of them. He was freed by your friends, the Chatgroves.'

'I know that. But your husband's father moved North.'

'Many freed Black people stayed in the South,' Gemma argued. 'Black freedmen who did not move to the North.'

'There were freedmen, yes, Mrs Rickers. But freedmen living in the South did not have equal privileges with White people. Do not forget freedom was a double-sided word in the South. Freedom meant one thing for Whites and another thing for Blacks. Let's hope that Freedom can mean the same thing for both people. But changes come slowly, painfully . . .'

Gemma asked, 'Did you lose anyone in the war?'

Sabrine shrugged. 'Alfred.'

'No brother? Father?'

'My father was active in politics before and all through the war. Father is not a young man. But he remains very political. He's a member again of the United States Senate. And as for my brother –'

Sabrine paused. 'I have one brother, Mrs Rickers. We call him Junior. And, no, Junior was not killed in the war.'

Gemma believed she detected that Sabrine's voice suddenly chilled when she spoke of her brother, Junior Dehasset.

Sabrine looked around the room in the process of being converted into a kitchen; she said in a brighter voice, 'Are you going to keep the old name? Candlewick?'

Gemma laughed. 'Warren and I haven't had time to talk about names. We're hurrying to get a summer garden planted for preserving and storing for winter. Warren's also

45

working hard to put in a little corn, a patch of late cotton, see what he can do about some wheat and maybe even a rice paddy down by the creek.'

'If you need seed or equipment, don't forget about The Freedmen's Bureau in Kettley.'

'Kettley?'

'A town about thirty miles to the north. The Union Army – we still call them Yankees – runs The Freedmen's Bureau. As you probably know, it's all part of the Yankee Reconstruction Program to get the South back on its feet. Our economy is in a shambles. Most everything was destroyed. The rest is in miserable condition. Hundreds of thousands of people are out of work, White people as well as Black. Planters are as destitute as the slaves they freed.'

Sabrine said more optimistically, 'But the Army hopes to remedy at least some of that hardship with their Freedmen's Bureaus. I'm certain they will help you.'

'Do the local White people fight them?' Gemma asked. 'These Yankee programs set up to help freed slaves?'

'Certainly there's a lot of gruff talk about Northern carpetbaggers trying to pass a Republican majority vote with the Negroes and get rich quick themselves off our problems. But so much of that talk is just political hot air.'

'You said your father's a Congressman. That is very impressive, Miss Dehasset. You must hear plenty of political talk at home.'

'Incessantly. Papa accuses me of being a Republican scalawag who'd give away the South to the first passing stranger. Papa says Mama is a dyed-in-the-wool rebel but only because Mama's a Creole and doesn't want to give up her aristocratic airs and graces. But as for my brother, Papa throws up his hands when it comes to Junior's political views. Papa says Junior is nothing but a redneck trash farmer who was left on our doorstep by –'

Sabrine jumped up from the chair. 'I've talked enough! Too much! I'm keeping you from your work! Your husband will be coming in from work and wanting his supper.'

'You've kept me from nothing, Miss Dehasset,' Gemma said, rising from the nail keg she had been using as a chair.

'And if you did keep me from a little work, who cares? This visit made me feel like a woman again!'

Sabrine squeezed Gemma's hand. She said, 'Welcome to Longchamp Parish, Mrs Rickers. But more important, welcome to this house which – once upon a time – was to have been my home. I only wish everything was in better condition for you and your husband. But never forget one thing. I will do anything to help make life easier, more comfortable for you. All you have to do is ask.'

'Thank-you, Miss Dehasset. I'll tell my husband.'

*   *   *

That night, Sabrine Dehasset's older brother, Junior, sat with five other White men around a table in the room above Fowley's General Store in Bossburg; the men played chip euchre by the light of a coal oil lantern hanging from the ceiling; they studied their hands of cards as they spoke in low, lazy voices about the Black Yankee couple which had settled on one of parish's oldest plantations.

'Go by the name of Rickers according to the story I hear tell. The buck's a kid of old Longrow Rickers who used to work for Charlie Chatgrove when I was just kneehigh to a mosquito leg myself.'

'Longrow Rickers? That the big coon who Chatgrove let be his overseer after Clancey Hewittson ran off with the Filburg floozy?'

'Same coon. Got his name from planting cotton in long stretches. Big long rows that niggers could pick here to breakfast. Charlie Chatgrove freed old Longrow, let him move North with the wench he'd jumped the broom with in the slave quarters.'

'Old Chatgrove always did have a reputation for being an abolitionist nigger lover. His wife, Miss Emmaline, she was a good, sensible woman. A man would've thought Emmaline Chatgrove would've come to her senses and changed Charlie's last will and testament once he'd widowed her.'

'Leaving good land to a coon. Crazy. Who's ever heard of such a crazy stunt? If that happened before the war, such a

47

paper could be contested and broken. But these damned carpetbaggers and no good Unionist scalawag trash, they'd fight it tooth and nail these days. Just the kind of muck Republicans like to stir up and rub like shit in our face.'

'Miss Emmaline had to sell off quite a chunk of land over the years to pay off her war taxes.'

'Candlewick can't be more than fifty, hundred good acres left now.'

'Fifty, hundred acres ain't nothing to sneeze at! More than me and Pearl farm over on Goose Hill. More than a lot of self-respecting White folks farm.'

'How long you think that Yankee coon's going to be able to hold onto that land? After taxes are payable?'

The men continued playing cards, discussing Candlewick Plantation and its new Negro owners as Rose Starett sat on the edge of the bed across the dimly lit room.

Rose Starett half listened to the men's discussion; she knew that they hated Negroes and Northerners.

Lately, though Rose Starett detected something destructive about these discussions of Negroes; the men guarded their words around her; they almost spoke in code about certain activities these days.

'Ha!' Rose Starett thought as she stitched a garment which Junior Dehasset had ordered her to sew for him. 'Ha! As if I care what these redneck clodhoppers do or think. I just want to get out of this town, get away from being their whore.'

Rose Starett cried whenever she thought how sex - not beautiful sex, not love, but sex besmirched with violence and domination and warped minds - had come to rule her life. Before the Civil War she had been blissfully in love with and married to a corn-haired young man with apple red cheeks named Glen Starett. Rose and Glen Starett had a healthy, chubby son, Frankie, and were planning a larger family when the Confederates fired on the Yankee flag at Fort Sumter; Glen joined the Louisiana Foot Brigade. Rose had stayed with little Frankie at the small farm until word came late one drizzly night that Glen had been killed at Shiloh. Glen's brother subsequently took little Frankie to live with his family in east Texas and Rose thought that she was going to die of heartbreak or go insane with loneliness in the cabin. She began sewing patchwork quilts to pass away the long hours.

Junior Dehasset visited Rose on the farm during her first months of widowhood; Rose had already sewn a pile of patchwork quilts, quilts pieced with intricate patterns called The Star of Texas, Georgia Sunset, Jerusalem Artichoke, The New England Tea-Cup, colorful needlework which kept her mind active but wore her fingers into bloody stumps.

Rose, a pretty and energetic young widow, welcomed Junior's first visits as diversions; she also welcomed his first sexual advances, accepting them as signs of badly needed flattery, attention; Junior insisted Rose take money from him when she needed to pay land taxes; he later suggested Rose abandon the small farm, asking her why she needed it when she did nothing there but sew patchwork quilts and make love to him.

Alone, dependent on Junior for advice, still despondent from the death of her husband and the loss of her child, Rose moved into one of two small rooms above Fowley's General Store in Bossburg.

Other local men immediately began paying nightly calls on Rose in her room above the store; she complained to Junior, innocently thinking he would defend her from the men and their prurient attention.

Junior's reaction had devastated her; he had scorned, 'What's the matter, woman? You too good to put out a little snatch for my friends?'

'Do what - for who?'

'Screw for my friends.'

'Why, I can't believe my ears, Junior Dehasset! You can't possibly mean, can't possibly be saying you want me to turn into a whore for every man in Bossburg.'

'Not every man. Just my buddies. Old friends and a few of the boys who fought with me in the war. We come home to Yankees giving orders. Least you could spread your legs for a few unsung heroes.'

'I don't believe my ears! You gave me money to pay off the

49

taxes on my farm. Next you said the farm was getting too expensive for me to keep, that the taxes were getting too high and I'd be smarter to move off the place.'

'I found you this room, didn't I?'

'Yes. But I'm not going to live here like a whore!'

'The boys, they offer you money?'

'They most certainly did!'

'Then you're a whore, ain't you? Living in a room where men come to visit you holding money in one hand and their dicks in the other – that makes you nothing but a no good whore, Rosie Starett!'

'But you promised me –'

'I promised you shit! I gave you advice. That's what I did. And if you were stupid enough to take it, then you can't afford no high-faluting ideas about being no . . . whore!'

Junior Dehasset's cruel laughter still rang in Rose's ears a year later; she had become increasingly deeply ensnared in Bossburg's seamy web of lust and perversion; she knew life could not become more despicable for her.

Sitting on the edge of the bed, Rose obediently stitched the shapeless white sheeting garment which Junior had entrusted to her; she listened to the hum of the men's conversation around the card table.

'Word is the Yanks are finally opening a Freedmen's Bureau in Bossburg.'

'The scummy bunch was supposed to be here by end of summer.'

'They cause any trouble for us, Junior? The Bureau?'

'Nope. One of our men can be appointed to work inside the Bureau.'

'But ain't the Army appointing all those carpetbaggers to run their Bureaus?'

'Army needs a deputy or two.' Junior lifted a whiskey jug from the table; he took a swig of the corn liquor, wiped his thin lips on the cuff of his shirt and said, 'Every Bureau needs men who knows the countryside. But if push comes to shove, carpetbaggers can be run out of the parish. Just like we did with that trash we found hanging around the nigger camptown.'

50

The men around the table remembered the White man they had lynched from an oak tree in the gulley; they glanced at one another and then looked at Rose Starett bent over her sewing on the edge of the bed.

Junior noticed the men were suspicious of him talking so openly about their secret late night activities in the presence of a woman.

'Hey, Rosie!' he called.

Rose looked up from her work.

'Ever hear the story about the coon who overheard his master whispering a secret?'

Rose shook her head.

Junior took another swig of corn whiskey, wiped his mouth, then explained, 'Well, the White master, he pulls out the coon's tongue with flaming red pinchers so the coon don't go around town blabbing no secrets.'

'That's one story I missed, Junior.' Rose returned to her needlework, saying, 'Folks credit me with hearing more than I do.'

The men sitting around the card table realized any secret would be safe with Rose Starett.

Junior confidently resumed, 'I've been in contact with a mutual friend of ours from Montgomery, the man we talked to before Surrender Day, the fellow who said for Southerners not to be in too much of a hurry to throw away our old nigger auction blocks.'

The men looked at each other in the lantern's yellow light; they knew exactly the man to whom Junior Dehasset referred.

Dave Cooper asked, 'He travelling through this neck of the woods?'

'Never know when he's going to show up,' Junior said. 'I got a letter. But that would be just like him, wouldn't it? Send a letter one day and show-up on your doorstep the next.'

'Got a name for him yet?'

'Only the code name. Cyclops. Wrote to tell me the progress of our bunch of . . . friends up in Tennessee and a new group over in Georgia.'

51

'What's his story now?'

'Wants to know if we got sure steps to map in on that railroad.'

'Johnny Reb's Line?'

'That's the one, Dwight. That's our baby. Rebel Railroad.'

The man at the table named Judd Gillman – known locally as Sheriff – said, 'I'm meaning to talk again to that big bozo up at High Hill. The only thing holding me back is that he's going to be asking about the old Chatgrove place. Planned on the parish auctioning it off for taxes. But the estate settled the taxes.'

Cooper said, 'Should be no trouble running off that Yankee nigger and his wife.'

'Cyclops writes to go careful. Says the south's full of carpetbaggers and scalawags. Not to make one false move and blow no plans.' Junior reached for the whiskey jug, took a long swig, wiped his lips on the cuff of his shirt. 'We got to be like the old cat playing with a dead mouse. Have a little fun. Maybe bat the dead mouse around a little. Don't do nothing drastic till we get word . . . or reason. Our *own* reason to make a move. But what the hell? We're men, ain't we? Time comes when we see fit to chase off the Yankee coon and his missus, we chase them off! Cyclops don't have to show us how to wipe our ass and tell us how many times a day to do it!'

The men sitting around the card table passed the corn whiskey jug in a circle and agreed with Junior's opinion.

*　　　　　*　　　　　*

By midnight Junior Dehasset still had not returned to Belrose Plantation from playing cards in Bossburg. The stableboy at Belrose, a nineteen-year-old Black boy named Paulie, waited dutifully in the stable to unsaddle Junior's horse.

Little had changed in Paulie's life since the end of the war; Paulie had been born at Belrose of slave parents; his mother, father, three brothers and two sisters had left the plantation after the Civil War and now lived nearby in one of the

52

makeshift communities for freed Negroes called 'camp-towns'. Paulie had stayed at Belrose, not wanting to risk going without a job or endure the squalor of a camptown, believing he at least could obtain food for his parents, his brothers, his sisters, if he remained working as a stable-boy.

There was one person at Belrose who kept reminding Paulie about a new life waiting for Negroes in the outside world where a man did not have to live in a camptown; he was the plantation blacksmith named Ken.

Ken, a brawny man with skin the color of cinnamon, a body tight with muscle and ten years older than Paulie, also worked for food and shelter at Belrose but planned to continue doing so only until he saw the right opportunity to make his move into a free world; he tried to convince Paulie to leave with him for a future in a new state.

Ken again visited Paulie late tonight in the stables; they sat side by side in the moonlight pouring into the barn. Ken said, 'We can leave together. Before winter sets in. Maybe go toward the Carolinas.'

Paulie lacked confidence; he scratched the black hair clinging tightly to his head like a skull cap, saying 'Master Junior, he'd be angry as a hornet if I'd run off from here.'

'Forget about that bully! He don't own you! He ain't your master. Not no more! You're free, free from the Dehassets! Free from Belrose! Free from all White people! What they do for you?'

'Miss Sabrine, she's good to me.' Paulie then thought about Ken's friendship with Sabrine's mother, Noele Dehasset, which earned Ken special favors. He asked, 'What about Mrs Dehasset? You go with her? And do more than husk corn!'

'What that old bag mean to me?' Ken sat studying his hands folded together across his bent knees; he said, 'Only person who means something to me is you, Paulie.'

Paulie lowered his head, nervously scratching one ear; he said, 'I can't forget about my kin. They ain't working. Not Pa, not Ma. Nobody working since they left slavery.'

Ken, reaching for Paulie's square chin, turned the younger

man's face toward him. 'That's the real reason, ain't it? Your folks?'

Paulie nodded.

'Don't be ashamed of it. That's fitting. I can wait for reasons like that. It means you're the good boy I thought you was.'

Slowly the two Black males moved their lips toward one another; their mouths met in a kiss.

Falling together onto the hay, Paulie and Ken embraced one another, their hug as athletic as two wrestlers. They held their mouths together in a prolonged kiss, their tongues pushing saliva from mouth to mouth, their penises swelling, their crotches driving against one another, their large hands gripping more strongly.

Ken reached down for the rope clinched around Paulie's tow trousers. Paulie likewise reached to free Ken from his clothing. They soon lay naked, gripping the strength of one another's manhood. Their mouths pressed more tightly together increasing the virility of their kisses.

Ken finally lifted Paulie's legs, flipped him onto his back and began spitting on his fingers to lubricate his bobbing penis.

But Paulie had his own ideas about tonight's sex; he moved back with agility, jumped behind Ken and grabbed him around the waist.

'You know I don't like taking pecker up my ass, Paulie.'

'It's your turn to take it.'

'I get to hurting back there when you cornhole me too much. And once you start cornholing, you just don't stop.'

Paulie, rubbing a handful of saliva on his hard penis, eased the full crown toward Ken's round buttocks. 'I'll go easy. But I can't promise you how soon I'm stopping. I start cornholing you, Ken, and I just don't want to stop.'

Nineteen-year-old Paulie did not find his attraction to another male, to a brawny man ten years older than himself, strange or perverse; he preferred having sex with Ken rather than young girls living in the work cabins on Belrose. He also learned many things from Ken, facts about freedom, life in the outside world, stories of people and places and ideas which Ken read about in magazines he got from Noele Dehasset. Paulie sometimes found himself becoming slightly jealous about the time which Ken spent with his White mistress but he tried to control himself. He knew that men did not love each other, not like husbands-and-wives, not with jealousy and emotions and feelings from the heart.

Ken whispered in the stable's darkness, 'We go away from here together, Paulie, we got all night for corn-holing, for love-making.'

Paulie eased his phallus into Ken's anus, holding him on the naked buttocks, feeling himself become excited by Ken's promise. It was deep excitement and he wondered if it was wrong to have such strong feelings for a man, if he should only be thinking about sex, about the act they called 'corn-holing', about a physical friendship. Was it even wrong for two men to kiss? Paulie did not know. But he did not feel that the act was unnatural, perverse, wrong for him to be doing when his lips pressed against Ken's warm mouth, when their tongues fought each other with masculine strength.

*   *   *

The sound of a horse galloping on the driveway disturbed Paulie and Ken.

'Junior!'

'Damn him to hell!' Ken grabbed for his clothes.

'We can do it later when Junior goes into the big house.'

'You horny bastard' Ken said, playfully rubbing his hand over Paulie's short hair. 'I'd like to but I don't think we can. I got to get at least an hour or two of sleep tonight. We've been at it all week.'

'Tomorrow night?'

Ken, stepping into his trousers, said, 'You run away with me and we never have to ask those kinds of questions.'

Kissing Paulie goodbye, Ken slipped away into the darkness while Paulie hurriedly shoved the evidence of his persistent erection between the legs of his tow britches.

*   *   *

Francey Dasher, wearing the ragged bridal veil on top of her straggly hair, stood alongside a chinaberry tree in the night's darkness and stared aghast at the imaginary stranger, a make-believe man who had come to bring her news of approaching trouble.

'A war?' she gasped as she stood alone under the chinaberry tree. 'You're sure a war's going to break out? A war between the states?'

The night was still; the windows of the small cabin were dark behind her; Broody Hen and Big Spanker had long ago gone to sleep.

Francey, nodding her head as if listening to a report, finally interrupted her make-believe visitor, asking, 'Does that mean my betrothed will go off to war? But what if he does not return to the parish? What if the Yanks kill him? Who will I marry? What will happen to me? I will be alone, I will have no one to marry.'

A dog barked in the distance.

'Listen!' she whispered. 'Listen! Yes. I hear other folks talking about it, too! The war! There will be a war!'

Turning, Francey Dasher grabbed the ragged tips of her bridal veil and ran across the weed field in the darkness, shouting, 'War! War! The South's at war with the North! War! War! Wake-up everybody. Send all your menfolk to war! War! War, everybody!'

*   *   *

Warren Rickers dipped the tip of his forefinger into a thick white puddle of sperm spread on his naked thigh, part of his minutes old erotic explosion after ejecting his penis from Gemma's womanhood. Gemma curled alongside Warren in the bed; Warren said, 'I understand what the Bible means about seed not being spilt on the ground. Those words were meant for olden days, for when all those tribes of Israel had to have lots of sons to be strong. But don't you think maybe we should start thinking about being strong, too?'

'You and me can't afford to have babies yet, Warren. Not a tribe. Not even a tiny little family. When we make our first baby we've got to know how we're going to feed him—or her.'

Gemma smeared a dab of Warren's sperm from his thigh; she licked it and promised, 'We'll know when the time's right, Mr Walnuts-and-Cream. We'll know.'

Rolling away from his naked body, Gemma said, 'But if you're worried about waste, let me take care of that problem now.'

Gemma knelt in the darkness and began licking the sperm from Warren's crotch, his thighs, the wiry hair between his thighs, tonguing the pearly white drops still clinging to the end of his limp penis, savoring every tongueful, enjoying it, wasting nothing, conserving every speck with the tip of her tongue.

The persistence of Gemma's quickly moving tongue - the warmth of her mouth criss-crossing his body - reawakened a sexual excitement in Warren.'

Pulling Gemma toward him, Warren plunged his tongue deeply into her mouth and tasted a flavor which was both hers and his.

Gemma's sexual excitement had also been refueled; she moaned, sighed, rubbed her furry patch against Warren's knee, feeling his penis growing harder against her, poking into her stomach as she rode his leg.

Gemma pulled away from Warren to resume licking him.

But Warren wanted to give Gemma satisfaction, too.

Turning quickly around on the bed, Warren knelt over Gemma's body and held his midsection high in the air so his long penis dangled down toward her face as he himself positioned his hands on her thighs and buried his open mouth between her legs.

Warren began poking his tongue in-and-out, in-and-out, in-and-out of Gemma's vagina; he worked her feminine lips with his mouth, tasting chewing, eating, licking - probing his long tongue deeper inside her.

The sensation made Gemma squirm, pump her hips, crease her vagina tightly like an exotic flower bud, then blossoming into fullness, pinkness, closing again; she held

57

onto Warren's penis with her stretched lips, working her own mouth to reciprocate satisfaction.

Warren concentrated on satisfying Gemma, wanting to taste, to know, to have the female juices meant to mix with his seed, to taste the orgasms flooding inside Gemma as she had tasted and swallowed his own emissions.

They locked themselves together in the darkness, their naked skin shining as their bodies pumped, moved, pressed closer, appeared to be part of midnight's blackness.

*   *   *

Black people. Negroes living on the old Chatgrove place. White people living on small farms and fading plantations of Longchamp Parish discussed the controversial subject as they lay in their own beds long after snuffing out candles, or turning off kerosene lanterns, and could speak about such matters in the privacy of night.

Marilee and Samuel Lintott, living on Cedar Breeze Plantation south of Kettley, agreed they must prepare themselves for more and more Black people owning their own land. Marilee Lintott snuggled against her husband's lanky body and said, 'The world's changing since the war and, honey, maybe it's all going to work out for the best.'

The Merriere family of Peachtree Farm had lost two sons in the war; Claude Merriere lay alongside his wife in their heavy carved walnut bed, both hands folded across his chest, saying, 'Junior Dehasset told me in Bossburg today about a Black couple living at Candlewick Plantation. I said to him, 'Junior, I'm going to give them young darkies a chance to prove themselves before siding with a soldier who spent the war hiding behind stumps and supply wagons!' He didn't like me for speaking out like that but I remember our boys saying Junior was nothing but a trouble-making yellow belly.'

The bachelor, William Tanet, was not so accepting of new people moving into the neighborhood; he heard his two spinster sisters gossiping through the wall of his bedroom and he shouted, 'Esmeralda! Lavinia! You two girls stop planning your welcome baskets! I absolutely forbid you to

58

pay social calls on darkies till they prove themselves to be fitting and proper people to live in the same community alongside White families!'

Louise Deauville, a chubby woman wearing her long black hair plaited into a braid for night, whispered to her husband, 'Maurice, you don't think those hooded riders will ride out to the old Chatgrove place now that there's colored couple living there?' Maurice Deauville cautioned, 'Shhh, woman! You don't know nothing about hooded riders, free Yankee niggers, nothing that's happening around here, understand?'

The Deauvilles. The Tanets. The Merriers. The Lintotts. Along with the Rowans who owned the new turpentine mills and the Dehassets who lived on Belrose Plantation. All families of Longchamp Parish, a patch of Louisiana state located in the wilderness to the west of the Mississippi River, south of the Arkansas state line, north of New Orleans, east of Texas. Pine forests. Cotton fields. Small farms enclosed by log fences. Plantations with slave-quarters sitting empty. White families. Black families. Everyone waiting, wondering, looking to see what changes tomorrow was going to bring them.

Chapter Four

BELROSE PLANTATION

Sabrine Dehasset wanted to share her excitement of meeting the new neighbors living in the old Chatgrove place; she approached her mother in the morning room at Belrose Plantation the day after she had visited Gemma Rickers.

Noele Dehasset, a handsome woman with high cheekbones and limpid grey eyes, was younger than her husband, Senator Dehasset, looking even younger than her age; she closely guarded her creamy complexion from the sun and her trim figure from rich, fattening foods; she possessed the elegance - and haughtiness - of her Creole ancestors, the Bonheurs.

She sat in a gilt-framed *fauteuil* in the yellow morning room modelled after a similar room in Thomas Jefferson's home, Monticello; she said, 'Sabrine, it's very generous of you paying housecalls on colored families who are trying to make a fresh start in the world. Your father would be very pleased with you. Do not be surprised if he even refers to your philanthropic activities in one of his speeches.'

'Mama, must you always be so ironical?'

'That's not irony, dear. It's fact. Pure, simple fact. Your father, like all politicians, is an out and out opportunist. Why, I declare, he'd drag you on a stump tour of the state if he thought you could win him a few votes.'

Sabrine knew that her father was no opportunist, that he was exactly the opposite from what her mother was accusing him of being; Senator Dehasset made many political - and social - enemies because of his liberal, often radical ideals; Sabrine said, 'Mama, the way you talk about Papa, I wonder if you love him.'

'Love? What does love have to do with your father and me, Sabrine? We're married. We're respected by our peers. We raised a family. Kept a home and our heads throughout the

60

war. Never at any time allowed cheap sentiment to rule us. Love, cherie, has nothing to do with a good match. Nothing.'

'I disagree.'

'Disagree if you will, Sabrine. But I don't want you getting overly friendly with too many freed Negroes. Try making a few calls on girls of your own age and class. Cathy Sue Lintott. Belinda Merriere. Perhaps those Rowan girls whose father is doing so well with those turpentine mills.'

'Mama, I swear! You talk about Papa being self-serving! I've heard you say the most scathing things about the Rowans being red-neck trash. But now that they start making a fortune from those awful new turpentine mills, you want me to make house calls on them!'

'The world changes, Sabrine. The world changes. Creole ways are - poof! Out the window! We must learn to live with people like the Rowans. They are the new elite. The South's new master class. The aristocracy *nouvelle*. The plantation system died at Fort Sumter. King Cotton is dead. Now money - plain, vulgar, filthy Yankee dollars - calls the tune!'

'But the Dehassets still survive, Mama. Belrose still prospers.'

'The only redeeming fact about Belrose's isolation from good society and the world is that even the Yankee Army passed us by. That's the one benefit of being stuck in the . . . sticks!'

'Maybe we do live in the sticks, Mama, but I will not befriend the Rowan girls.'

'Now listen to who's a snob!' Noele Dehasset pointed her ivory backed fan at Sabrine. 'Maybe there *is* hope for you, cherie.'

'Mama, the Rowans sold sick slaves from the back of a wagon before the war. During the war they profited from the Georgia blockade. Now they pay dirt cheap wages to all those poor people working at their awful turpentine mills.'

'Those "poor people" are Black men and women lucky to have jobs. What else could they do?'

'Mama! Sometimes I think Junior gets his redneck ideas from you!'

'Sabrine! Watch your tongue!'

61

Sabrine felt ashamed for the anger she showed to her mother. But was not her mother the only woman who could awaken such anger in her? Sabrine wondered why – why did her mother always trigger such arguments, such outbursts of emotions?

'I'm sorry. Mama. I didn't mean to go so far. Not to call *you* a redneck. But –'

'Apologize right now for what you said about your brother.'

'Mama! Junior's got a red streak down his neck a mile wide! The simple fact of the matter is that he's actually proud of being a small-minded person. He's never tried to improve himself. He refused to go away to school. He stayed in a tent all through the war and played poker with bounders. He consorts with army deserters, turncoats, woodrats. He's vindictive, petty, a drunk . . .'

'Sabrine, it wouldn't make your father happy to hear you slandering your brother. And I do not enjoy acrimony between my children.'

'Then let's talk about something else . . . like Mrs Rickers.'

'Gladly, Sabrine. If you tell me who she is.'

'Rickers. The new people at Candlewick.'

'You poor darling,' Noele Dehasset comforted, patting Sabrine's hand. 'You're being brave, aren't you? Candlewick was meant to be your home.'

'I somehow think the Rickers family will be happier there than I would have been.'

Noele looked startled; she studied her daughter's oval face. 'What a curious thing to say, Sabrine. Unless you mean the house itself. It is small. A small, dark, little house. Much too small for weekend house parties. Impossible for entertaining on any decent scale.'

'I'm talking about Alfred. I'm sorry he was killed at Bull Run. But I'm not sorry we didn't marry.'

'Love! Amour! You're thinking about romance again. Well, don't wait around for Prince Charming, my dear, or you'll never get married.'

'There are worse fates.'

62

Noele Dehasset arose from the *fauteuil*; she gathered the crackling skirts of her emerald green dress; she said, 'The one fate worse than spinsterhood is being a spinster – in Longchamp Parish!'

Moving toward the double doors, Noele called, 'I'm going down to the pergola to read, Sabrine. Don't bother me, promise?'

'Do I ever bother you in the pergola, Mama? Does anyone?'

*   *   *

Noele Dehasset had borne her husband three children, the last having died at childbirth; Noele allowed the world to think that she – like many other Southern ladies of gentility – had performed her wifely obligations and continued dutifully in her role of mother, hostess, and social figure.

Sex, nevertheless, played an important role in Noele Dehasset's life at Belrose Plantation; she had developed an early taste for sex as a young girl in New Orleans; she had discovered after marriage that her husband was not a sexually robust man; she never divulged her own voracious sexual appetite to Senator Dehasset as his own sexual requirements began to wane into nothingness; Noele had always managed to have a clandestine affair at Belrose; the Senator's absences enabled her to enjoy these erotic trysts.

Noele's current lover was the plantation blacksmith, Ken. She enjoyed how Ken seldom spoke to her, only when she commanded him to speak, always appearing promptly at their usual meeting place, the pergola built in a willow copse at the end of the small lake located in the grounds of Belrose Plantation.

Another fact which Noele enjoyed about Ken was his masculinity and the cleanliness in which he kept himself. Noele enjoyed oral as well as vaginal sex; she also enjoyed how Ken – silent, concentrating on his role – rode her in a fashion which he had discovered in the reading lessons he had begun since freedom allowed Negroes the opportunity to read; Ken looked through magazines for new words and had seen a drawing of the popular machine called a bicycle in a magazine.

Ken met Noele Dehasset again this afternoon, remembering how his meeting last night with Paulie had been disturbed, and he was able to produce a quick, firm erection for Noele.

Noele, licking the crown of Ken's stiff penis with her thin tongue, held his bulging scrotum in her hand; she sucked one testicle, then the other; she finally announced, 'You may ride me now.'

Ken did not enjoy but neither was he repelled by having sex with Noele Dehasset; they had started before the war and he was still able to perform the duty without a loss of erection; he thought of Paulie when he drove into her.

'Stir inside me,' Noele commanded.

Ken obediently stirred his penis, secretly amused how properly, how lady-like Noele Dehasset behaved at the outset of each sexual rendezvous, so completely opposite from his lusty romps with Paulie. Their man to man encounters began with earth-shaking sexuality and completed with gentle, erotic, love-filled emotion.

Slowly, gradually, steadily, Ken began pressing deeper into Noele Dehasset, moving one leg, then the other, lifting the first leg, pressing the other, moving, pumping, working his legs between her open thighs as if he were riding the bicycle he had seen in the magazine.

The bicycle movement was Noele's favorite position because it made Ken's penis sink deeper, harder, more steadily, more satisfyingly into her womanhood.

'You are doing it . . . you are reaching me . . . you are getting there . . . now, touch my breasts. Touch my breasts, hold my breasts.'

Ken kept riding the imaginary bicycle as he groped for Noele's small, ivory-like breasts which, in his mind, were the handlegrips of the bicycle had had seen in the magazine.

'Yes,' Noele assured him. 'You are getting there.'

Then came her next command, always the same order. 'Now grab my wrists . . . grab both of my wrists with your hand . . . grab my wrists and hold me helplessly . . .'

One of Ken's large hands could easily accommodate both of Noele's thin wrists; he obediently grabbed her wrists as he kept moving his legs, pushing his penis, riding the bicycle, pressing deeper into the feminine hole.

Tossing her head back and forth, Noele Dehasset began exploding under Ken's masculine prowess, enjoying the grip in which he held her, gentle but firm.

She whispered, 'I am helpless . . . I am helplessly yours.'

Ken knew what he was meant to reply; he said the three words, 'You are helpless.'

'Helpless . . . I am helpless . . .'

Noele shook with explosions of excitement; the thought of being dominated thrilled her; she was ecstatic at the thought of being held helpless by a Black man, a man who, in her mind, was still nothing but a Black slave, a potent Black slave working on her aging, impotent husband's plantation.

*   *   *

Senator Dehasset, a short man, with a stomach bulging his brocade waistcoat, and white hair yellowing with age, had seen the Civil War approaching and made preparations for his slaves to receive weekly pay for their work if abolition was achieved. The foresight of this gesture meant that Belrose did not go through a period of inactivity like other Southern plantations, that a work force had remained on the land, that Belrose was not only a profitable, productive plantation after the war but made more money than it had in the ante-bellum years: few plantations could immediately begin shipping to Northern and English mills left hungry by the war's embargo and paying high prices for crops.

Many Negroes had abandoned the plantation after freedom was granted to them, giving up their homes in the slave quarters for a life in the free world. But their numbers at Belrose were quickly replaced by other migrant freed slaves looking for work, people eager to receive food and shelter.

Senator Dehasset, prospering from the conditions of the times, was also troubled by the uncertainty of these days; he paced Belrose's front verandah lined with six Doric columns and considered the problem of four million freed slaves wandering the South, industry at a virtual standstill, fields lying fallow, inhumane conditions in the growing number of camptowns, and unrest among the uneducated White people complaining that freed Negro slaves were getting all the new government's money.

The Reconstruction program, Senator Dehasset knew, was rife with pitfalls. The trouble had all started with the assassination of President Lincoln. Senator Dehasset cursed the madman, John Wilkes Booth, who had shot Abraham Lincoln last April and he cursed the Southerners who had thought the assassinations would help the South. The assassination had only worsened conditions. Vice-President Andrew Johnson – now President of the United States – was a less generous, less visionary man than Lincoln, and definitely no friend to the South. President Johnson's plans for Reconstruction were more severe than Lincoln's and many Southerners were beginning to realize this.

Senator Dehasset knew that the South's attitude made every Confederate state a potential powder keg. White people – mostly small farmers – were forming vigilante groups all over the South. He knew that there was a vigilante movement in Louisiana, with chapters springing up all over the state.

The Senator had just received a letter this morning from Montgomery, Alabama about another problem evolving from the vigilante movements, a letter alleging that a member – or members – of the former Confederate cabinet was organizing a 'Rebel Railroad', a system by which Negroes could be worked in slavery, taken from one spot to another in the South by a system modelled after the network perfected by Abolitionists before the war to run slaves to freedom in the North – the Underground Railroad.

One of the organizers – according to Senator Dehasset's letter – was a Confederate officer known to his new colleagues only by the code name – a title like a name from a child's game, or a college boy's fraternity ritual – Cyclops, the mythological giant with one eye.

Cyclops? A man with vision only for violence? Senator Dehasset feared that that might prove to be the reality.

*   *   *

The Black amazon, Big Spanker, could never remember Broody Hen's names for local farms, plantations, towns – the names which the old crone correlated to the numbers on a clock face. But Big Spanker remembered that Belrose Plantation was two o'clock on Broody's map and she complained again tonight about Junior Dehasset and his friends taunting her to have sexual relations with them; she said, 'I wouldn't touch that man from two o'clock with a ten foot board!'

'Them trash knows better than to come on this here land,' assured Broody Hen as she stood in front of the iron cookstove in the cabin. She had always been an oddity in the neighborhood but was also respected as a midwife by people both Black and White; no person dared step foot on the property where Broody lived and risk evoking an outcry from people in the community.

Broody said, 'I gets me a gun and I fill his tail with buckshot!'

'White trash like them, they don't have a good word to say for colored folks until they want to pester with us.'

Then, suddenly, Spanker changed the subject from herself to Francey Dasher.

She said, 'Miss Broody, we got to do something with that poor girl. She's forgotten about the dog. Now she's jabbering about war breaking out between the states.'

Broody chewed on her clay pipe. 'I heard the poor tyke ranting and shrieking about war. She's scared of being left here alone.'

Spanker remained serious. 'Miss Broody, we got to send Miss Francey away from here.'

'No place to send Miss Francey away. No Dasher kin left to send her to. All the Dashers dead and buried.'

'So far, folks are good and don't poke no fun at Miss

Francey. They just let her be. But she might get hurt some way bad.'

'I agree with your ideas, Spanker. We can't pretend Miss Francey's craziness ain't happening. The fact of the matter is her crazy ways sooner or later always come round to pestering. Fooling around with menfolk. I just don't know where this war talk is going to take her. How it's going to fit in with that notion of hers about finding a husband.'

'What we do, Miss Broody? What we going to do about Miss Francey's deep ways?'

Broody Hen ignored the question; she was looking out the cabin window. She called, 'You better be thinking about your own deep ways, big girl.'

Spanker snorted. 'Nothing deep about *my* ways! Fact is, since the war I ain't had no ways to be thinking about. Nobody comes around here wanting me no more.'

'You better think again, big gal.' Broody kept looking out the small window toward the field. 'I see a right pretty buck traipsing through the weeds. I do declare I think the buck be one of your old-time visitors.'

'A visitor!' Spanker ran to the window and saw a tall, broad-shouldered young man with brown skin.

'Why that be Matthew!' she gasped. 'Matthew who used to live with his folks up at Belrose. They moved down to Two Forks Camptown.'

'Probably too many folks in camptown for Matthew to get him the kind of loving he wants from a gal,' Broody Hen suggested. 'Too many folks living near and around those tents. They can hear all the ruckus.'

Broody turned to look at Spanker; she asked, 'You up to dishing-out hard cooking to that buck, girl?'

'Me?' Spanker's face broadened into a grin. 'I'm always ready to cook up something for a pretty buck like that Matthew. He's young but he's a man in lots of other ways.'

'Then hop to it, gal! Give that boy some enjoyment he'll never forget. You enjoy yourself, too. I'll save your supper on the back of the stove.'

'You sure, Miss Broody?'

'Dang right I'm sure! You get your tits out in those weeds

68

and has a good time. You never know how many years you got ahead of you!'

*   *   *

Big Spanker sat alongside Matthew on a log at the edge of the weed field in the evening's fading light; Matthew bashfully told her about life in the settlement for freed slaves, how he and his parents and brothers and sisters hoped to find work soon and leave the camptown.

Spanker knew Matthew was ill-at-ease; but she was considerate of a man's ways, a man's masculine pride; she gently said, 'Everybody needs somebody to takes care of them. Even big strapping boys like you, Matthew.'

Matthew bashfully hung his head. 'Guess I might do.'

'Needs somebody strong.'

'Guess you be right.'

'Somebody strong,' Spanker repeated. 'Somebody know what . . . she's doing with a big boy like you.'

Matthew nervously shrugged his wide shoulders.

Pulling him toward her, Spanker slowly lowered her arm, beginning to pat her hand against his arm, the side of his chest, then his buttocks.

'Yes, boy,' she said, 'You need somebody big, strong, hefty to look after you.'

Matthew sighed, nodded his head, snuggled closer against Spanker's warm breast.

Increasing the firmness of her pats on his buttocks, Spanker felt Matthew's penis harden against her thigh; she remembered him being mature in many ways for his age but not so generously endowed.

'You sure be a big boy,' she assured him. 'But big boys need a strong hand lots of times, too, don't they, Matthew?'

'Uh-huh.'

He was beginning to quiver with excitement inside her firm hug.

Spanker also was becoming excited; she moved one hand to the front of his tow trousers; she pulled the knot on the rope belt; she pushed down the trousers from his waist and

69

began rubbing the palm of her hand in circular motions over the roundness of his bare buttocks.

Feeling Matthew quivering and shaking against her body, Spanker said, 'Just slide yourself over my lap, boy, and let me take nice, good care of you.'

Matthew soon lay across Spanker's knees; his bare brown buttocks stuck-up into the air; Spanker's hand came down in sharp slaps; she continued in a steady rhythm and, then, she changed the direction of her strikes, slapping one buttock with the front of her hand, using the flat of her hand to slap the other naked cheek; she next made his buttocks shake like jelly as she increased her rhythm, intensified the force of the spanking.

Beginning to whimper, Matthew nevertheless lifted his buttocks higher for Spanker to smack him with all her might.

'You sure do need this . . .' Spanker brought her hand down harder and harder against the arched nakedness of his buttocks. 'You sure do need this . . . and need this one . . . and this one . . . and this one . . .'

Matthew's gasps quickened; he rolled his naked buttocks to enjoy the full aim of her hand.

Spanker spread apart her knees; she ordered, 'I gives you room now for your hand, boy. Go on. Plays with your pudd while I heaten your tail.'

Matthew, moaning gratefully, remained spread facedown across Spanker's knees, but reached to push his penis long and hard from under him so he could firmly grip it with one hand.

Spanker kept spanking him, smiling as she listened to him pleasurably groan, watching his arm move up and down, up and down, masturbating himself as she slapped his buttocks.

Waiting for him to start gasping, to approach his orgasm, Spanker then grabbed him by the neck and lowered him to the ground between her spread legs.

She pulled up the hem of her dress and, pushing him toward her open thighs, she ordered, 'Now, boy, you pull that pudd and eat my brown muffin, understand!'

Matthew, kneeling obediently, gratefully between Spanker's

spread thighs, voraciously – noisily – gobbled her wet vagina as he pulled on his long, hard, inky black penis.

'Pull that pudd, boy! Pull that big pudd and chew that brown muffin! Pull! Pull! Pull! Let me walk on your spunk like rain! Rain down your spunk so I can walk, slipping and sliding my bare feet all over your cum, boy! Cum, boy! Cum!'

*   *   *

Big Spanker's infatuation with fat-bottomed boys was child's play, Broody Hen knew, compared to other acts of domination and submission in Longchamp Parish.

Broody Hen, uneducated by books but schooled in the ways of Southern people, had seen for many years that the men and women of Longchamp Parish lived a remote life, and that they often indulged in pastimes which outsiders considered to be strange, perverse, against nature's grain.

Broody Hen had seen prosperity come to Longchamp Parish before the Civil War and watched it give swaggering confidence to White landowners; she had seen the Civil War beginning, first giving courage to Confederates, then obliterating their hopes, frustrating appetites and dreams.

Southerners were like spoiled, pampered children, and if something was taken away from them – something important like slavery – they would insist that they got it back, even if they had to be slaves themselves, even if they had to be slaves to one another, even to Black people.

The roles of 'master' and 'slave' had always gone farther than the slave-quarters and work fields of Southern plantations; perverse lusts crept into the haylofts of barns, moved up the staircases of mansions, spread like a ground fog through parishes and towns, engulfing White people, Black people, married couples, bachelors, widows, proving that a Civil War might reunite the South with the North in politics, but that Southern sexual cravings would always be distinct, unique, against nature's grain – and cursed as the slave system on which the Confederacy had been built.

Sex. Domination. Submission.

Broody Hen, in her earthy wisdom, in crude terms and

thoughts formed over the cookstove, knew that participation in sexual perversions was one way by which many Southerners – both Black and White – accepted the reality of slavery, and its abolition, giving a continuation to the local tradition of bondage . . . shackles . . . flogging . . . humiliationn . . . the punishment of one person by another.

Big Spanker was part of a love pattern. And Broody Hen just hoped she did not get involved with White people, would make love only to other Black people and not risk getting hurt – by hurting the wrong people.

Chapter Five

KU KLUX KLAN

'Okay, whoever you are, state your name, get slowly up to your feet and don't try no monkey business or I'll jab this pitchfork right through your gizzard!'

Warren Rickers stood holding the prongs of a pitchfork against the chest of the White man he found sleeping in the corner of the barn.

The White man blinked his eyes in the early morning light cutting in bright shafts through the boards of the barn. He realized with a start that a Black man was standing over him, that a pitchfork was being held against his chest; he raised both hands for Warren not to stab him, to have patience, to give him a chance to speak.

Warren, holding the prongs in position against the White man's chest, demanded, 'You a carpetbagger?'

The man, youthful and handsome, with coal black curls tumbling over his forehead, shook his head to deny he was a carpetbagger.

'A Black man's got enough troubles without harboring no carpetbaggers.'

The stranger again motioned for Warren to withdraw the pitchfork.

Warren threatened, 'Don't try no tricks, understand?'

The man finally spoke; his voice was thin, halting. 'I was just trying to get some . . . sleep.'

Warren lowered the fork. 'You better not try nothing smart.'

'Mighty grateful,' said the curly-headed man, his forehead covered with beads of perspiration. He forced a laugh, saying, 'You had me thinking there for a minute I had died, woke up in Hell and was looking at the old devil himself pointing his pitchfork at me!'

'The Devil's red.'

The man smiled.

'What's your name?'

'Cramer Crowley. I travel through these parts selling Firefly Water. My wagon broke down. The bottles broke in the accident. I had no place to sleep. So –'

'Firefly water? What's that?'

'Sir, you'd probably call me a liar if I told you.'

'Some kind of cure-all? Like snake medicine? You some kind of travelling flim-flam man, mister?'

'I could take offence at your words, sir, but I won't. I follow the Good Book and will turn the other cheek.'

Warren irritably replied, 'What do you say about putting yourself on your feet and getting the heck out of here?'

'You don't need some work done around the place? Something I might do in exchange for a bite or two of breakfast?'

'There's a lot of work to be done around here. But by a man a lot huskier than you.'

'I'm strong!'

Warren smiled at the stranger's boyish indignation; he stood back and, nodding his head toward the open barn door, he said, 'Okay, strong man. I'll tell my wife to put something more in the skillet. But I warn you, she's a suspicious gal and not likely to invite you to come inside and sit at her kitchen. Not that we're uppity, understand. On the contrary. But we're new here, we've got reasons to be suspicious of strangers.'

'And I don't blame you one bit,' said Cramer Crowley as he jumped to his feet. He began brushing the straw from his long trousers and his black deacon's coat, saying, 'Especially not after the stories I heard about the Knights of the Camellia riding in this part of the state.'

'The who?'

'The Knights of the Camellia. A vigilante group. They operate here in northern Louisiana. They're like the Ku Klux Klan who ride the backhills of Tennessee, Alabama, Georgia.'

'The who, what kind of clan?'

'Ku Klux Klan. Another vigilante group. White men who

74

fancy themselves as custodians of White orderliness in the South. Neither the Klan nor the Knights of the Camellia take too kindly to carpetbaggers, Black people, Catholics, Jews, freed slaves, anything they think might pollute their precious White blood.'

'You be White,' Warren said, his fingers firming on the pitchfork handle. 'How come you know so much about these types of men?'

'I'm Irish. The son of Irish immigrants. The Klan and the Knights don't look too kindly on immigrants either. They say immigrants take good jobs away from the American people.'

'They got a bone to pick with almost everybody, don't they? What makes them think they're so privileged?'

'Good question.' Cramer Crowley nodded and repeated, 'Good question. The answer seems to be that they are men who have nothing else to distinguish themselves in the world except for the color of their skin.'

'These so-called Knights,' Warren asked, 'they wear white robes and leave white camellias wherever they go?'

'They wear white robes, yes. So do the Klan. But as for leaving white camellias . . .'

Cramer stopped. 'Why you ask that? You've had some kind of trouble here?'

'Nope. Just heard about doings like that.'

Warren turned and beckoned him from the barn. 'Come on. I'll show you where you can get washed. I'll tell Gemma to put on more breakfast.'

The White man smiled behind Warren's back.

*   *   *

Cramer Crowley sat with Warren and Gemma at the scrubbed pine table in the kitchen. Gemma had prepared a panful of ham and grits but no eggs because, so far, they had no chickens in the hen coop. Cramer Crowley animatedly jumped from subject to subject like an overly excited child; he charmed Gemma but she had to remind him to stop talking and eat his breakfast before it got cold.

'You folks are doing a fine job here,' Crowley praised as he looked around the kitchen after Gemma and Warren had told him in what condition they had found the old house. 'I can't believe you haven't been here for even one month. It's a lot of work for one man and his wife.'

Warren patted Gemma's hand. 'She does the work of four, five people.'

'Good cook, too,' Cramer said, adding, 'I fancy lots of folks would work just for a taste of this cooking and a roof over their heads.'

Gemma answered, 'Thanks for the compliment, Mr Crowley, but we're not able to be very generous yet. Not enough money. Not enough food. Not enough knowledge of local ways.'

Warren elaborated. 'We both figure we need more time to get to know who – and who not – to trust.'

Cramer nodded. 'Wise, wise.'

Gemma tried a leading question. 'You seem to be a trusting soul, Mr Crowley.'

'Me? I'm no different from anybody else, no wiser, no more trusting. I travel the backwoods selling Firefly Water. But maybe I'm only running from my own problems.'

'Firefly Water?' Gemma looked from the personable but mysterious guest to Warren.

'Mrs Rickers, I'd tell you about Firefly Water but you probably wouldn't believe me if I did.'

'Some kind of snake medicine,' Warren explained. 'He sells it from the back of a wagon.'

'No, no, no, most emphatically no! I told you before, Mr Rickers, that is not so. But if you're happy believing I deal in cure-alls, we can leave matters at that.'

Warren said, 'Do you care to talk about your problem then, Mr Cowley?'

'No more than any other man cares to talk about his problem, Mr Rickers.'

Gemma and Warren exchanged amused glances.

Warren said, 'So tell us more about that white camellia bunch and them – what did you call that other gang up in Tennessee?'

'The Ku Klux Klan.' Cramer Crowley held his tin mug to

Gemma for more coffee, asking, 'You don't have a wee touch of milk or cream, do you, Mam?'

'Afraid not. We've found wild turkeys, wild geese, wild rabbits. But so far no cows, Mr Crowley.'

'I'll keep my eyes open for you, Mam.'

Cramer then proceeded to answer Warren's question.

'The Ku Klux Klan started in Tennessee just after the Civil War. Rumor has it that it was a private club, like a fraternity, started by college kids during one Christmas vacation. They called it the Ku Klux Klan, saying that the word '*kuklio*' in Greek meant a circle. Their secret circle. So they rode like a secret club, or clan of friends, through the night - quite harmlessly, so it's told - wearing white sheets and hoods as part of the rites of their secret circle. Then one night they were seen by an old colored man who ran to tell his master that he had just seen ghosts riding through the countryside on horseback. That's how the Ku Klux Klan supposedly learned that colored folks were frightened by hooded riders. Or so that's the story people tell.'

Cramer Crowley took another sip of coffee, then continued. 'Now, as for the group here in Louisiana, The Knights of the Camellia, they are not as organized - nor as famous, yet - as the Ku Klux Klan. But often obscurity leads to viciousness. Violent people revel in acclaim. The Knights also want to protect the South from pollution, to return life here to as it was before the war. But I suspect the Knights are just one more group of cowardly men looking for some kind of recognition, going to all ends to gain notoriety.'

Gemma stared at her own tin coffee mug. 'I guess they aren't too pleased with freed slaves.'

'I'm afraid not, Mrs Rickers.'

'Black people in general?'

'None.'

'Let's just hope there's no clan around here,' Warren said, toying with his spoon. 'No clan. No Knights of those camellia trees. No riders who wear sheets or white hoods.'

Gemma could not look at Warren; she knew he was remembering their first night in Longchamp Parish, the lynching they had seen, the man they had buried.

She asked, 'Mr Crowley, why do things like this happen? In more than one place, but at the same time?'

'I'm no scholar, no wise man, Mrs Rickers. But my answer would be – fear. Anger. Loss of position. Seeing another man taking your place, maybe your property. Then you go for their weak spot.'

'That's happening here? And Tennessee and Georgia? The same thing in all different places?'

'In all the states suffering from the war. Mostly small farmers. Maybe some planters who can use farmers to their advantage. But, all here in the South. You don't hear about such groups forming in Philadelphia, Boston, New York. Men work there. They get rewards. Men work here and get nothing. The Lord doesn't give here at the moment. He just taketh away.'

*　　　*　　　*

'That tall guy ain't a bad-looking fellow, Gemma, but there's something suspicious about him.'

'I know what you mean, Warren. Maybe because he's Irish. We knew lots of those Irish people in Philadelphia who had – I won't say 'bad' ways – but I just wouldn't trust them, that's all.'

'Smart, though. All that Greek talk. Able to translate all those Greek words like Ku . . .'

'Ku Klux Klan.'

Gemma and Warren, lying in bed, discussed for the first time all day the facts which Cramer Crowley had told them about vigilante groups of White men forming in the South; Crowley had left after breakfast; Gemma and Warren had each separately brooded all day and all evening about the stories and theories he had told them. Now, the tallow candle was snuffed out for the night, blankets hung on the windows of the dining-room which served for their temporary bedroom. They both ventured to discuss the subject of vigilante groups, at least to ease their minds for a night's sleep.

'Gemma, you ain't scared, are you?'

'Of those clan people?'

'Them or those Knights?'

'Wouldn't do much good to be scared, would it? If they're going to come get us, Warren, they're going to come get us. We can't stop living. We can't stop working. Stop trying to make a home.'

A silence followed.

Warren finally said, 'Maybe I better visit that Freedmen's Bureau in Kettley again. Just to make contact with somebody around here. Let the Army know we're still here.'

'Don't think about it tonight, Warren.' Gemma rolled over against his warm nakedness. 'You won't be able to sleep.'

'Gemma, you're right, you know that?'

'About what?'

'About worrying. No amount of worrying is going to keep trouble from our door.'

She brushed her lips against his shoulder. 'I still do my share of it.'

Warren turned on the mattress. He lifted one leg and, laying it across Gemma's naked hips, his erect penis poked into her bare skin.

'You know I love you, gal.'

'I love you, too . . .'

They began kissing.

Warren, wrapping one arm around Gemma, pulled her closer toward him, pushing open her legs to make a movement toward the moist patch between her thighs.

Neither Warren nor Gemma spoke as they made love tonight; their embraces were desperate. Warren drove with deep, almost angry passion. Gemma revelled in his fury, she understood his feelings, she shared his vehemence, she welcomed the long, hard, deepening drives.

Warren's penis swelled larger, thicker, became more persistent inside Gemma. They still did not speak, not even when Warren's penis finally exploded white fertile seed deep inside Gemma's motherhood.

*   *   *

79

Warren's whisper eventually broke the long silence.

'We did it.'

'I hope so.'

'We made our baby.'

'You've been planting lots of seeds around here lately, Warren Rickers. Let's just wait and see which ones the Good Lord lets take root and grow.'

'You sorry?'

'Me? Sorry?'

'You sorry we didn't stop this time? Sorry I didn't pull out?'

'I'll show you how sorry I am, Mr Walnuts-and-Cream.'

Gemma slipped down under the sheet; she began working Warren's spent penis with her mouth, tasting the residue of his seed, her own sexuality; she kept working, sucking, pulling his penis with her mouth and hands until she coaxed it back into an erection. She sat on his penis this time, straddling it as she worked herself up and down over his thighs, pumping, pressing, working for a second load of seed, taking it inside her vagina; then slipped down under the sheets to excite him again . . . and again . . . and again . . . to show him she was not sorry.

*   *   *

A map of Longchamp Parish, Louisiana hung among other maps, charts, lists, papers on the walls of an attic room in a grey shingled house on Park Street in the city of Montgomery, Alabama.

The four-storey house looked little different on the outside than it had done during the four-year-period when Montgomery had been the capital of the Confederacy; the recent changes happened on the interior, in the rooms of the various tenants.

Daryl and Edna Stuks recently moved into the basement apartment. Daryl Stuks had worked as a roustabout in the Confederate munitions depot in Montgomery during the war; he had met an officer, Colonel Pat Fenton, and discovered that social – and educational – differences did not

80

alter racial opinions in certain men. Both Stuks and Fenton believed in the superiority of White men, a survival of a society promulgating the enslavement of all Negro people.

Colonel Fenton arranged for Daryl Stuks and his wife, Edna, to move into the house on Park Street at the conclusion of the war. Fenton hired Stuks to travel occasionally through the South and compile a list of Confederate prison camps now being put into disuse, to make notes of their conditions, capacities, accessibility; he also hired Daryl and Edna Stuks to serve as caretaker and housekeeper for the house on Park Street which had long-ago been converted into apartments.

Lieutenant Jeff Ames, another Confederate officer, had originally rented the ground floor apartment for sole occupancy. But Jeff Ames had moved his Negress lover into the apartment with him at the end of the war. Daryl and Edna Stuks, using a basement stairway which had been sealed shut from use during the house's conversion, listened to, and peeked through cracks at, Jeff Ames and his mistress; they discovered that the lover was a transvestite – a delicately-featured young Black man dressed to look like a woman on the street – but at home would only wear bits and pieces of feminine clothing, allowing his penis to dangle in full view, and often beat the army officer with a riding crop, making him perform acts of obedience.

The apartment on the next floor was vacant but had previously been occupied by a short, pudgy, porcine man named James Hirsch, a postal worker who had been discovered molesting a Black school girl in a graveyard and had been lynched by a mob of angry Negro parents. No relatives appeared to claim Mr Hirsch's belongings on Park Street, but, slowly, his possessions – an overstuffed chair, a pair of curtains, a set of china dishes – could be seen in the basement apartment of Daryl and Edna Stuks.

Colonel Pat Fenton occupied the top two floors of the house on Park Street; his living quarters were on one floor and he used the attic rooms for his study, a workshop, a space to keep his extensive library, a small printing press, reports on the Confederate prison camps, lists of names, of the clubs, groups, societies believing in the promulgation of slavery in North America.

Fenton traveled extensively – frequently under assumed names – and spent most of his time in neighboring states in what he considered to be a political, almost religious cause.

Daryl Stuks warned his wife not to snoop in Fenton's possessions. Edna regularly cleaned both the living and office quarters, always hurrying in her job as the rooms frightened her.

Edna Stuks glanced at the maps tracing routes through the thirteen Confederate states. She saw drawings of men hanging from trees, nailed into coffins, crosses burning with large flames. Edna Stuks was semi-illiterate and had tried to read snippets of paper pinned to the wall until she realized they were either Biblical quotations condoning slavery, or theatrical reviews which – her husband explained – came from the pre-war days when Pat Fenton had appeared on the stage as an actor.

Finding the attic rooms eerie, uncomfortable, disquieting, Edna Stuks especially disliked one small room with a wall niche in which set a marble bust of a man – a man with a chin, a mouth, a nose, two ears, but only one eye, a staring, all-knowing eye centered in the middle of his forehead, and seven letters chiselled into the marble base: C-Y-C-L-O-P-S.

Chapter Six

THE WHIPPING

A loud pounding on the kitchen door disturbed Gemma and Warren as they sat eating their breakfast at the scrubbed pine table.

Warren looked up from his strips of fried corn pone. 'Who's that so early?'

'Maybe the tall Irishman looking for more breakfast.'

Gemma was uncharacteristically quiet this morning; she was beginning to realize the obligations of becoming pregnant, having a baby, raising a child in a house that was not yet even a home.

'The Irishman said he might be coming back this way.'

Gemma went to the door and, surprised to see Sabrine Dehasset standing on the doorstep, she said, 'Miss Dehasset! What brings you here this early?'

Sabrine glanced at a horse and buggy parked behind her in the dirt yard and then looked up the driveway leading to the parish road.

'Oh, Mrs Rickers, I'm so sorry to bother you but –'

'Miss Dehasset, what's the trouble?'

Sabrine blurted, 'Please help me!'

'Honey, you come right in!' Gemma moved to wrap her arm around Sabrine and lead her into the kitchen.

Sabrine raised her arms, shook her head in confusion, again glancing at the buggy. 'A boy called Paulie, Mrs Rickers. He's in trouble. I've got to find some place to hide the poor boy. My brother's just threatened him with a whip. Just this morning.'

'Slow down, girl.'

'Maybe I'm doing the wrong thing, Mrs Rickers, by coming to you for help –'

Gemma turned and called, 'Warren, come here.'

Warren had already risen from the table and stood behind

83

Gemma in the doorway; he had only met Sabrine briefly but was pleased that his wife had found a friend in the neighborhood.

Sabrine said, 'Good morning, Mr Rickers. I'm sorry to bother you and your wife so early. But I'm here about a boy working at Belrose. My brother accused him of mistreating his horse. My brother threatened to whip Paulie, and Paulie, he ran to the house to get me to help him. I was up early –'

'Whip him?' Warren felt anger rise in him.

Gemma asked, 'Is the boy Black?'

Warren said, 'Makes no difference what color the boy is. War's changed that.'

He looked at Sabrine and asked, 'Why don't this boy just quit and look for another job, Miss Dehasset?'

'I wish it were that simple, Mr Rickers. But it's not. Paulie's got no place to go. His home, his job at Belrose is the only security he's ever known. I haven't told you much about my brother, Mr Rickers, but Junior is so ornery –'

The loud thundering of horse hooves on the driveway attracted their attention.

Warren, Gemma, and Sabrine looked down the avenue of yellowing cypress trees and saw six White men galloping toward the yard.

'Something tells me, Miss Dehasset, we're going to meet your brother.'

Gemma whispered, 'Warren, get your gun.'

'Do no good, honey. There's more men than me. And, look, they've got their own guns.'

*　　　*　　　*

Junior Dehasset rode with five companions, Dave Cooper, Billy Collins, Sheriff Judd Gillman, Dwight Pine, Ron Wilkie. The men carried guns across their saddles or in long holsters hanging from the sides of their horses. Junior Dehasset carried a gun as well as a long leather whip curled around the horn of his saddle; the six White men drew to a halt between Sabrine's buggy and the back door of the house.

Junior Dehasset pushed back a black felt hat on his head. 'Okay, little sister, where's the kid nigger?'

Sabrine showed mettle. 'Junior Dehasset, you watch your filthy tongue.'

'I ain't got much patience, little sister. Where's the kid nigger?'

'I don't know what you're talking about.'

'Paulie. That's who I'm talking about. And you damned well know why.'

'Paulie? Why would I know anything about Paulie?'

'So you want to play games?' Junior pulled the leather whip from his saddle horn; he unfurled it with a loud snap and a cloud of dust rose from the ground.

Sabrine, standing in front of Gemma and Warren, shrilled, 'You aren't going to whip anybody here, Junior Dehasset!'

Warren stepped forward and put his hand on Sabrine's shoulder. 'I don't know your brother, Mam, but maybe you better let me talk to him.'

'The name's Dehasset, nigger,' Junior called from his saddle. 'Remember it if you're planning to stick around this country longer than five minutes.'

Warren returned Junior's stare. 'If you care to remember my name, it's Warren Rickers.'

'I know who you are . . . nigger.'

Low, wicked laughter spread among the White men mounted on their horses.

Gemma cautioned, 'Warren, hold your tongue, honey. Just hold your tongue.'

Junior danced his horse around the yard; he ordered, 'Dave, you and Judd take a look under that buggy robe and see what you can find.'

Sabrine rushed forward. 'Leave my buggy alone!'

Junior sneered down from his horse, 'You never were good at playing games, little sister. Always were too fair.'

Dave Cooper and Sheriff Judd Gillman rode to either side of the buggy; Cooper pointed his gun at the buggy's tufted leather seat while Sheriff Gillman leaned from his saddle to pull back a maroon woollen robe.

85

'Pull back the robe now!' Junior ordered.

Sabrine ran forward. 'Leave my buggy alone!'

But she was too late; everybody stared at Paulie crouching on the buggy floor.

'Keep talking, little sister, and you'll find yourself arrested. Don't forget Judd Gillman is Sheriff around here. He can arrest you for interfering with justice.'

'Whipping is not justice, Junior!' Sabrine shrieked at her brother. 'It's just another way for you to feel important.'

Junior turned to Cooper and Gillman. 'Take the kid nigger to that hitching post over there. Strip off his shirt.'

Turning to the other men, he ordered, 'Dwight and Billy, you bring some rope to tie up his arms good to the post.'

Warren moved forward to protest.

Gemma grabbed his arm. 'Be sensible, Warren. Be sensible.'

'But that boy!'

'Be sensible.'

Junior snapped his whip; he called to Sabrine, 'Little sister, get your nigger friends in the house. Tell them not to try anything smart. The same thing can happen to them. Maybe worse.'

He swung his leg over the saddle, dismounting with whip in hand.

*   *   *

The White men shoved Paulie face down across the hitching post then knotted his wrists to both ends of the post with rope. They ripped the shirt from his back.

Junior stood silently behind them, watching as the men secured Paulie into position; he finally took a stance behind Paulie. He snapped the whip in the dirt. Dust rose and before it settled he hurled the whip lashing Paulie across his bare back.

Junior struck again. Again. His face became sober. He regripped the butt of the bullwhip. He kept his boots firmly planted. He struck a fourth, fifth, sixth time.

The men, closely watching each strike, began to talk to each other.

'Maybe we should take bets,' Sheriff Gillman suggested. 'See how many stripes the nigger can take before passing out.'

'I say no more than twenty and he's gone.'

'You got a bet, Dwight.'

'Give it to him, Junior!' called Dave Cooper. 'Remind him of the good old days when White men were masters.'

'White man's still master - least around here.'

'Going to get tougher for other niggers, too.'

Junior no longer listened, nor spoke, to his friends; he concentrated on the aim of his bullwhip.

Swinging his body with each stroke, Junior discovered that - by pivoting his stroke from the waist - he could put more strength into each lash, make the whip fly more quickly through the air, catching Paulie's skin with neater, tighter, sharper stings.

Paulie's back was bleeding, laddered with welts and open cuts, covered with a deep redness across his shoulder blades, down to his waist.

Junior listened to the hypnotic strike of each blow, like a metronome of leather, snapping, cracking, striking in rhythm. He gauged after the twenty-third lash that Paulie had lost all consciousness.

But Junior felt the urge to send a few last singing lashes against the dark body. Seeing that the tip of his whip was tangled with skin, he pulled back the whip over his shoulder with a loud crack - he cracked it over his shoulder again, and again, to clean off the tip.

Then, repositioning his boots in the dirt, Junior took aim to make his last few marks on Paulie's bleeding body.

Behind Junior, the other men were arguing, laughing, cursing about who had won the wager about how many lashes it had taken to make the Black man unconscious.

*   *   *

Warren rushed to cut Paulie's bleeding body from the post as soon as the men galloped down the driveway.

He called, 'Gemma! Get water! Clean rags!'

87

Gemma, her heart beating with terror, her fists tightened with anger, shouted, 'I found herb salve in the barn last week. That'll help, too!'

Sabrine Dehasset, standing helplessly in the yard, was only now beginning to realize the mistake she had made in bringing Paulie here.

She watched Gemma and Warren hurriedly working to untie Paulie, balance him between them and lead him toward the house. She did not notice another White person coming over the hill.

*   *   *

'What's happening around here?'

The voice startled Sabrine; she jumped and looked over her shoulder; she saw a tall, curly-headed man leading a cow by a rope and balancing a crate of cackling chickens on his shoulder.

'What's all the fuss going on?'

'Who are you?' she asked.

'Name's Cramer Crowley. Where's Gemma? Warren?'

'You know them?'

'Well enough to bring them a little present.' Cramer Crowley lowered the crate of chickens to the ground and dropped the rope by which he had been leading the milk cow. 'Pardon me for saying so, Mam, but you look a little bit ruffled. Disturbed.'

'My name's Sabrine Dehasset and –'

Sabrine stopped; she looked from Cramer Crowley, to the crateful of cackling chickens; to the milk cow with its watery big eyes; she impulsively threw her arms around Cramer Crowley, burying her face in his chest, crying, 'Oh, help us! Please help us!'

Cramer Crowley patted Sabrine's golden hair. 'Everything's going to be all right, Mam. All right indeed.'

He smiled. He guessed that Sabrine Dehasset must be the daughter of Senator Dehasset, the sister of Junior Dehasset. He kept patting her golden hair and smiling to himself.

*   *   *

Junior Dehasset did not explain the sexual excitement he
still felt hours after whipping Paulie; he could not explain the
feeling of power which made his penis swell hard and remain
erect without the coaxing of words or the manipulation of
squeezing fingers. Junior Dehasset stood with his trousers
dropped down to his ankles and held Rose Starett to her
knees in front of him on the floor; he pressed her head
against his groin with the force of both hands, driving his
small but firmly erect penis farther, deeper, more violently
into her mouth, ignoring the gagging sound she was
beginning to make. Rose could not breathe as Junior selfishly
drove his penis into her mouth; she began to retch; bile rose
in her throat, then came the vomit, first in short spurts, next
in full gushes; vomit soon surrounded Junior's penis but he
did not stop pushing the small organ harder and faster into
her stretched mouth; he felt as if his penis was twice, three
times, five times, even ten times larger than its actual size, he
felt like a man brimming with masculinity, a man who was
White and strong and hung like a stallion who had authority
over all inferior people . . . over slaves . . . over women . . .
over Black people . . . prostitutes . . . females who knelt in
front of him and had to vomit when they sucked him because
his penis was so big, so thick.

89

Chapter Seven

THE FREEDMEN'S BUREAU

Cramer Crowley did not divulge to Gemma and Warren Rickers where he had found the milk cow, nor the crateful of chickens, which included one rooster with a majestic red comb. Gemma and Warren were pleased to receive such important - and useful - gifts and did not press him for details.

They had agreed to keep their mouths shut about many things after the morning Junior Dehasset had flogged Paulie; they concentrated on their own world, which now included making a cabin habitable in the slave quarter for Paulie. The herb salve worked its miracle on Paulie's back and he showed signs of a quick recovery. But Gemma and Warren suggested to Sabrine Dehasset - and received her immediate agreement - that Paulie should not move back to Belrose Plantation, never again be subjected to physical punishment. Paulie gratefully accepted the offer of a new home in one of the few habitable cabins in the old slave quarters. Gemma and Warren less graciously accepted Sabrine's gift of the horse-and-buggy. But Sabrine insisted on bestowing the gift; the buggy, the horse remained at the old Chatgrove place along with Paulie to care for it.

Paulie pledged to work in the garden, the fields, the barn in exchange for a cabin and food; he began planting, fertilizing, weeding, hoeing, and eventually harvesting crops on acreage which lay behind the slave quarters and in front of the pine-covered hills bordering the back of the property.

Warren devoted much of his time in the passing days to mend the roof on the house for the approaching winter months, to repair the barn for the treasured milk cow, to fix the springhouse for storing milk, butter, cream. Warren and Paulie together propped up the old chicken coop for the cackling hens and their strutting rooster. Warren still promised Gemma that he would try to convert an upstairs bedroom by winter. Warren and Gemma were still sleeping in the dining-room. Gemma tried not to grumble about the temporary sleeping arrangements; she longed for the time, though, when she could cover the dining-room walls with colorful paper, hang velvet portieres from the tall windows, serve piping hot food from china dishes set with silver cutlery on a shiny mahogany table, and pour cool lemonade from a cut-glass Waterford pitcher. Gemma was nevertheless grateful for the white iron bedstead which Warren dragged down from an upstairs bedroom and reassembled in the dining-room near the fireplace.

The mornings were becoming touched with autumn coolness; Gemma was feeling sickly. Her monthly bleeding had long ago stopped; she was pregnant. Gemma and Warren accepted the pregnancy with a calmness, a matter-of-factness which surprised both of them. But Warren tried to force Gemma to lessen her work load. He could not keep her from boiling a daily stewpot, though, in the backyard for the increasing numbers of beggars – itinerant freed slaves – approaching the house for food.

Gemma could not turn away anyone hungry; she argued with Warren that their land was proving fruitful and that they must share good fortune with less fortunate people.

Gemma welcomed the freed slaves – men, women, children dressed in rags, carrying no more than a few soiled bundles – with enthusiasm, warmth, a ready ear to listen to each sad story.

A young mother, no older than twenty years, arrived with three little boys – all under six-years-old – who had shaven heads to protect them from lice.

The mother explained, 'My man and me, we picked cotton side-by-side in Alabama. Freedom came and we heard work was going here in Louisiana. But Tiger – he was my man – got sick in the belly one night and never woke up the next morning. I just don't know what to do now, Missy, except to walk and walk and walk, take my little boys here and walk till we come to the end of the world. Oh, why, Missy, why did Freedom day ever have to come?'

A young couple, Sara and Todd, told Gemma they were not yet wed and had planned to jump the broom on their old plantation near Natchez. Todd explained, 'We hears broom-jumping now outlawed, now no way for colored folks to get hitched. So we got no money to pay a preacher and we don't know what to do. My Sara here is knocked up and we wonder if we're going to end up buried in some camptown starving to death. Or should we forget about jumping the broom and just jump over the cliff, Sara, the baby in her belly, and me - all of us jump over a cliff and meet happy in Heaven? Is that what the Lord means us to do now?'

Gemma had never before heard so many people speak about suicide; she encouraged men, women, young people to try to live for the future, the spirit of Black people, the families they would raise. But she could never provide an adequate answer for the one inevitable question - 'What we do for food, Missy? For home? For shelter? For work?'

Warren did convince Gemma, though, not to try to harbor homeless people, not to give refuge to the lame, the sickly, the blind; the line would be endless straggling down the drive, he told her, and they would soon be just one more camptown dotted on the bleak map of freedom. He also cautioned her of the diseases she could contract from the wandering free slaves and risk the health of the infant growing larger inside her womb week by week, month by month.

Also, during these days when frost began to cover the ground and branches became barren shapes against a grey sky, Gemma and Warren were laughing less with one another. They stopped calling each other playful nicknames. A youthful silliness, a childlike spirit had disappeared from their lives. The sombre change was fueled by the migrant slaves, the constant talk of suicides, hopelessness, starva-tion, but it dated from the summer morning when the White men from Bossburg had tied Paulie to the hitching-post in the backyard and Junior Dehasset had whipped him into unconsciousness.

Gemma and Warren had come to face the bitter fact that

they had moved to, were building a home in a hostile land, that they would be raising their family in a country where White people still whipped Negroes as if they were slaves.

*   *   *

'Every nigger in the parish has to register.'

'Rubbish. Only freed slaves register.'

'That's how it is in Kettley, Pa. But the new Bureau in Bossburg's going to be different – a hell of a lot different!'

The Dehasset family lingered over coffee, cognac and small silver trays of *petits fours* in the dining-room at Belrose. Senator Dehasset and his son, Junior, again argued about the new Freedmen's Bureau scheduled to open by the late winter, early spring time in Bossburg.

The after dinner conversation bored Noele Dehasset and, toying with the opals dangling from her long filigree gold necklace, she waited until it was time to take an evening stroll down to the pergola.

Sabrine sat oblivious to her father's and brother's increasingly heated argument. She thought about the handsome young Irishman she had met – '*Has three months already passed?*' – at Gemma and Warren Rickers on the morning that Junior had whipped Paulie.

Senator Dehasset, sitting at the position of *pater familias* at the head of the fruitwood table, asked his son, 'What if some people were born in freedom? Not in slavery, but in freedom? Do they register in Bossburg?'

'They Black?' Junior picked at a crescent of dirt under one fingernail.

'For the sake of argument, say they are Black. But were not slaves at the time of freedom. Say they had already been manumitted, or born free.'

'If they're Black, then they register.'

The Senator banged his fist and shook the crystal wine glasses, 'But that contravenes Federal law!'

'Federal or not, that's law around here far as I'm concerned, Pa.'

'But Junior! Men must answer to a higher and greater

93

authority than friends of yours like Judd Gillman – that man who calls himself Sheriff.'

'Nobody around here said Gillman ain't Sheriff!' Junior grinned at his father.

'I agree. Nobody's complained. But most people are probably too frightened to speak out!' The Senator glanced at his wife and, seeing her slip away from the table, guessed that she was bored. He saw that Sabrine was daydreaming and not listening to the conversation; he chanced to mention a subject he had avoided speaking about before now to any member of his family.

He said, 'That so-called Sheriff Gillman's no better than those . . . Klansmen running riot in Georgia, Tennessee and the Carolinas in their white robes and hoods.'

Junior nonchalantly replied, 'No Ku Klux Klan around here, Pa.'

'One small blessing in our favor,' said Senator Dehasset. Then casually, slowly, he said, 'How you heard about the Klan, by the way? I didn't know their existence was public knowledge.'

'Keep my ears open.' Junior himself wondered if his father was testing him, parrying with him, trying to learn how much he knew about vigilante groups.

'A damn bunch of trouble-makers,' grumbled the old politician.

Junior chanced, 'You have the same low opinion about the Knights of the Camellia?'

'Knights of the Camellia?' The Senator played ignorant, he did not want to betray he had learned of the group. 'Who in tarnation are the Knights of the Camellia?'

'Another police force. Like the Klan.'

Senator Dehasset could not hold back the explosion. 'Police force? The Ku Klux Klan's nothing but thugs and bully-boys. Cold blooded killers and terrorists who trample on human rights. Men who make mockery of justice.'

'You talk high and mighty about justice, Pa. But there's also something called law and order. Citizens are meant to live in an orderly fashion. That means keeping track of possible troublemakers. Keeping pins on them.'

'Junior, you're no better than a tyrant! A despot!'

'If despot's another word for a red-blooded man willing to fight for law and order, then I guess I just might be a despot, Pa.'

Senator Dehasset gripped the edge of the table; his face reddened with fury.

Junior teased, 'You look like you're going to bust a gut, Pa. I'd hate to have you kick the bucket before you get the chance to add your name to a good cause.'

'Good cause? What good cause?'

Junior did not want to be too specific. 'Times are changing, Pa. So's prosperity. Belrose might not always be so rich. Ever consider that? Niggers and Yanks getting too much power?'

'I manage Belrose, Junior. And as long as I do, this land will prosper.'

Senator Dehasset knew his son was challenging him – like a young bull – but he could not keep from performing a father's duty and warn Junior for his own safety; he said, 'You involve yourself in Reconstruction politics, Junior, and the Union army might make trouble for you. Bad trouble. So go cautiously in Bossburg.'

Junior leaned back on the back legs of his chair. He boasted, 'I already talked to the Army in Kettley, Pa. They're glad to get a local man like me, ease their burden.'

'Nevertheless, don't forget the Freedmen's Bureau is a branch of the War Department, an official Union agency.'

'Official! Every man with a brain knows the Bureau is only as official as the political party in office at the moment. Today it's Republican. They're trumping up nigger votes for the Republican party. Matter of fact, Pa, that's exactly why they're buying my idea of getting every nigger in the parish to register with the Bureau. Registering could mean more votes for them, and more ways of keeping count of niggers in the parish.'

'Pernicious!' Senator Dehasset believed in total freedom for everyone, an equality among people if the Government recognized them as citizens. 'Foul, pernicious despotism!'

95

'Call it what you want, Pa, but Republicans are going along!'

'Republicans! The party system is a necessary evil of government.'

'You say that, Pa, because you're in a minority now. There's no way you can interfere to stop the new Bureau, the registering, not even folks calling Judd Gillman "Sheriff".'

'Junior, I never thought I'd see the day a son of mine would divide this family.'

Junior held his challenging eyes on his father; he said, 'Lots of things I do might surprise you, Pa. Don't forget, you always called me a redneck. The bad apple in the Dehasset barrel. It's Sabrine – lovely, sweet, do-gooder Sabrine – who's the apple of the old man's eye. Face it, I'm just your embarrassment. I don't squat to pee. I don't tuck a hanky up my sleeve. I just a red-blooded, hairy-chested, wild-living . . . man!'

Junior Dehasset, leaning forward in his chair, pounded a fist into the palm of his other hand; Senator Dehasset sat across from him shaking his head, wishing Sabrine were his heir instead of this bully he called 'Junior'.

*   *   *

Autumn chilled the evening air as Noele Dehasset hurried across Belrose's moonlit lawn which sloped to the lake and slipped into the pergola where Ken had come to meet her.

Ken, usually visiting Paulie at the old Chatgrove place during these night-time hours, resented a late rendezvous with Noele Dehasset. He was pleased that the weather was cold, that she seemed to be uncharacteristically anxious, eager to finish love-making tonight with little foreplay.

But she was also uncharacteristically talkative; she lay on her cushions and asked, 'What do you think about when you lay on me like this?'

Noele's question startled Ken; the words broke his concentration on imagining he was making love to Paulie.

'Think? I guess I think of that bicycle I seen in that picture book.'

'No. Apart from the bicycle. A bicycle could not make you . . . hard in me.'

'Freedom makes me hard. I think of being a free man and I get hard and could stay hard all night.'

'Freedom?' Noele crossed both wrists in front of her, confessing, 'I think the opposite - bondage.'

Ken reached to grasp her thin wrists with one hand as he had always done in the past.

'No,' Noele whispered. 'Tie me.'

'Tie you?'

'Instead of gripping me, tie me.'

'Tie you with . . . what?'

'Rope . . . chains . . .' Noele reached for the long golden chain still hanging over her bare neck. She said, 'Tie my wrists with this. But not too tight. Don't mark me.'

Ken held the gold chain dangling with opals and studied its preciousness; he said, 'This might break. It looks thin, expensive.'

Noele fleetingly thought that Ken might tie her up and steal the heirloom opal necklace. But she put the idea from her head, thinking, 'The darkies here have always been honest. Lazy, stupid, and honest.'

*   *   *

The talk of the Freedmen's Bureau at the supper table made Sabrine Dehasset think even more of Cramer Crowley; she had become obsessed with the tall, dark-haired Irishman since she had met him at the old Chatgrove place.

Was she a fool, she wondered, to love a man yet know so little about him? She had heard talk of dangerous strangers since she had been a little girl. Especially about pedlars. But Sabrine still could not believe that Cramer Crowley was a pedlar. She had never seen his bottles of Firefly Water. She never heard him talking about selling it anywhere specific. But why would he lie to her? Why else would he be in Longchamp Parish? And keep disappearing, then coming back?

The beeswax candle in the pewter candlestick on Sabrine's

bedside table threw strange shadows across the blue and yellow canopy of her bed. She inched the finger of her right hand down the flatness of her stomach toward the furry delta between her legs as her brain revolved with images of the only man who had ever excited her appetite – the curly hair, the long lashes, the boyish grin.

'Stop it,' she told herself, pulling back her hand and pushing her white nightdress of broderie anglaise down over her naked legs.

Sabrine snuffed the candle out next to the bed, pulled the sheets over her shoulder and told herself to go to sleep.

But she could not get the image of Cramer Crowley out of her mind. She wondered if he thought about her. He had not even made a pass at her.

'Maybe he's a carpetbagger,' she thought, smiling at such an absurd idea, 'or some radical politician. Maybe he really hates all Southerners, even us women!'

Sabrine tossed in her bed, telling herself to go to sleep, to stop thinking about Firefly Water, politicians, and, especially, to forget her gnawing sexual desires.

One last thought floated through her brain: 'Maybe he's an actor just pretending to be partial to me, to be Irish, to be a traveling pedlar . . .'

She rolled over in bed, telling herself. 'Stop it! Go to sleep!'

*   *   *

Cramer Crowley also thought about Sabrine Dehasset the same night despite the fact he met two other young women for love-making.

But Cramer did not have his usual interest in the two young Black girls, Sari and Dina, when he met at their new rendezvous located in a birch copse beyond the Bossburg crossroads.

Sari and Dina, both girls who enjoyed making love with one another, or together with a man, sidled against each side of Cramer's bare chest and tried to find out what bothered the usually ebullient, sexually voracious White man – the man they called Pedlar Man.

'What's the matter, Mister Pedlar Man?' asked Sari. 'You found yourself a sweetheart?'

'Maybe you already made love today?' said Dina.

Cramer Crowley, holding an arm around each of the girl's necks, pulled them toward him and reassured, 'My mood has nothing to do with you two brown beauties. I'm just thinking about some other people I met.'

'Who they be, Mister Pedlar Man? You meet new girls?'

Cramer did not want to talk about Sabrine; he answered, 'I meet many people. Two people I met are a young couple. The husband and wife settled in our old meeting place.'

'The two darkies at the old Chatgrove place?'

'They're the ones,' he said.

'We seen them too,' said the girl named Sari. 'We seen them come there with their carpetbags and bundles.'

Dina announced, 'We were making love in our old shed there when we seen them hugging and laughing and swinging each other round in circles like two crazy people.'

The two brown-skinned girls, moving to squat naked in front of Cramer, wrapped their arms around one another; Dina eagerly asked, 'Why you thinking about them? They don't ruin nothing. Not for us. We found a new place to meet.'

Sari added, 'The only person who gets angry about them new niggers being there is our master.'

'Your . . . master?'

Sari explained, 'Mister Herc likes his privacy. Something like you, Mr Pedlar Man. Master Herc don't want nobody living close on that land, I guess. He gets rightly jealous about everything, even land.'

Cramer considered the fact; he said, 'I know you told me you could get punished for meeting me.'

'Our master has other girls besides us. But he's jealous of us all.'

Sari nodded. 'Master Herc would especially punish us for seeing another man!'

'But we still take the chance, Mr Pedlar Man. We like you. You make us feel real good. We still don't know much about you. But we like you, Mr Pedlar Man.'

Cramer did not want to tell the two girls - or anybody in the parish - too much about his private life, the true nature of his travels in the South.

Wanting to change the subject from himself, Cramer reached toward Sari's breast and fingered a small golden ring he saw pierced through her nipple; he asked, 'What's this?'

He looked at Dina kneeling alongside Sari; he saw she also had a ring pierced through her nipple. 'You've got one, too. Why have you pierced your nipples?'

'Our Master did it,' answered Dina.

'Master Herc did it,' said Sari.

'Master Herc? He pierced your nipples?'

Sari nodded. 'And put rings in them.'

Cramer was intrigued. 'Did it hurt?'

'A little. When he first put in the hot pin to make the hole.'

'Does it still hurt?'

'When Master Herc pulls them.'

'Pulls them?'

'Master Herc gets mean. But not as mean to the Black girls living with him as he does to the White woman. You should see the way Master Herc treats poor White mistress at High Hill. She is more slave sometimes than all the Black girls in the house.'

High Hill. Master Herc. A White woman living with a virile ex-slave. Cramer Crowley had never been to the isolated plantation called High Hill, nor had he ever seen the Negro named Master Herc, nor the White woman there who was his lover.

Cramer Crowley had met these two young Negresses from Herc's harem, Sari and Dina, on a back country road little more than a year ago; he had made love to both of them; they had told him about the strange, isolated place - High Hill - where they lived in a big redbrick house with the Negro named Master Herc who kept Black girls living inside with him and his White mistress. Cramer had subsequently met Sari and Dina on his visits to Longchamp Parish; he told them his usual story - that he was a pedlar - and tried not to show too much interest in the strange place where they lived.

100

But he wondered now why their master, the Black man named Herc, might be upset about Gemma and Warren Rickers moving on to the old Chatgrove place, why their presence on the land would trouble . . .

The sound of wet licking disturbed Cramer's thoughts; he saw both girls laying head-to-foot on the ground, tonguing one another's vagina.

He sat watching the two lithesome girls making love to one another and the image of Sabrine Dehasset popped into his mind; he imagined Sabrine being one of the girls; he next visualized himself laying head-to-foot with Sabrine; they were savoring one another's sexuality. Cramer's penis hardened with the thought. He knew that the roundabout position would only be foreplay, that he would do what he wanted to do since the first morning he had seen Sabrine at the old Chatgrove place, that he would lay upon her body, that he would feel her gentle femininity under him, satisfying him, feeling her becoming satisfied by him being on top of her, inside her, alongside her, around her.

Cramer put the thoughts out of his head. He knew it would not be that easy. Not yet. If at all. He had his work. She had her family.

*   *   *

Ken left Belrose Plantation after Noele Dehasset returned to the big house and the autumn moon shone brightly in the night sky; Ken ran through the backwoods, following a path he had come to know well, jumping over fallen logs, hurrying to enjoy at least a few hours with Paulie in his new home. Paulie waited anxiously for Ken's visit; he greeted him in total nakedness, both arms outstretched; they gripped one another, hugged in a tight embrace; Paulie immediately began to undress Ken's body, to taste the perspiration from the midnight run beading the skin tightly covering his athletic frame, to wrap his lips around the penis already firm and ready for the meeting. But Ken reached down to Paulie sinking to his knees in front of him; he did not want the younger man to taste his penis, to put his mouth on it, not

101

tonight. And Paulie guessed the reason why Ken was protesting, that Ken had been with Noele Dehasset again tonight and did not want his lover to dirty his mouth, to soil his lips, to taint his tongue with any hint of a woman's sexuality, not that woman's. Paulie rose to his feet, chewed Ken's ear, whispered that nothing he did could soil him, and, soon, the two men lay naked, head-to-foot, on the cotton mattress spread on the cabin floor; they lay mouth to midsection, two muscular black shapes in the darkness; one pair of large veined hands squeezing the other male's buttocks, pressing them to bring the penis deeper into his mouth; the other pair of workman's hands gripping his male partner's thighs, also taking his manhood into his mouth, hungrily wanting closeness, love, working for a crest of passion before the time quickly arrived when Ken had to get dressed, hurry back through the woods to Belrose, and Paulie had to get a few hours sleep so he could arise fresh, full of strength in the morning to work alongside Warren. It was after these meetings – after nights of love-making with Ken which always culminated with them being separated by the distance between Belrose and the old Chatgrove place – that nineteen-year-old Paulie began to realize perhaps two men could in fact live together as Ken wanted; two men could maybe share the same cabin, exist as lovers, not ever be parted from one another for longer than a work day, maybe even working side-by-side, building a home, becoming one another's family. Was such an arrangement possible between two men? Between a nineteen-year-old boy and a man ten years older? Was such a wish doomed?

*   *   *

Autumn in Longchamp Parish. Rose Starett welcomed the turn in the weather, the daytime's clear blue skies, the nights being too chilly for the majority of her male visitors to leave the snug warmth of their homes to ride into Bossburg and satisfy their lust with her. Rose Starett sat on a straightback chair alongside her upstairs window in Fowley's General Store during the light hours of day, watching wagons creak

102

along the street turning into mire from the autumn rains; she saw sickly White families bringing their few pennies to spend in the store, or toting small sacks of vegetables and withered fruit to barter for a slice of salt pork, a piece of smoked beef. Rose Starett seldom saw Negroes on the main street; the freed slaves avoided White settlements, passing instead through the woods as they moved from camptown to camptown, fearing the residents of small towns like Bossburg where White people were often as impoverished as the freed slaves themselves; the poor Whites cursed Negroes, threw stones at them, sicked dogs on them, did everything in their power to remind themselves that they might be poor but at least they were White.

Wrapped in the warmth of her patchwork quilts, Rose Starett looked out the window into the night and saw clouds drifting in front of the harvest moon, heard owls hoot in the branches of barren trees, listened to squirrels, chipmunks, rats scamper across the moss-covered roof.

Night hours without men dominating her body became a luxury for Rose Starett. She had finally stopped crying for her dead husband; she also cried less and less for her child, Frankie, taken from her by his uncle. Time - and mistreatment - had taught Rose Starett that she must now begin to fend for herself; she saw, she heard, she learned in the night how other creatures protected themselves from predators.

Rose Starett watched the field mouse run from the owl swooping from a barren branch; she heard hens squawking to raise an alarm against the fox sneaking from the soggy woods; she heard the haggard, bedraggled mother of fourteen children who lived next door cry and scream at her whiskey drunk husband to leave her alone in bed; she watched a snake slither out of the path of a rusty wagon wheel rumbling along the muddy street.

Sitting in her chair by the window, wrapped in her patchwork quilts, Rose Starett studied the world of night creatures and kept her hands busy, occupied, constantly working, sharpening the blade of a knife on a whetstone, persistently rubbing the long blade against the whetstone,

103

working the knife into a long, narrow shaft – almost as thin as a hatpin.

Rose Starett did not know when the time would come. She did not know if it would be soon. She did not know if she would have to wait for years. But she knew she would be able to protect herself, to be like the snake, the hen, the field mouse, the mistreated woman next door, one of the many little insignificant creatures of the night threatened by larger, stronger, more important predators.

Chapter Eight

A GIRL FOR A GIRL

The wind shook the window panes, whistled down the chimney and made the flames dance wildly across the sputtering pine logs heaped on the iron grate in the fireplace. A torrent of rain drummed against the roof and the deluge formed small lakes in the dirt yard, as forks of lightning streaked across the sky and the hills shook with thunder.

Warren Rickers ran back and forth from the bedroom to the kitchen, opening the door to see if Paulie had come back yet in the horse and buggy, pushing the door shut against the force of the wind, bolting it, then running back to the fireside to check on Gemma's condition.

The birthing time approached; Gemma tried to be brave, tried not to make Warren more nervous than he already was by asking if Paulie had come back yet with Broody Hen.

Warren and Gemma had debated all autumn about asking the old midwife, Broody Hen, to deliver their child; Warren wanted a doctor to bring their first child into the world, but the nearest doctor was thirty miles away in Kettley. They finally had decided that they must put their trust in the old black crone who had directed them to this house by explaining the countryside as if it were a clock. The old woman who had bragged she'd never lost a mother nor a child.

The decision made less sense to Warren as the storm became more fierce; he paced the floor, complaining, 'Who needs a midwife anyway? I can do anything she can.'

Beads of perspiration lined Gemma's forehead; she tried to smile, saying, 'Watch your bragging, Big Papa. You might have to play doc!'

The seriousness of the occasion – and its excitement – brought back the air of playfulness, of nickname-calling to the house which recently had been so heavy with gloom.

Warren's eyes widened. 'You close, honey?'

'Getting closer and closer . . .'

'Hold it!' Warren fell to his knees alongside the bed, pleading, 'Oh, hold it just a few more seconds! I know that crazy old gal might not be the best I could get for you, Buttercup. But she's the only one in the parish.'

Gemma reached for Warren's face. 'Don't apologize, Mr Love. Don't apologize . . .'

She stopped; she rolled back her eyes.

'What's the matter? It coming?'

'Baby's threatening, Warren. She threatening to come.'

'*She?*' Warren jerked his head. 'I gave you strict orders for a boy.'

The pain eased. Gemma gulped for air; she answered, 'You get what me and old Broody Hen gives you.'

'Where is that crazy old coot?'

Warren jumped to his feet, dashed from the bedroom, opening the kitchen door again to see if Paulie had returned from the Dasher place.

*   *   *

Broody Hen, wrapped in a brown blanket dripping water, burst into the kitchen door with Big Spanker following her with a worn leather black satchel in her hand.

Broody immediately set Big Spanker busy in the kitchen boiling water and tearing the sheets while she herself began carving a peg of wood.

Broody Hen, standing alongside Gemma's bed, handed her the small peg of wood, explaining, 'Bite hard on this thingamabob when you feel the pain bad. Don't fight the pain. Just fight, bite, talk back to this here thingamabob I makes for you. Understand, gal?'

Gemma nodded, perspiration now running in rivulets down her face.

'You ain't going to get feisty and make things tough for me?'

106

Gemma shook her head.

'Feisty gals have more trouble birthing than sweet ones. Feisty gals always think they know better.'

Warren pushed between Broody Hen and the bed; he leaned over Gemma, saying, 'If I can make things easier, Sugar Top, you just tell me.'

'I know . . .'

Broody Hen cocked her head at Warren. 'You want this bozo nigger buck hanging around acting like a stump in a plowing field?'

'He's the Pa.' Gemma's voice was weakening.

Broody snorted. 'He's got the stomach to watch?'

Warren flared, 'If my wife's got the strength to have the baby, then I sure in heck got the strength to watch!'

Broody chewed her toothless gums, finally saying, 'Men! Think they're so strong! But you know what folks say, don't you? Folks say the Good Lord made women do birthing because men are too . . . weak for it!'

Turning to the kitchen, Broody Hen called, 'Spanker! What you doing out there? Snooping through all the cupboards? Looking for hard candy and peach jam? Bring me that water, big girl!'

Gemma let out a scream.

Warren fell back to his knees alongside the bed.

Broody Hen pushed him aside and ordered Gemma, 'Bite, honey! Bite on that peg!'

She called, 'Spanker! Get yourself in here, big gal!'

*   *   *

Warren squinted his eyes, covered his ears, tried not to hear, to see Gemma suffering birthing pains eased by no medication, no liquor. Gemma grasped Warren's hand for reassurance but Broody Hen kept shooing him away, repeating for Gemma not to fight the birthing, to let the baby flow from her body.

Broody Hen, after six hours of lightning, thunder and screams, coaxed Gemma into giving birth to a small brown infant; Broody Hen grasped it by the feet, smacked it with her hand, waited for squalls to fill the room, then announced, 'You got yourself a daughter!'

Gemma smiled weakly from the bed.

'A daughter,' Warren said, 'Emmaline.'

Gemma and Warren had agreed to name a girl in honor of the woman – Emmaline Chatgrove – who had willed them this land.

Broody Hen snorted, 'Emmaline? Pretty enough name. But more likely she should be called Friday Night.'

'Friday Night?'

'That's the only night of the week you sodbusters get around to doing any bedwork, ain't it? Friday night?'

Warren and Gemma ignored Broody Hen's eccentricity; they stared in awe at their little daughter.

'After you two get over oohing and aahing over Friday there, I'd like to talk to you about payment.'

Warren turned from the bed; he was eager to call Paulie to take Broody Hen back to her house. The storm had slackened and he hoped the sky was clearing.

Broody dropped her head, suddenly mumbling, 'I don't know if it's right, me asking now.'

'Go ahead,' Warren ordered. 'Ask.'

Broody chewed her toothless gums; Big Spanker stood in the kitchen doorway, admiring the newly born infant.

Broody Hen slowly proceeded to explain, 'Maybe this is the right time to ask then. I just helped give you a girl's life. I'm asking you for a girl's life in return.'

*　　　　*　　　　*

Broody Hen studied her gnarled brown hands clasped in front of her round stomach as she explained. 'Miss Francey Dasher, she's got no kin left in the world. It ain't my place, nor Big Spanker's here, to go jawing to you about the poor girl's private life. Her folks were our old masters. But, well, it just ain't fitting and proper for no girl – regardless who she be – to go on living and acting and behaving so queer like that little gal does since the war.'

Warren remembered the Dasher girl, her ragged white

108

wedding veil flowing in the breeze, the big white dog trotting alongside her in the weeds.

'You folks come from up North,' Broody said, her head still hung from embarrassment. 'We was wondering, Spanker here and me, if you'd put your mind to thinking of somebody decent up North who might be willing to give Miss Francey a chance, to take her and maybe give her another start in life. The war kind of took the last chance away from her.'

Warren asked, 'And that's all you're asking for tonight's work?'

Broody jerked her head. 'All? That seems to me, buck nigger, like a heck of a lot to be asking.'

Gemma, weak and tired, called from the bed, 'You get your wish.'

Broody turned to the bed. 'May the Good Lord bless you, Missy, and your little Friday.'

'We'll find your little lady some place nice and respectable,' Gemma promised.

Big Spanker moved forward from the kitchen doorway; she lowered both large hands to her thick thighs; she gripped her thin cotton skirt and whispered, 'Thanking you rightly, Missy,' and dropped into a curtsey.

Chapter Nine

THE LOVE DOLLY

'**S**he looks like a princess.'

'Don't get me started about little Friday, Miss Dehasset, or you won't be able to shut me up!'

'Little . . . Friday?'

'Oh, we're all crazy around here. Everybody's got a nickname. Friday's just one of our silly nicknames for Emmaline.'

The birth of Emmaline Rickers revitalized Gemma's and Warren's spirits; they concentrated the majority of their energies on the healthy infant and threw the rest of their strength into planting a spring crop and resuming the renovation of the old Chatgrove house.

Warren made a cradle from a bureau drawer, padded the inside with a goosedown quilt and put it on rockers. The cradle set in the kitchen during the day next to the table and, at night, Warren carried it upstairs to the bedroom he had finished for Gemma and himself.

Gemma, having just finished breast-feeding Emmaline, rocked the cradle as she visited with Sabrine Dehasset in the kitchen.

Gemma leaned over the cradle and playfully pushed a colorful rag doll against Emmaline's stomach. 'Look how she loves her new toy!'

Sabrine Dehasset had brought a rag doll as a present for Emmaline; she had made it herself, using brown cotton for the doll's face, arms and legs, stitching dark brown yarn for hair and tying the yarn into two pigtails with strips of red calico. The little brown doll wore a yellow gingham dress, with puffy bell sleeves and a full length white apron bordered with lace.

'I plan to make more doll clothes,' Sabrine promised. 'Party dresses and petticoats and sunbonnets. But I just couldn't resist bringing little Emmaline her first toy as soon as I finished it.'

'Miss Dehasset, you do so much for us. You bring so many little treats. Jams. Jellies. Cookies. I'm not even going to mention that horse and buggy, and now you make Emmaline a doll! I sure wish there was some way to pay you back for being such a good neighbor.'

'You repay me in more ways than you know. I'm also happy seeing Paulie settling in so well here with you and Mr Rickers.'

'Paulie's a good boy. Nice mannered. Hard working. But he's quiet, very quiet. Almost moody. As if he's hiding some secret from the world.'

'Paulie's mother and father left Belrose after the war. They're a large family and I understand they aren't doing too well at the moment. The poor things live in one of those camptowns. They're too proud to come back to Belrose.'

'We've all got our pride, for better or worse. But those poor camptown folks-' Gemma shook her head. 'The sad sights I see coming to the back door begging for food. Enough to make me cry some times, I tell you.'

'I think Paulie's family would virtually starve if it weren't for him. I often think Paulie stayed at Belrose for the food I gave him to take to his parents on weekends. I honestly think the food was the only reason Paulie put up working in the stable for my brother.'

'Excuse me for saying so, Miss Dehasset, but you watch out for that brother of yours too.'

Sabrine reached to rock the crib. 'Junior's doing something I should warn you about, Mrs Rickers.'

'Warn me?'

'As you know, I hear a lot of political talk at Belrose. I have reason to believe something is finally coming to a head, a plan evolving which could affect you and your husband. I don't want to alarm you, Mrs Rickers, I just want to keep you informed. Please understand that.'

'Miss Dehasset, stop beating around the bush! Tell me what you've heard.'

'The Freedmen's Bureau. I know very little about those

agencies. Except that they have been set up by the Union Army since the war and meant to help freed slaves get a new start in life.'

Gemma nodded. 'Warren got some seed corn and wheat from the Kettley Freedman's Bureau. They were good enough to him in Kettley. But Warren didn't go back. We weren't in slavery. Neither of us. So we don't want to take away things from folks who might be needier than us.'

Sabrine hesitated, finally divulging. 'There's a new Bureau opening in Bossburg, Mrs Rickers. It's for all local Black people. Every one of color.'

'*Every* one?'

'Yes Mrs Rickers. All Black people in this vicinity must register in Bossburg. Give full details about themselves. How many people are in their family. Names. History. How much land they own, till or sharecrop. The crops they grow. Make a complete accounting of themselves and possessions. Regardles of their backgrounds.'

Gemma, pulling herself upright in the wooden chair, said, 'Nothing against your brother, Miss Dehasset, but he must've heard wrong.'

'I'm afraid not, Mrs Rickers. You see, my brother is rather highly placed in this new . . . venture.'

'How high?'

Sabrine meekly said, 'Junior is in . . . charge of it. Co-chairman with the Union officer, Captain Flannery.'

Gemma slumped down in the chair.

'I didn't mean to upset you, Mrs Rickers. I just thought you should know.'

Gemma stared blankly at the small crib, at her precious little baby girl chewing on the rag doll.

'Mrs Rickers, please! There's no need to get depressed.'

Gemma reached into the pockets of her cotton apron; she shook her head, 'Law's law.'

Then, suddenly, Gemma pulled one hand from her apron; she had found a blue tissue envelope in her pocket and she handed it to Sabrine; she said, 'I forgot. A letter came for you.'

'A letter? For me? Here – at Candlewick?'

'Came two days ago in Kettley. Warren had to send a letter to a friend of ours in Philadelphia, some word about finding a new home for a girl from around here. The Kettley postmaster gave Warren two letters waiting for us. One letter from my brother, saying he's coming down the river on a boat. Then this other letter for you - or, at least, I *think* it's for you.'

'Your brother's coming? How exciting!'

'We're excited,' Gemma nodded at the blue envelope. 'Go on. Open your letter. See who it's from.'

Sabrine looked at the name and address printed on the envelope - *Miss Pretty Neighbor Lady, Rickers Farm, Nr. Kettley, Longchamp Parish.*

Blushing, Sabrine stammered, 'Somebody must be playing a prank. I wonder who it could be?'

'One way to find out.' Gemma rose from her chair, saying, 'Keep an eye on Friday. I'm going to make some coffee.'

Sabrine, opening the blue tissue envelope, was unable to hold back her instant excitement.

'It's from Cramer! It's from Cramer Crowley!'

Gemma was not surprised. She and Warren had both noticed how smitten the young couple had been with one another since their first meeting.

Standing by the stove, Gemma remained silent as Sabrine read her letter and she thought about Sabrine's news of Junior Dehasset running a new kind of Freedmen's Bureau where every Black person had to register.

'What's that no good skunk up to now?' she wondered.

*   *   *

The morning after Sabrine Dehasset brought the rag doll to Emmaline, Warren Rickers found a broadside sheet nailed to the trunk of a pine tree across from the gate to their land. It announced, in bold black letters: NEGROES! ALL MEN WOMEN CHILDREN OF COLOR! REGISTER NAMES AND POSSESSIONS! BOSSBURG FREEDMEN'S BUREAU! FOWLEY'S GENERAL STORE! NO EXCEPTIONS TO ARMY LAW! ALL FREE PEOPLE OF COLOR!

113

Warren ripped the poster from the tree, hopped into the buggy and, snapping the reins on the mare, bounced down the avenue of cypress trees to the house.

He found Gemma in the kitchen; he waved the ragged edged piece of paper, shouting, 'Army! My ass! It don't take no genius to guess why this poster was put up in front of our gate!'

'Warren, don't get so het up.'

'Don't get so het up? Gemma, this is their way of changing the rules. Their way of pretending the war never happened. The damned Southerners lost the war, the planters had to give up their slaves! This is just another sneaky way of trying to hang onto slaves. To get us back in their shackles!'

'We were never slaves, Warren and we'll never be slaves.'

'Then why are damned White trash troublemakers trying to treat us like slaves? You wait and see if I'm right or not.'

'Don't condemn all White people, Warren Rickers!'

Warren, pacing the kitchen, threatened, 'I just won't register us. That's what. I won't go to Bossburg. Ugly little shithole of a town. And there's no way nobody can make me register there neither.'

'Paulie was a slave,' Gemma reminded him. 'Will Paulie have to register in Bossburg?'

'Paulie is a grown man. He can do what he wants. I'm not his master.'

Warren spun round, waving the broadsheet, shouting, 'But God damn it! Neither is Junior Dehasset his master!'

'Oh, Warren. Maybe it wouldn't hurt none just to go peacefully to Bossburg, to report we live here –'

'No, Gemma! NO!'

'But we got to think about more than ourselves now, Warren. We got to start thinking about Emmaline.'

'I *am* thinking about Emmaline!'

'Then send our names in a letter. Be polite. Write our names on a piece of paper. Send them to Bossburg, saying –'

'No, Gemma!' Warren thundered. 'We do that and, before long, Junior Dehasset would have us picking cotton at Belrose as he lashed our backs with a whip!'

'Warren, now you're getting hysterical. Such a thing

couldn't happen. Slavery's over. The war's ended it. Black people are free!'

*   *   *

'The dolly? Where is it?'

'The dolly? What dolly?'

'You know what dolly I mean.'

'Junior Dehasset, did you really want me to make you such a thing as that . . . doll?'

'You'd better have sewn me that little doll, whore –'

Junior Dehasset pulled back his hand to slap Rose Starett across the face.

Rose turned toward the small bureau in the room; she reluctantly pulled open the top drawer and lifted out a small doll. She said, 'I made it.'

'Let's see it.' Junior grabbed for the doll which was no longer than a corncob.

Soon Junior Dehasset and Rose Starett sat on the edge of her bed; Junior looked with fascination at the phallic shaped rag doll which Rose had sewn according to Junior's precise instructions.

She asked, 'Junior, where did you get such a . . . peculiar idea?'

'I seen one. I seen somebody making one.'

Junior did not want to divulge that he had seen his sister sewing a rag doll at Belrose and had got the idea of having Rose make one for him with a few alterations.

'But, Junior, dollies like this usually have hair. Little button eyes, embroidered smiles on their faces. Women-folk make little dresses for them. They're toys for little children.'

Rose had cried when she had been sewing the doll, had cried about how she might have made such a doll for her daughters if the Civil War had not happened, if Glen had not been killed, if her life had been different. Rose Starett had dried her eyes, though, and made a resolution to be strong.

She asked, 'What do you need a toy for, Junior?'

115

'What do you think? For playing sex games.'

Rose's suspicions had been correct; she had known for a long time that Junior Dehasset possessed a very demented mind; she knew him so well by now that she could even anticipate his next words.

'Now, undo your wrapper.'

Rose untied the sash on her kimono.

'Lay back on the bed and spread open your legs. Let's see you press this dolly in your twat.'

Rose pretended to be surprised. 'Press . . . where? How?'

'Yeah, you know, push and rub it like a pecker in your God damn twat!'

'Junior Dehasset, some times I think you've taken leave of your senses.'

Junior Dehasset ignored Rose's show of disgust; he freed his penis from his trousers and began working himself with the tips of two fingers.

Rose obediently lay alongside Junior on the bed, following his prurient instructions.

Junior had now also unbuttoned his shirt; he glanced from his penis jutting like a red stamen from his crotch to look at the hair between Rose's legs; he held the canvas doll, prodding it toward her vagina, saying, 'This dolly should really be made out of leather. Nice, slippery leather. Easier to slide.'

'Leather's hard to work with,' Rose casually commented. 'Tough going with a needle.'

Rose reached to take the doll from Junior's hand. 'Let me grip it . . . please.'

Junior lay on the mattress; he watched Rose rubbing the doll between her thighs, rotating its round head shaped like the crown of a phallus.

'Yeah, bitch,' Junior encouraged in whispers as he worked his penis into a harder erection. 'Screw yourself with that . . . pecker.'

Rose began to sigh, to moan, to grip the doll as if she were feeling a real phallus.

She confessed, 'This does feel good, Junior. This little love dolly does feel - oh, so good!'

116

Next Rose ran the doll up to her stomach, between her breasts; moaning, 'This is some good feeling . . .'

Junior grabbed for it. 'Let me do it.'

Rose did not release the phallic doll from her grip; she knew what excited Junior; she teased, 'Don't you want your whore to rub this love dolly over your big naked body?'

'Hey, gal! You really like that cloth pecker, huh?' Junior laughed.

'I sure do,' Rose said, slowly moving the doll toward Junior's unbuttoned shirt and trousers.

Rose lay on the bed alongside Junior but she did not see him. She was momentarily seeing a picture in her mind of a snake, of a field mouse, of all the night creatures set upon by predators.

Junior Dehasset was the fox lurking in the woods. He was the owl swooping down from the barren branch. The rusty wagon wheel crushing through the mud to smash everything that got in the way.

Rose Starett - determined not to be like the hen, the mouse, the bedraggled woman next door - sprang to her knees and poked the rag doll with a sudden rush of strength toward Junior's bare chest.

Junior grabbed her hand.

Rose fought his strength.

'You bitch!' he said, struggling to press back her pushing hand. 'You gone crazy or something?'

Junior then saw the blade, the long thin blade of a knife poking through the top of the rag doll's head - the blade which Rose Starett had sharpened as thin as a hatpin and sewn into the rag doll which Junior had ordered her to make for him.

Junior wrenched the doll from Rose's hand; he cursed, 'You bitch! You tried to . . . kill me!'

He slapped her again, shouting, 'You tried to . . . kill me!'

Junior, then pushing Rose's naked body to the mattress, gripped the rag doll in one hand and began driving it - the long, sharp blade poking from the doll's head - into her body,

117

repeatedly stabbing her with the blade, piercing her breasts, slashing her shoulders, slicing her neck, cutting into her abdomen, pushing the doll's head toward her vagina, pushing in the long blade, pulling it toward him, opening the orifice, making it wider, slashing at her innards, her intestines, her womb and her bowels.

The sheets ran red with Rose Starett's blood.

'Tried to kill me,' Junior kept repeating as he continued cutting, stabbing, hacking the woman's lifeless body.

'Dirty, stinking, no good whore tried to . . . kill me!'

Rose Starett's patchwork quilts provided the necessary wrapping for her corpse; Junior waited until darkness before he threw her quilt-wrapped body over his shoulder, carried it down the back stairway of Fowley's general store, tossed it across his horse, still muttering to himself.

'Tried to kill me. Dirty, stinking no good whore tried to . . . kill me. Me! ME!'

                    *   *   *

Junior Dehasset's temper had calmed by the time he reached the isolated section of Longchamp Parish called Water Oaks; his brain had cleared and he had perfected a story about why Rose Starett would suddenly disappear from the room above Fowley's General Store.

A Negro had killed her, Junior decided. A young Negro had raped her and killed her.

Junior threw Rose Starett's body in a ditch; he threw a few branches over her; he still muttered to himself, 'She had to be killed anyway . . . Knew too much about Knights . . . Cyclops . . . Our meetings and plans . . . Bitch had to die anyway . . .'

Yes, Junior decided as he grabbed a handful of dewy leaves to wipe the blood from himself. *A nigger killed poor Rose Starett. Killed and raped the poor widow. And I know just the nigger who did it, too. I can kill two birds with one stone with this story . . .*

Kill two birds with one stone!

Junior Dehasset threw back his head and laughed at the

118

idea; the sound of his laughter in the night's stillness made mice scurry through dried leaves, owls flutter their wings in flight from barren branches, snakes slither over the branches covering Rose Starett's corpse.

Chapter Ten

NIGHT RIDERS

Gemma and Warren, drowsy from a long and hard day's work, lay in bed facing one another in the darkness of their new upstairs bedroom; today again had provided too few hours for them to visit with one another, and they seized these last moments to discuss their favorite subject, little Emmaline; the baby slept nearby their bed in her crib; Gemma and Warren spoke softly, debating, wondering, even joking about a young child already showing signs of stubbornness, temper, natural independence, they jokingly began accusing one another about being the parent responsible for those personality traits when - suddenly - they heard the pound of horse hooves on the driveway; they both sat up in bed; the horses came closer to the house; the galloping became louder; the noise awakened Emmaline; she began to cry.

Gemma moved to soothe the baby but, next, she and Warren heard a strange sound outside the window, a swoosh in the night's stillness - and the night's darkness was suddenly lit with a blinding light.

Running to the window, Gemma and Warren stared down at a tall cross of fire blazing in their yard.

'Grab Emmy!' Warren ordered.

He dashed for the gun he kept on the wall.

'Grab baby and run down the stairs to the back!'

'Warren! Don't take the gun!'

Warren checked the gun's chamber for ammunition; he pulled on his clothes, repeating, 'Just grab baby and get out of here!'

Gemma, cradling Emmaline in her arms, hurried down the stairs from the bedroom.

Warren, more angry than frightened, ran down the stairs in bare feet, unbolted the front door and threw it open.

120

He stood facing a line of hooded men mounted on horses.

The horsemen sat calmly, motionless, looking at Warren, the house; the light from the burning cross intensified the starkness of their white clothing.

Warren gripped his gun. 'What you want?'

One hooded rider spoke. 'Sign, nigger!'

'What you doing on my land?'

'You ain't registered, nigger.'

'Get off my land!'

The rider danced his horse from the line of other hooded men; he dropped a piece of paper and a lead pencil to the dirt in front of Warren's bare feet; he danced back his horse and pulled a long bullwhip from the horn of his saddle.

He repeated, 'Sign, nigger!'

Warren raised his gun. 'Get off my land, whoever you are.'

The other riders raised their guns; they pointed the barrels at Warren.

The first rider, gripping his long bullwhip, ordered two of the other men, 'Ride around back and get that kid nigger brat who raped poor Rosie Starett!'

'Paulie!' Warren shouted. 'Paulie's ain't done nothing! You leave Paulie alone!'

'Nigger, you got more important business to worry about than a kid nigger accused of murder and rape.'

The rider snapped his whip, ordering, 'On your knees, Rickers and sign . . . that . . . paper!'

'I know who you are!' Warren shouted. 'You don't scare me no more than . . .'

The hooded rider reared his horse; Warren dropped his rifle; the rider jumped from the horse and, first, began to beat Warren with the leather butt of his whip; he next drew a rifle from his saddle holster and began to swing the rifle by the barrel, like a club, losing his temper, hitting Warren with growing fury, calling, 'Dumb . . . thick-headed . . . nigger . . . slave . . .'

*   *   *

Gemma dashed down the stairs from the bedroom, raced

121

through the dining-room and into the kitchen, and looked out the back window before opening the door.

Her hand froze on the latch.

She held Emmaline close to her breast when she saw two white-hooded riders galloping from the old slave quarters and dragging Paulie between their horses.

Holding the blanket around Emmaline's head, Gemma ran back through the dining-room, through the archway into the parlor.

      *   *   *

Gemma, clutching Emmaline to her breast, stopped in the parlor when she saw more hooded men outside the front door, one hooded man holding Warren down to the dirt in front of the door, holding a boot to Warren's neck, pointing the long barrel of a gun into Warren's bloody head.

The hooded man threatened, 'Now sign, nigger! Sign that piece of . . . paper! Or do you want more of a working-over?'

Gemma felt her heart beating, her knees becoming weak, as she looked from the hooded man, to Warren, to a piece of paper lying on the ground in front of Warren's head.

'Sign, nigger!' the hooded man repeated.

Gemma opened her mouth – she wanted to shout, to protest – but no words came out of her mouth.

The hooded man pulled back the hammer of his gun; he said, 'One last time . . . sign, nigger!'

Warren's hand slowly moved in the dirt; he reached for a pencil laying beside the paper; he moved the pencil across the paper; he dropped the pencil, his hand, his head back down to the ground.

The hooded rider scooped the paper from the ground, turned to the masked riders sitting on horseback – two riders holding Paulie between them – and he shouted, 'Let's get out of here!'

The hooded men galloped away from the house, up the driveway, toward the parish road.

      *   *   *

Gemma dropped to her knees alongside Warren's body. 'Warren? You okay?'

The towering cross still blazed in the night; a white camellia lay on the ground a few feet away from Warren.

'Warren!' Gemma screamed as she clutched Emmaline to her breast. 'Warren, say something . . .'

Gemma thought she saw Warren move. She thought she heard him whisper. She listened closer. She begged, 'Yes, Warren? *Yes?*'

Warren asked in a faint whisper. 'Baby . . . she's fine?'

'Baby's fine. I'm fine. But what about you?' She saw blood.

Warren's voice was weakening. He gasped. 'Coffee Cup . . . take care of . . . baby.'

He slumped to the earth.

PART TWO

HARD DAYS

Chapter Eleven

SHOWBOAT!

Cramer Crowley drove Gemma Rickers, her baby, Emma-line, and Sabrine Dehasset to Palmetto Landing in a carriage to meet Gemma's brother, Jay Greene, arriving on a Mississippi riverboat called *The Southern Breeze*.

Gemma, Sabrine, and Cramer sat in the open carriage parked with other wagons, buggies, barouches, crowding the river bank where the gaily painted gold-white-and-yellow paddlewheeler was moored. *The Southern Breeze* was a showboat which entertained audiences on the Mississippi River between Cairo, Illinois and the port of New Orleans.

Banjo plucking. Fiddle playing. Tap dancing and lively songs. A platform festooned with red, white and blue bunting was built on the stern; performers danced, sang, shouted jokes to the audience seated in wagons, sprawled on the grassy river bank or perched in the stout branches of old trees.

Two minstrels dressed in candy-striped trousers and purple swallow-tailed coats, high-kicked their way across the small stage, followed by a brightly painted blonde actress who sang a repertoire of comic songs.

This afternoon's show was free, an enticement for the longer entertainment produced for a fee every evening on a gaslit stage inside the showboat; the minstrels concluded their brief act with a catchy popular tune, beckoning the audience to join in the song. A few women and children began singing but, soon, the crewmen aboard the riverboat picked up the tune – '*The morning sun shines bright, but the cat comes out at night, in good old Ken – tuck – eee.*'

The minstrels stopped, staring with surprise at the boat's crew singing along with them. The crewmen themselves then paused for a young Negro – a waiter who had emerged from

127

the passengers lining the riverboat's deck – who began a smart tap dance which drew instant applause from the audience squatting on the shore.

'That's Jay!' Gemma squealed with delight, pointing at the tap-dancing waiter. 'That's my brother, Jay!'

'Gemma, are you certain?' asked Sabrine in awe.

'I'm positive!'

Gemma lifted Emmaline to see her uncle dancing on the riverboat's deck.

'Your brother's very talented,' whispered Sabrine. 'I bet he doesn't stay working as a waiter very long. He should be one of the players!'

The audience cheered for the tap dancing waiter but the stage minstrels resumed their performance, introducing a White man with shoulder-length red hair who wore a shiny white satin frock coat, the riverboat captain and showboat impresario – Dr 'Red' Harte.

'Ladies, gentlemen, lovers of music and good cheer!'

Dr Harte extended both arms to the audience crowding the river bank and shouted, 'You've just had your first whiff of the sweet *Southern Breeze!*'

*   *   *

'You see the little turn I did for you, Sis?'

'Oh Jay! Jay! I knew that was you!'

Jay Greene, two years younger than his sister, Gemma, had a trim build, narrow hips, sturdy shoulders and a gregarious personality.

He stood alongside Cramer Crowley's open carriage, holding his niece in his arms, saying, 'The only thing that kept me from knowing for sure it was you, Gemma, was I didn't see Warren.'

'Warren's been feeling poorly, Jay.'

'Sick?'

Working hard,' Gemma answered stiffly. 'Planting season's coming on.'

Sabrine and Cramer exchanged quick glances; everyone in the parish had heard about the masked riders putting a

128

burning cross in the yard at the old Chatgrove place, but few people spoke about the incident.

The night-riders had also taken away Paulie and no one had seen him since. Gossip still spread through the parish that Paulie had raped and killed a widow in Bossburg, that the night-riders had been determined to avenge the poor woman's death. But details were sparse, all facts shrouded in mystery.

Sabrine heard no talk of the incident at Belrose; her father refused to discuss it; her mother spent more and more time in the privacy of her pergola. Junior Dehasset was the only member of the family filled with good spirits and boundless energy; Sabrine somehow suspected that Junior himself was involved in the ugly matter but she knew better than to approach him. Sabrine feared Junior might take revenge against Gemma and Warren; also she no longer discussed the situation with Gemma because Warren had withdrawn completely inside himself.

Consequently, Sabrine was grateful for Cramer Crowley's more frequent visits to Longchamp Parish; she thrilled at the first signs of romance developing between them in these warm days of springtime.

'Planting season?' Jay scoffed at Gemma's reply to his question about Warren's whereabouts. He joked, 'My brother-in-law just don't want to see me! Well, bad luck for him! The boat's not staying here for long. But I'm coming to see you in your new place even if I have to – walk!'

Gemma beamed. 'Can you come back today? Ride home with us?'

'We got a show tonight, Sis. But maybe I can get away for a few hours tomorrow.'

Cramer Crowley offered, 'I'm coming this way around midday tomorrow. You can ride with me.'

'That's very kind of you, Mr Crowley. But I'll have to be back early tomorrow night, too, for the show.'

Gemma asked, 'You're in the show? They're putting you in the show, Jay?'

Sabrine said, 'I told your sister they'd make you part of the show.'

129

'I've always been part of the show,' Jay said, modestly adding, 'Mind you, not a minstrel. They're all White actors. Painted black with burnt cork.'

'Burnt cork?' Sabrine grimaced. 'But why?'

'A new craze.' Jay thumbed toward the flamboyant Dr Harte still urging the riverside audience to attend the show tonight in the gaslit theater.

'Doc Harte there is a crafty old coot. You see, color laws don't allow Black folks on the same stage with White folks.'

'Is that true?' asked Gemma.

Jay nodded. 'In the South. Below Cairo.'

Gemma began to understand. 'That's why you pretend to be a waiter?'

'Pretend? I *am* a waiter! I do two jobs! Same as the crew you heard singing. The crew does two jobs, too.'

Cramer smiled. 'Pretty crafty.'

'Indeed, pretty crafty!' Jay explained. 'The law also makes it cheaper than hiring all those entertainers. Crewmen and waiters get a lot less money than dancers and singers. Doc Harte just makes sure all his laborers can sing, dance and play at least two musical instruments'.

'That's exploitation!' cried Sabrine.

Jay shrugged. 'It's also called life on the river, Miss Dehasset.'

Gemma sniffed, 'And sometimes on land, too.'

Jay, handing Emmaline back to Gemma, said, 'You tell Warren I'm coming visiting tomorrow and I don't want to hear no more of this "it's planting season" talk, hear me now?'

Spinning around in front of the carriage and clicking his heels together in a high jump off the ground, Jay mimicked his employer, saying, 'Tell Warren I'm coming like the sweet *Southern Breeze!*'

Gemma knew Jay was joking but, nevertheless, she already believed his visit, however brief, would serve as a much needed tonic.

*   *   *

130

The moon was a searing white sphere in the Louisiana sky as Cramer Crowley rolled from the naked body of one Black girl – Sari, who had sneaked away tonight with her friend, Dina, from High Hill Plantation – and mounted the waiting body of the other girl.

Sari, watching Cramer Crowley's white buttocks move up and down as he drove into Dina, said, 'We never expected to see you no more, Mr Pedlar Man. We haven't seen you for weeks – months!'

Cramer Crowley did not reply; he positioned his hands on the ground and dipped his phallus deeper into the heat settled between the out-stretched black thighs.

'We was surprised to find your sign on the road, Dina and me. We was surprised to see that pile of three stones telling us to meet you here tonight.'

Cramer grunted.

'You be thinking of somebody else, ain't you, Pedlar Man? You be thinking of one gal while you pestering another.'

'Yep.'

'Is she pretty, the gal you be thinking about?'

'Very.'

'Is she . . . hot?'

'Warm,' he corrected as he pursued his steady rhythm. 'She's warm and sweet and . . . delicious.'

'She's a White gal, ain't she? The gal you be thinking about when you pumps away on Dina, she be a White gal, ain't she?'

Cramer did not reply; he wanted to concentrate on Sabrine Dehasset, imagining that he had not left her at the old Chatgrove place a few hours ago with Gemma Rickers after he had driven them back from Palmetto Landing.

He fantasized that Sabrine had remained with him in the wagon, that he was making love to her here on the ground, that he no longer had to copulate with every woman he saw, that he no longer had to satisfy his lust with strangers, females dotted around the countryside, that Sabrine Dehasset was the only woman who could satisfy him, gratify him, fulfill all his manly needs and still remain the beautiful, lovely, alabaster . . .

131

Sari again broke Cramer's fantasy; she said, 'Don't be too bashful to talk, Mr Pedlar Man. The moon is full. There's a big full moon out tonight. Folks say a full moon makes a brain crazy. So you do and think and say anything you want to because there's a full moon in the sky, Mr Pedlar Man.'

'Shhh. . . don't talk . . .'

'I'm spoiling your wishes, ain't I? I'm sorry, Mr Pedlar Man. The moon makes me crazy too, I guess.'

Sari pulled her bare knees up to her naked breasts and began to plait her hair into small braids as she waited for Cramer Crowley to reach his orgasm with her girlfriend. She plaited her hair and began to sing, '*Moon makes me crazy, Moon makes me sad, Moon makes me lazy, Moon makes me bad* . . .'

*   *   *

The full moon burned brightly in the night's dark sky as the young White girl, Francey Dasher, sat in the field of weeds beyond the cabin where she lived with Broody Hen and Big Spanker.

Francey Dasher was pleased to have all the ladies from farms and plantations dotted around Longchamp Parish to take time from their busy schedules to come and bid her good-bye and best wishes on her pregnancy. The ladies had gathered together in the imaginary parlor of Francey's home to give her a surprise baby shower.

'Charles is worried, of course, about me traveling alone. But we all have to be brave during war time. I tell Charles I worry about him off fighting with General Lee. I only expect him to have deep concern about me and . . . baby.'

Charles was the name of Francey's latest imaginary husband, Charles Alphonse LaSalle. The ladies who had come to Francey's make-believe tea party all knew Charles LaSalle, many of the women still being envious that Francey had won the heart of such a handsome, rich, eligible young man.

'No, no, no. I don't see Hiram anymore,' Francey confided to the ladies from Tulip Hills Plantation. 'Hiram was not for me. He's like so many White men in this parish. He has an

132

incurable weakness. An illness. What? Is he sick? Why, yes. I would say that Hiram is sick. Very, very sick. He is obsessed, absolutely obsessed with rolling in the grass with - excuse me, ladies, for being so blunt - black wenches! I'm not telling secrets out of school by divulging to you ladies that Hiram has actually knocked-up that Lulubelle wench again! I swear to it! Lulubelle - that high yellow slut - is pregnant again with Mr Hiram's child and her belly's hanging near enough down to the ground! I swear to it! I swear!'

Shaking her head, Francey Dasher mused, 'Those Black wenches! My, my, my! It's so easy for those Black wenches to have babies. I'm of a highly delicate nature myself. That's why Charles insists on me going North. Boston, you know. Charles has people there. In Boston.'

Francey, pausing in her conversation with the imaginary guests at her baby shower, rested both hands over her stomach as she had seen pregnant women sit in chairs. She sat proudly in the field of weeds, listening to her lady friends compliment her on the beautiful appointments in her parlor, the rosewood settee upholstered in scarlet velvet, the emerald green portieres tied back with golden ropes, the china tea service painted with delicate pink-and-blue flowers.

'Yes, it's going to be difficult to leave all these beautiful things behind,' Francey Dasher confessed to the imaginary ladies dressed in full crinoline skirts. 'But Charles will buy me all new things when we get to Boston. I will miss a few things, of course. And what I will miss most of all is that big old chandelier up there. It's been in the Dasher family for years, literally hundreds and hundreds of years.'

Francey raised her slim hand over one shoulder and pointed at the full white sphere of the moon.

'I hate leaving it behind in Longchamp Parish.'

133

Chapter Twelve

MR LOU GLOOM

The temporary settlement of five thousand freed slaves called Two Forks Camptown was located fifteen miles south of the Longchamp Parish borderline. A cloud of bonfire smoke hung low through the surrounding pine forest and the bent figures of Black people moved, or stood, like dark shadows among the peaked, flat and sloping tents of the makeshift town.

Two Black people, a portly woman named Stella and a lanky man named Lou, spoke in low voices in front of their small tent pitched on the edge of the camptown.

Stella and Lou were discussing their eldest son, Paulie, who had not visited them for two months.

Lou said, 'We ain't going to see Paulie no more, Stella. Paulie be that boy them White folks catched and hanged up in Longchamp Parish for raping that White war widow.'

Stella disagreed. 'Paulie raped no White war widow, Lou. Our son's no raper and killer. Paulie's still working for them sweet Yankee niggers same he tells us the last time he's here bringing us food. Paulie's working, selling vegetables, putting pennies aside to buy that little place for all of us to live together like a big family again.'

Lou was not so optimistic. 'Our family's never going to live together no more, Stella. This camptown be the last time we're living together. You. Me. Our boys. The girls. Freedom took away slavery, Stella. But freedom also took away family living together. A man used to be scared to death of being sold away from his wife and kids, sold down the river by his master. A man didn't think life could get worse than on plantations. But look around you, woman. You hear laughing? You smell good cooking? You hear singing in this camptown like you heard in the old slave quarters at Belrose? Singing and laughing and gospeling?'

Stella understood what her husband, Lou, meant, but she did not like him to complain about the miserable conditions of life in the camptown. Stella wanted Lou – as well as their three other sons and two daughters who lived in the camptown with them – to trust that life here was only temporary, that Paulie would soon find a cabin and a small plot of land for them.

Lou sat on a log in front of the tent; he continued, 'Nothing left in life to do except screwing and killing, pestering and murdering. The wenches who ain't opening their legs for every buck in the camptown be stabbing their husbands with a knife. The bucks who ain't screwing every hole they sees is busy fighting, scrapping, beating one another to a bloody pulp. Nobody's got no respect no more. Nobody's got no pride no more. Nobody's got no gumption. No get up and go. Freedom comes and takes away gumption from everybody. The White man says a nigger's no good for nothing but screwing and fighting. Maybe that's why the White man gives niggers our freedom. To prove the White man right. To show the world a nigger's good for nothing but screwing and fighting.'

'Freedom takes the gumption away from you, old man,' scolded Stella as she stood in front of a smoking bonfire and stirred a long wooden spoon around a small black pot.

The woods had long ago been hunted empty of rabbits, squirrels, possum; the bushes had been picked bare of nuts and berries. The men, women and children who lived in this particular settlement had little more to eat these days than leaves, bark from the trees, handfuls of clay.

Stella, who had managed to save a small cache of root vegetables from Paulie's last visit, stewed them with leaves to make their food last longer. She continued preparing the frugal supper and said to her husband, 'Black folks weren't going to get nothing if we stayed slaves to White people.'

'Black folks are starting to talk different about White people, Stella. Black folks aren't all happy with freedom. Not the freedom we sees. This ain't freedom. This kind of life. I hears men talking, good, hard-working nigger men like me talking right here in camptown about White men changing

135

back to old ways. White men looking for bucks who can do hard work, special work. Keep their mouths shut about it.'

'What kind of special work?'

'Plantation work, Stella.'

'Why Black men got to keep their mouths shut about plantation work? I hears talk too. This new work's called share-cropping.'

'Share-cropping's something different. Share-cropping means each family gets little patch of land, Stella. But there be a whole lot of free niggers in a whole lot of camptowns. Not that many White folks have that much land for no share-cropping. This here other work for niggers is more like the old days of slaving. But it's work. It's knowing there's going to be work tomorrow and the next day and the day after that.'

'Old days of slaving? Lou, what foolishness you wishing for?'

'Get food. That foolishness? Signing Matthew, Mark, Luke up with me for a job? That foolishness? Making sure we all got jobs for tomorrow and the next day and the day after that? That foolishness, too?'

'Signing?' What you signing, old man? You can't even read!'

'I can listen and put my mark to what I hears read to me, Stella.'

'You can listen and mark yourself right back into slavery, that's what you can do, Lou!'

'A man can do worse, Stella. A man can do a lot worse. Like starving to death here in camptown.'

'You do what you want with your own life, Lou, understand? But don't you do nothing with our boys. Don't you go signing up Matthew, Mark, Luke or Paulie for no slaving jobs.'

Lou did not listen to his wife; he continued to explain his ambitions, his hopes.

'I maybe find work for Hetty and Willa, too. Work in one of those turpentine mills.'

Stella scoffed at the idea of their two daughters, Hetty and Willa, securing work in a turpentine mill.

136

'Every gal in this camptown wants one of them jobs. But turpentine jobs all got taken months ago.'

'Not in new mills, Stella. Not in new mills opening across state line over in east Texas. Fact is, I heard a White man's fixing to come soon to this camptown and sign up a whole bunch of black gals. Sign up enough black gals to fill a whole wagon train and take them away to work in new turpentine mills in east Texas.'

The prospect of her two daughters leaving in a work wagon appalled Stella. She waved the long wooden spoon at her husband, commanding, 'Don't you go signing up the girls to take them no place like pigs to a market, understand me?'

'A body's got to eat or die, Stella.'

'You're eating. You've been eating food what Paulie brings us from those sweet Yankee niggers. So don't you go putting your mark on nothing.'

'Paulie ain't going to come back here no more, Stella. Paulie's the poor boy all the folks are talking about, I tell you. The White men hanged Paulie for raping that White war widow up in Longchamp Parish.'

'That hanged boy ain't our Paulie. I knows it. I just knows it.'

Stella continued stirring her pot, saying, 'But it ain't no good for me to talk sense to you. You do nothing but moan and talk gloom talk. All the light's gone out of your day. You and me, Lou. We used to think about a pretty word, a pretty name to take for our new family name now that we're free people. You and me and the kids used to talk and consider names of Presidents, names of famous generals, names like Washington, Grant, Lincoln, Davis. Well, I tells you right here and now what name you can take. You can take . . . Gloom! Mr Lou Gloom! That's a good last name for you to take. All the light's gone out of day. You see nothing but darkness and storm clouds and more slavery and . . . gloom! Yes, sir, that's who you are! Mister Lou Gloom!'

*　　　　*　　　　*

137

Junior Dehasset kept Paulie's whereabouts a secret between himself and a hired White man working on Belrose Plantation named Clyde Quine. Junior Dehasset and Clyde Quine moved Paulie from place to place on Belrose, connecting him to a post with a chain and slave collar.

The slave collar was no more than a thick, rusty chain wrapped around Paulie's neck, a chain which had rubbed his skin raw. Another rusty chain - a long one - was wired to the slave collar and nailed to the top of the post planted in a patch of tall weeds. The long chain creaked on a nail driven into the top of the post as Paulie crawled in a circle, pulling grass and weeds from the ground for Junior Dehasset's horse.

Junior Dehasset, returning to Paulie's secret whereabouts with a bucket of pig slops, dumped it on the ground for Paulie to eat and threatened, 'Don't you stop crawling, coon. Don't you stop crawling and pulling grass. If I come up the path and I don't hear that chain squeaking on the end of the post, I'm going to whip your ass into a piece of raw beef.'

Junior Dehasset had been keeping Paulie captive for two months on Belrose Plantation, since the night that the hooded riders had galloped into the old Chatgrove place and taken Paulie from the cabin in the abandoned slave quarters.

Junior Dehasset and his friends subsequently spread the rumor in Longchamp Parish that a young Black man had been hanged for raping and killing the White widow, Rose Starett. The story provided Junior with an explanation for the sudden disappearance of Rose Starett as well as the opportunity to use Paulie as his own personal slave.

Junior only hoped that Paulie would not die too soon. He liked to stand over him and remind him, 'Don't forget I can do whatever I want to you. Even kill you. I could've hung you, tarred-and-feathered you, stuck a burning poker up your asshole, done whatever I wanted the night we dragged you from your Yankee friends. But I'm just keeping you around like a tomcat keeps a dying mouse alive, batting you around, having my fun, letting you know, pretty boy, that nobody wants you - not your pretty face, not your tough little body, not your big nigger pecker, nobody wants you for nothing

138

but to whip . . . to punish . . . to keep chained like my very own slave!'

*   *   *

Belrose Plantation, a vast empire of fields, rolling hills, forests, many secret places, also provided Noele Dehasset with a retreat from scrutiny. Noele lay in her lakeside pergola protected by the willow copse and enjoyed the evening air as she contemplated how far she had progressed in the last six months as Ken's mistress.

Slut . . . Bitch . . . Whore . . .

Noele repeated each name of denigration which Ken called her these days. The harsh sound of the titles excited her; she also remembered the threatening expression on Ken's face as he hurled – sometimes literally spat – the insults at her when she knelt in servitude at his feet.

'Beg for that cock.'

'Did I tell you to lick it yet?'

'What are those balls doing in your mouth, bitch? Did I give you permission to suck those balls yet?'

'I said suck, don't chew. Suck like a little piggy.'

'The feet now, slut. I want to see you down on the ground, kissing my feet.'

Six months had made Ken more talkative, more inventive, more domineering as a lover.

First, Ken, had used the golden jewelry chain as a restrainer for Noele. He had progressed to strips of cloth. Ken next tied her with thin black leather thongs. He also used leather thongs as a lash for Noele, had begun by teasing her with the leather thongs, making her wet them, chew them, take them into her mouth, squeeze them inside her vagina. He rubbed the moist leather thongs over Noele's thighs and slowly, slightly, not too harshly, he began to lash them against her delicate skin.

Noele Dehasset lay in the lakeside pergola and waited for Ken to join her again tonight; she never knew what to expect, what she wanted from him, how much punishment she could accept.

Noele could not remember the last time Ken had ridden her like a bicycle; she only wanted him to dominate her, restrain her in bondage, surprise her with new thrills. Tonight – what was he going to do with her tonight? How much farther could he take her into the realms of perversion? How much more could she endure? She felt as if Ken was slowly pushing her to the edge of decency.

*   *   *

Ken pursued his own secret dreams in the early morning hours in the stable loft where he and Paulie used to make love. Ken bent his head forward against his clasped hands and prayed, 'Lord, Paulie's some place on this plantation. I know it, Lord. I know Junior Dehasset's got Paulie hidden some place on Belrose and so, Lord, please help me find Paulie and I promise you, Lord, I won't try to get no revenge by killing Junior Dehasset, by killing any of the Dehasset family. I do bad things, Lord, but I promise you that, whatever I do, I won't kill no member of the Dehasset family if You only help me find Paulie.'

*   *   *

Sabrine Dehasset turned in bed and unexpectedly felt the warmth of a naked body curled alongside her on the snug feather mattress; she did not scream, did not sit upright in bed, did not immediately move to jump out of bed, did not even reach to light a candle. She intuitively knew she was not in danger.

The naked body snuggled closer to her. An arm spread over her body. She felt a light kiss on her cheek. A voice whispered in the darkness of her bedroom, a kind voice assuring her, 'I love you, Sabrine.'

Still not alarmed nor frightened, she whispered, 'Cramer?'

Another kiss answered her question.

'What on earth are you doing here, Cramer?'

The room was totally dark; she could not see him smiling,

but she knew he was smiling as he answered, 'What do you think I'm doing here?'

'How did you get in here?'

'Didn't you know? I'm a magician. That's what I really do. I'm not a pedlar. I'm a magician.'

Cramer kissed her again, rolling closer against her; his knee moved gently between her knees; he spread open her legs as he rolled on top of her body; she felt a heat, a burning presence, a large and burning presence between her naked thighs, inching its way into her vagina, a presence that was satisfying, fulfilling, tantalizing, unlike any sensation she had ever felt before, completely engulfing her body and felt as if it were also touching her soul.

Cramer's voice was as warm, as satisfying as his body as he asked in the darkness, 'You enjoy being with me like this, don't you, Sabrine?'

Sabrine was too bashful, embarrassed at first to reply to the question, to speak as Cramer was moving to take her virginity, to make love with her.

'Don't be afraid,' he assured her. 'Sex is nothing to be frightened of, nothing to be ashamed about.'

He pressed his penis deeper into her vagina, saying, 'There . . . your hymen is gone . . . broken . . . and you did not even feel it . . . you like doing this, don't you?'

She still did not reply; she lay on the mattress, looking up at the outline of his head, his curly hair, his broad shoulders, his naked torso tapering above her in the darkness.

He repeated, 'You love doing this, don't you, Sabrine Dehasset? You love having sex?'

Silence.

'Sabrine Dehasset, you love sex, don't you? You want sex, don't you? You want sex if it's love-making, don't you, Sabrine Dehasset?'

Cramer intensified his drives into Sabrine's vagina as he asked the questions.

His voice became louder, demanding, 'Tell me, Sabrine. Tell me that you like sex!'

Sabrine opened her mouth to speak, to answer.

But it was then – at the moment of feeling heat engulfing

her body, the moment she was prepared to confess her desire, her need, her enjoyment of sex – that Sabrine awoke from her sleep and sat upright in bed.

It was a dream.

Sabrine had dreamt that Cramer Crowley had crept naked into bed with her and made love to her and asked her questions about sex.

Sitting upright in bed, Sabrine felt a hunger, a physical need in her groin instead of the satisfaction, the heat she had enjoyed in the dream.

'I don't know if I can bear this,' she said to herself. 'I oh so desperately want him to make love to me. I'm sorry. But I can not help it. I oh so desperately want him . . .'

Sabrine reached toward her nightdress. She touched one breast. She felt her nipple standing hard, erect, taut under the thin fabric.

She whispered. 'I do love sex, Cramer . . . yes, I do love having sex . . . with you . . . if it's love-making, making love with you . . .'

Chapter Thirteen

THE BLACK MYTH

The showboat, *The Southern Breeze*, was scheduled to leave Palmetto Landing in two days' time - on Friday - and continue sailing on its scheduled trip down the Mississippi River to New Orleans.

Jay visited her sister, Gemma and his brother-in-law, Warren, again on Wednesday for the third consecutive afternoon. Gemma had improvised a table in the dining-room for Jay's first visit to their new home but the warm weather and Jay's insistence on casual reunions, gave Gemma the idea to serve the next lunches on a table laid under the leafy oak tree beyond the kitchen.

Gemma killed a chicken for the outdoors meal, made potato salad and draped the table with a cloth which swept the grass. They devoured the special feast and washed it down with peach wine which Warren had made last fall.

Then Gemma took little Emmaline inside for her nap before preparing coffee and bringing out a wild raspberry cake she had baked for dessert. Gemma seized the moment to tell Jay finally about the hooded riders coming to the farm, planting the burning cross in the yard and taking Paulie from his cabin. Gemma excluded the detail about the hooded men forcing Warren to sign a document for the new Freedmen's Bureau in Bossburg; Warren, still affected by that night, had spoken little about it and had not once referred to the incident of the hooded man holding him down to the dirt with the barrel of a gun and the sole of his black leather boot.

The story shocked Jay; he had heard about masked vigilante groups beginning to harass Negroes in the South but he thought it was wise not to mention this fact to his sister and brother-in-law. He waited for Gemma to finish her account before saying, 'Sis, I won't try to convince you and Warren to leave Longchamp Parish. If you wanted to move back to Philadelphia you would've done it by now. But let me ask you this. Don't you think you should make a few more friends around here?'

Gemma quietly answered, 'We have Sabrine Dehasset.'

'A nice enough person,' Jay said, 'but don't you think you should have other friends than her? Don't forget it was Sabrine Dehasset who brought Paulie here in the first place and maybe started all the trouble for you.

'But Sabrine was trying to protect Paulie!'

'From her brother,' Jay reminded Gemma, adding, 'the Dehasset family don't sound like ideal neighbors.'

'You've met Cramer Crowley,' Gemma said. 'We see him, too.'

'Cramer Crowley,' Jay repeated the name and visualized the tall Irishman with the easy smile and friendly manner. 'He's pleasant enough, Sis, but what do you really know about him? That he's a pedlar. Even you admit you don't know what Firefly Water is! Can't you understand what I'm trying to say?'

Gemma looked at Jay, waiting for some advice, at least an explanation.

Jay went on, 'I'm talking about people like you. Like Warren. Young people. Married people. People trying to make a home. People working the soil, raising families, fighting the same battles. Black people.'

Warren spoke. 'There's a Black man working High Hill.'

Gemma and Jay both turned to look at Warren; this was the first time he had spoken since he had sat at the draped table under the oak tree.

'High Hill?' Gemma asked. 'What's that?'

Warren held his eyes on the red and white plate in front of him as he slowly explained. 'High Hill's a plantation. I heard about it when I first went to Kettley. A man named Phillippe Summers used to own High Hill but he was killed in the war. His widow lets a Black man run the plantation for her now - a fancy big Black man named Herc.'

Gemma suspiciously raised an eyebrow. 'I suppose Herc is short for Hercules and this big Black man's got himself a real pillar of Hercules dangling between his legs.'

Warren's eyes suddenly came to life. 'How you know that?'

'I don't know it for a fact, honey. I'm just guessing.'

'Why say so?' Warren pressed.

'A White widow? A fancy Black man named Herc? Come on now, Warren. Use a little imagination.'

Warren's anger increased; his attitude suddenly totally differed from the somnambulistic manner he had had up to this point of the lunch. He demanded, 'Gemma, how do you know about a neighbor being built like a bull?'

'Don't look at me like I've been up there sampling it, honey!' Gemma pleaded.

'Tell me how you know!'

'I guessed – that's how! I remembered the old rumor about why White women chase Black men, the old story about Black men all supposing to have a pole between their legs.'

'I don't hear you complaining, woman!'

'Nobody's complaining, Warren. I'm just talking about that old rumor of Black men being built like stallions and –'

Jay interrupted. 'Excuse me, kids, but will you stop arguing.'

Gemma turned on him. 'Embarrassing you, baby brother?'

Jay raised himself to full height in the chair; he answered in a mock tone, 'Indeed not. In fact some of my best White friends are people who wanted to verify the very same myth of which you speak.'

Warren put his hand on Gemma's forearm; he warned, 'Don't try to use Jay to change the subject, gal. How do you know about Herc?'

Gemma stared at Warren. She blurted, 'You're jealous!'

'Damned right I'm jealous!'

'Walnuts and Cream is jealous!'

'What do you expect?'

Gemma jumped up from her chair; she threw her arms around Warren's neck and, squeezing him, she said, 'My big baby wine-presser is jealous . . . just like the good old days!'

Jay watched his sister hugging Warren, seeing Warren slowly break into a smile, the first smile Jay had seen since he had arrived here. He said, 'Warren, rumor or no rumor, something tells me that you don't have anything to worry about. Your wife looks pretty content to me.'

*   *   *

Gemma explained in detail at lunch the next day the reason why she was always angered about White people constantly equating Black people with sex, complaining that it seemed to her that all White men believed every Negress was a virtual little hot furnace of love, that White women chased Black men for the reputed size of their manhood. Warren and Jay both agreed with - and laughed at - Gemma's stories, her complaints, her theories.

Friday afternoon's lunch was Jay's last visit at the farm, though, and Gemma crowded in many anecdotes which she had not been able to tell Jay in their fleeting hours together. Vignettes about her trying to find a bull in a nearby field to mate with their milk cow; about the midwife, Broody Hen, asking them to locate some place for the White girl, Francey Dasher, to live; about Gemma writing to the woman in Philadelphia, Dorothy Bliss, for the name of a family or an institution which might give a home to the demented White girl; about the migrant freed slaves who used to come down the driveway for food but whose visits had suddenly, mysteriously stopped immediately after the hooded riders had put a burning cross in the yard, and Gemma believing that word spread quickly through the homeless Black people about where danger lay; and, again, Jay urged his sister and brother-in-law to find more friends in the neighborhood apart from Sabrine Dehasset and Cramer Crowley, to concentrate on making a circle of Black friends.

Warren hitched the horse to the buggy and brought it from the stable to drive Jay back to Palmetto Landing. Gemma stood in the yard as she held Emmaline in her arms and kissed Jay goodbye. Warren watched from his seat in the buggy and said, 'Jay, always remember you've got a place at our table.'

Jay took his niece from Gemma to hold for the last time; he played with Emmaline's chubby brown hand and answered, 'I know that, Warren. You can't imagine how many times the thought has been a consolation to me.'

Gemma struggled to hold back her tears; she said, 'We're expecting to hear some day that you're settling down yourself, baby brother.'

'It's too early for me to plant roots, Sis. I've got a lot of travelling to get out of my blood.'

'Where do you go after New Orleans?' Warren asked.

'West.'

'West!' Gemma was impressed.

Jay nodded. 'San Francisco, California. The gold camps. The silver mines. Nob Hill and Chinatown and the Pacific Ocean. All the excitement of the last frontier.'

'Knowing you, Jay,' Gemma said, 'it's not so much the gold and silver as the excitement.'

'That's right, honey! The rainbow's got a whole lot of flavors in it – lemon, strawberry, orange, huckleberry – and I want to taste a little bit of each.'

Warren called from the buggy, 'Break off a chunk and send it back here to us.'

Jay looked up at his brother-in-law. 'You know, Warren, you probably have a big chunk of rainbow right here in –'

He stopped. He looked at Gemma. He asked, 'What name does that old midwife call this house?'

'Three o'clock.'

'Three o'clock,' Jay repeated.

Looking back to Warren, he said, 'The end of the rainbow is probably right here at three o'clock, Warren, and you just don't realize it yet. So don't give up.'

Gemma stood in the dirt yard holding Emmaline in one arm and waving her other arm at Warren driving Jay down the driveway between the yellowing cypress trees. She called one last time, 'Bye, Jay! Be careful, baby brother!'

She was crying now, tears rolling down her cheeks, but she did not forget to add, 'You be careful too, Warren, on the way home!'

Rainbows or no rainbows, Gemma never forgot for one moment how vulnerable they were here in Longchamp Parish.

* * *

Warren returned home safely from Palmetto Landing
before sunset. He and Gemma talked all through supper
about Jay's visit, laughing about the showboat and its
flamboyant entrepreneur, weighing up snippets of Jay's
advice to them, debating about Jay's wanderlust, possible
reasons for his not getting married.

Gemma put Emmaline to bed and then returned upstairs
with Warren to their own bedroom. But neither of them
were tired enough to go immediately to sleep.

They had also discussed the subject of Black people's
sexuality at supper. Warren felt romantic, erotic, even
daring after the conversation; he placed a small mirror on the
bedroom floor and set the candlestick alongside the mirror.
Gemma undressed and Warren gripped her around her
naked waist to move her back and forth on his erect phallus,
looking into the mirror on the floor to watch himself
penetrating her, admiring how she surrounded his slickly
moving phallus.

Gemma at first concentrated on Warren; she did not look
down to see the act of copulation reflected in the mirror.

Warren said, 'This is for you, too. For both of us.'

Gemma always listened to Warren's desire; they had long
ago agreed that if one of them had a sexual desire he – or she
– must simply confide in the other, to have no shame, no
reluctance to satisfy themselves; however, Gemma still did
not look in the mirror.

Warren, holding her by the waist, coaxed, 'Look over your
leg and see . . .'

Gemma finally looked. She saw Warren's erect penis and
her accommodating vagina in the mirror but she did not
speak, neither did she remove her eyes though, when Warren
began to bounce her body against him, to show his penis
swollen inside the wetness of her womanhood.

Finally, she whispered, 'It does look good, honey.'

'*You* look good – taking me!'

'You look good – pushing in and out, in and out . . .
hmmmm.'

148

Gemma continued to look down at Warren pulling out his phallus to its crown, then stirring himself in circular movements.

'Like that, little one?' he asked. 'Like it like that?'

'Love it like that, big one.'

'Feel this?' Warren asked and he pressed deeper inside her with sudden strength.

Gemma groaned; she threw her arms around Warren's neck; she began kissing his lips, his cheeks, his eyes, his forehead, saying, 'This is the best, you are the best.'

Warren increased the force of his thrust. 'You aren't going to go to no other man?'

Gemma suspected why Warren had wanted this little scene - that he did not like her talking about another man, another Black man. She answered, 'I love just you, Mister. Just you.'

'I'm big enough for you, gal?'

'I don't know what I could do with anything bigger, honey love.' Gemma chewed on his chin, promising, 'And I never want to find out.'

Warren, holding Gemma against his midsection, walked her to the bed and lay her on the mattress. He continued to drive into her saying, 'I love you, Coffee Cup. I love you . . . I love you . . .'

Gemma clung to Warren's chest; she felt herself exploding, realizing that tonight was the first time since the hooded riders had left the burning cross in the yard that Warren had made love to her.

Gemma listened to Warren panting, taking deep breaths, grunting as he reached his orgasm.

'That's my man!' she praised, taking his seed. 'That's my own big mahogany man!'

*   *   *

The young Black boy, Matthew, who lived in Two Forks Camptown with his mother, Stella, his father, Lou, his two sisters and two brothers, also was sought out for the size of his penis - but by a Black instead of a White woman. The idea embarrassed – even repelled the young boy and he tried to ignore the Black woman's comment about his sexuality. Matthew was not proud of his large penis.

Sex – every kind of sex – troubled Matthew; he especially sought for the courage to sneak away from his family to visit Big Spanker on the Dasher place; Matthew was thrilled by Spanker's masterly treatment of him, how she made his naked buttocks feel warm with the palm of her hand, how she held him to the ground between her sweet-smelling thighs and kept speaking, saying exciting words to him as he licked his tongue inside her vagina. But he constantly feared somebody in the camptown would find out about his strange sexual habits and make fun of him for not enjoying the tender kisses and games of a young Black girl.

Matthew noticed, though, that ideas about sex in the camptown were quickly changing. Especially after the Black woman, Belle, arranged for a makeshift bordello in the woods where men could pay food, bits of firewood, a jar of whiskey to have sex with a woman. Belle moved among the women and nubile girls in the camptown and told them they were foolish to make love for free when they could receive payment for their bodies; Belle also explained how she would take a small part of the payment as her services for guarding their love-making from intruders, and for finding more interested partners.

Belle was the woman who sought out Matthew for the size of his penis. She said, 'You got a big pecker in your pants there, boy.'

Matthew gaped at the crude remark; he did not know Belle as a friend, only hearing that her husband, Romer, was the foreman at a turpentine mill and that the Black couple had more money than other people in Two Forks Camptown.

Belle studied Matthew's body. 'Lots of wenches would like to play with you, boy.'

Matthew nervously backed toward the trees so nobody criss-crossing the camptown trails would hear the embarrassing conversation.

'What's the matter?' Belle demanded. 'Don't you like pestering?'

150

He shrugged, gripping one of the wooden whistles he spent his time whittling because he had nothing better to do since freedom had been given to slaves.

'Shame all that meat in your pants going to waste!'

Matthew was shocked by hearing a woman speak so rough; his mother was strong-minded, strong-willed, but she never spoke crudely, like a man.

'You be a pansy boy?'

He quickly shook his head.

'Maybe you like hard treatment?' she suggested. 'What if I find somebody who'll pay a little something for you to drop your pants for a spanking? What do you say about that?'

Matthew's eyes widened; he immediately wondered if word about his sexual preferences had spread among the people in camptown. If this woman, Belle, had heard gossip that he liked to be spanked by women. Or were there other people in the world with the same appetites?

He mumbled, 'Got to go now, Miss Belle.'

Turning, he moved away from her.

She called, 'Nice cheeks on your ass, pretty boy. Nice big cheeks on your ass.'

Matthew tried to keep control of himself but he wanted to run through the woods, to hide from that woman, Belle, who had seemed to be able to look into his soul. Matthew wondered if her husband was as evil.

Chapter Fourteen

HIGH HILL

Warren, invigorated by his renewed love-making with Gemma, finished the chores early in the morning after Jay's departure and he set out through the pine forest to visit the back country plantation named High Hill.

'Hold it right there, stranger!'

Warren stopped on the path at the sound of the command and stared at a broad-shouldered Negro sitting on a chestnut mare.

'Where you going?' asked the man.

Warren tried to be friendly. 'My name's Warren Rickers. My wife, Gemma, and I live down below on the old Chatgrove place.'

The Negro, dressed in a brocade waistcoat, white breeches and a white linen long coat which strained against a muscular frame, replied, 'I know exactly who you are. I asked where in hell you think you're going.'

Warren kept forcing his smile, saying, 'You must be Herc. I thought it was about time we met.'

'Why?'

'There aren't that many neighbors around here –'

'I don't have time to be neighborly.'

Herc's eyebrows were black lines against cocoa-brown skin; his nose was small and well shaped; his teeth were a clean white line and his jawline firm and square.

Warren studied the tall man and finally said, 'You know, mister, I don't exactly expect a red carpet to be rolled out for me everyplace I go. But I at least expect a man to be civil.'

'What you expect is your own business.'

Warren told himself not to let his anger get out of control; he looked Herc straight in the eye and continued. 'I heard about a Black man farming up here. Gemma and me, we're

Black and work the land next to you. I thought it might be good for us to know one another.'

'What you want from me, Rickers?'

Warren struggled harder to keep his anger from exploding. 'I don't want a thing. But my wife and I have been here for more than a year and haven't made friends with anyone nearby who –'

'If you want friends, Rickers, go to the Freedmen's Bureau in Bossburg.'

Warren kept his voice under control as he replied, 'I already met the men from Bossburg. They came to me wearing white robes. You might have seen the burning cross they brought.'

Herc pulled a pistol from inside his jacket; he pointed it at Warren, saying, 'I don't know nothing about burning crosses or men wearing white robes and I don't want to know. I think you better get moving, Rickers.'

'You're obviously a man who think he can make it alone in the world.'

Herc motioned the pistol, saying, 'Just turn around, head down the hill the same way you came up.'

'Sorry to have troubled you.'

Warren turned to go back home to Gemma and report he had been repelled by Herc of High Hill.

*   *   *

Herc reined his chestnut mare in front of the large red brick house at High Hill, left the horse with the groom and angrily stalked through the white columns fronting the Federal-style house; he entered a large foyer from which a circular staircase rose, curving graciously for three stories above the ground floor, topped by a stained glass sky-light.

Herc, planting his knee high leather boots on the shiny parquet floor, looked up and shouted, 'Hey! Get out here! All of you!'

Pretty young girls began to appear along the circling banister; their skin ranged from the color of rich honey to a

153

purple blackness; they wore thin cotton shifts and their breasts showed nipples pierced with golden rings.

'We just had a visitor,' Herc called to the girls.

The girl named Cora asked, 'A visitor, Master Herc?'

A second girl, Suebelle, called, 'Like those Yankee soldiers who used to come snooping around here, Master Herc?'

Herc answered, 'This was no soldier. This was a Yankee coon living down at the old Chatgrove place.'

'What he want?' asked the girl named Sari.

Sari's secret lover, Dina, stood alongside her by the banister and innocently called, 'We got neighbors now, Master Herc?'

Herc ignored the questions; he asked, 'Any of you girls been talking to strangers?'

There were seven Black girls lining the circling banister and they chorused, 'No, Master Herc.'

'You wouldn't lie to me?'

The seven girls shook their heads.

'You know what happens to girls who tell lies to their master,' Herc reminded them. 'They get more than their nipples pierced!'

The Black girls lowered their heads.

A door opened behind Herc in the foyer and a brittle female voice said, 'If anybody's been talking about High Hill, it's probably your friend, Junior Dehasset.'

Herc turned; he saw Marisse Summers standing in the doorway to the parlor.

Marisse Summers, a White woman in her late twenties with high cheek-bones and auburn hair tumbling in loose ringlets around her pale face, stared defiantly back at Herc.

He demanded, 'What shit you talking, woman?'

Marisse Summers ignored the question. She continued, 'If anybody gossips about you it's Junior Dehasset or that trash farmer, Judd Gillman, who is now calling himself Sheriff.'

Herc glared at her.

Marisse smirked. 'And you think those bastards are your friends! You poor pathetic thing!'

Herc pulled back his arm and struck Marisse across the face; she fell back but, catching herself on the edge of the

154

parlor door, she stopped herself from completely slumping to the floor.

'I warned you, woman,' Herc towered over her, his chest heaving with anger.

Marisse supported herself on the door but kept her head lowered; she stared at the tips of Herc's black leather boots and mockingly asked, 'Are you going to punish me now by making love to your . . . babydolls?'

'Yeah! I'm going to make love to my babydolls. But I ain't going to let you watch. No matter how much you beg!'

Marisse kept her eyes on Herc's shiny black leather boots. 'You'll let me watch you sooner or later. You like showing off too much and you know I'm the only woman who really appreciates you.'

'You've got a lot of confidence, don't you, White Bitch?'

'That's why you need me, Herc.'

'I don't need nobody, understand? Nobody!' Herc raised his foot to press Marisse down to the floor.

But, grabbing his boot, Marisse held onto it and said, 'I love you, you big black elephant . . . prick!'

Then she leaned forward, kissed the toe of the boot, protruded her tongue to lick the sole, and fingered the golden rings piercing her own nipples showing beneath the silk wrapper.

'Horny bitch.' Herc pulled away his boot.

'That's how you like me - horny.'

'Slut. Dirty, evil . . . slut.'

'You don't get my kind of love from your sweet little . . . babydolls.'

Marise Summers slumped to the floor and, reaching again for Herc's black leather boots, she said in a teasing voice. 'You'll be back, Herc. You like what I do for you. You like to be the kind of big man I make you. No babydoll can make you into what I make you . . . Master Herc.'

*   *   *

Marisse Summers, a widow and mother of a half-caste son sired by Herc, knew that the people of Longchamp Parish gossiped about her. But gossip had always surrounded Marisse's life, ever since she had come from Richmond, Virginia, to marry Phillippe Summers and become the mistress of High Hill.

Phillippe Summers, a dark man with decadent tastes nurtured by extensive travels in Europe and Asia, had considered Marisse to be a suitable match for his own lusty perversions. She was insatiable in love-making and as inventive as himself.

It had been Marisse who had first suggested to Phillippe that they bring the young slave, Herc, into the big house. Marisse had heard her parlormaids gossiping and giggling about the size of the young man's phallus.

Herc surpassed his reputation among the housemaids; his manhood even impressed the calloused Phillippe Summers who kept a collection of engravings picturing outsize genitalia. Marisse herself had been spoiled all her life by generously endowed men in Richmond. She shared Herc with her husband, obediently playing subjugated roles which Phillippe invented for her.

Phillippe and Marisse's marriage quickly became dependent on a third party in their love-making, and always the third party was a man who could make love to both of them.

Herc, becoming accustomed to hearing praise for his penis, suggested that Marisse and Phillippe bring a Black girl from the slave quarter into their bed to add to the enjoyment; Phillippe eagerly brought one, then two Black girls, and enjoyed watching Herc move from Marisse to the Negresses, joining in the squabbles himself for a few inches of Herc's potent manhood.

Marisse finally realized she was pregnant. But she did not know if her husband or Herc was the father. Phillippe did not want his wife to give birth to a black child and he went to New Orleans to bring back a doctor to perform an abortion. But, becoming drunk in a poker game, Phillippe Summers joined the Confederate Army which was beginning to recruit soldiers for the Civil War and he never returned to High Hill.

The decision to allow Herc to remain in the big house had not been difficult for Marisse to make; Herc had already

156

proved to be a good lover; he also quickly resumed the role of overseeing the plantation. Marisse had noticed early that Herc was ambitious to own his own land, that he wanted to be something more than a stud.

The memory of the morning she had invited Herc to move permanently into the big house was still one of Marisse's favorite erotic memories, the height - or depth - of her sexual submission to him, her interview for being his full-time love slave.

Marisse had asked Herc to join her in the study; she sat on a buttoned maroon leather chair in front of a large desk and stared at the pigeon holes of papers, documents, work orders; she said, 'This is a big desk, Herc.'

'High Hill is a big plantation.'

'Too big for a woman to run alone.'

'What about Mr Summers?' Herc had stopped calling Phillippe Summers 'Master' since they began having sex together.

'I didn't invite you here to talk about Phillippe.'

'Why did you invite me here?'

'Why do you think you were invited into the big house in the first place?'

Herc stared at her.

'For your cock,' she answered. 'That's why. But I think you're more than a cock.'

'What do you think I am?'

'What do you want to be?'

'Depends on who we're talking about?'

'What do you want to be to me? To High Hill?'

'Could be it's the same thing.'

'Say it then. Why don't you say it? Are you scared to admit it? What you want to be here?'

'No. I just don't want to scare you.'

'I like your confidence.'

He nodded. 'I *am* confident about myself. But you've got to tell me what you want before I tell you if I will give it to you.'

'I might want more than you can give.'

He laughed at her. 'Don't worry about that. You just tell

157

me what you want. Need. How you need to . . . serve me. How Phillippe and you both need to serve me.'

'What if I told you that Phillippe is never coming back to High Hill? That he was killed in the war?'

'Then you'd just be speaking for yourself, wouldn't you?'

'Cold bastard!'

'I've got no time for feelings. And neither do you. You want a man who's hard. Tough. Who's going to control you with iron. A man who's going to control all of your life. Your business. Everything.'

'Are you man enough to do that?'

'Man enough to do a lot more.'

'How much more?'

'As much as you can handle.'

'Herc, I'm a strong woman.'

'And I'm a strong man. I can hurt you in a lot of ways. Keep you in line, in tow, under my thumb like some no-good whore . . .'

Herc suddenly grabbed Marisse by the hair; he pulled her head toward him, looked down into her eyes, saying, 'You're going to be my slave, bitch! And I want everybody to know it. The whole parish. The whole state. The whole world. I want everybody to say "See that woman there! She licks that man's boots! She's his slave!"'

Marisse, staring up into Herc's eyes, did not speak.

Herc pulled back his hand and slapped Marisse sharply across the face; her eyes widened but she did not cry nor scream.

Herc slapped her again, a third time.

Marisse's breasts began to heave with excitement; she opened her mouth to speak but she hesitated.

'Say it!' Herc ordered.

'It's Phillippe. He *is* dead. I got word this morning. He was killed.'

'And you don't give a damn, do you? Because now you've got me, got me all for yourself!'

'You smug . . . bastard!'

He slapped her again.

She began to speak but, again, she hesitated.

158

'Say it!'

'Can I . . . finger myself?' Her voice was weak, suddenly servile.

'Sitting in the chair?'

'Yes. Can I lift up my skirt and finger myself?'

He slapped her across the face. 'Horny bitch!'

'Please may I finger myself while you –'

He slapped her harder, then ordered, 'Go ahead, play with your pussy, bitch. But never do it without asking me, right? From now on, I give orders around here! *I* am the master!'

Marisse quickly lifted her long skirt with one hand and used the other to gratify her moist womanhood; Herc stood alongside the leather chair, rubbing his clenched fist across her face, letting her lick, kiss, rub her cheek against the fist, pushing his bulging crotch against her breasts, but slapping her when she moved to kiss his penis swelling beneath his trousers.

'Bitch!' he murmured. 'Nothing but a bitch whore who has to crawl on her knees to get her master to move in the same house with her. So play with yourself, bitch, play with yourself and think how you're going to devote yourself to me, how you're trapped – like being trapped in irons, handcuffs, manacles – tied to me and there's no getting away, no escape, no way to unlock yourself ever from being slave to me and this . . . prick.'

Gossip quickly spread in Longchamp Parish about Herc moving into the big house at High Hill Plantation immediately after Phillippe Summers' death. But the rumors did not trouble Marisse. She considered the local White men to be trash and far inferior to herself; she knew the White women were jealous of her sexual life. She furthermore realized that she was not the only White female in Longchamp Parish who made illicit love to Black men. Marisse had seen the proud Creole lady, Noele Dehasset, literally lick her aristocratic lips as she stared at Herc's bulging crotch. But Marisse Summers doubted if pompous Noele Dehasset had the courage to pursue her secret desires.

Marisse also was amused when she watched Herc becoming aware of her devotion to him, how she acted as his slave but still retained a unique, definite power over him. Marisse Summers knew that many Black people had survived slavery, even prospered during their years of bondage to White people. She knew there was an art to being a slave, especially for a White woman to be an expert slave, controlling her master as if he were a puppet for her deep desires for his manhood. Marisse Summers knew that, ultimately, she was still in command of High Hill.

*   *   *

Herc believed he controlled the seven Black girls living inside the plantation's big house at High Hill but he worried that he still did not dominate Marisse Summers, not totally, not as he wanted, not as his male pride demanded.

Herc knew many women craved him merely for the size of his masculinity; he had known that fact since boyhood, since girls and older women had first begun chasing him - even occasionally men - and since White people gossiped in town about his penis, so evident inside his thin trousers; Herc came to cherish his penis like a treasure. He measured his penis in softness; he manipulated his penis and measured it in hardness; a foot rule was too short; few women could encircle his penis with their hands; only a man like Phillippe Summers' mouth could comfortably accommodate it. Herc suspected that his penis could serve him - his ambitions - better than a fine education to climb in the world.

Adoration. Desire. Need. Herc saw his penis awaken those feelings in people. But men - especially White men - often showed jealousy, even hatred for Herc and the sexual reputation which surrounded him like an aura. But lately Herc was learning how to win White men's trust; he knew that the trust of White men was important if he was to achieve status as a landowner in Longchamp Parish.

Nevertheless, Herc hated the sight of certain White men, especially the two White men whom he had recently begun meeting in secrecy to pursue a private business matter.

One man was Junior Dehasset, the other was Judd

Gillman. Herc planned to meet Gillman for business again today in the far corner of High Hill Plantation.

Herc saw Judd Gillman waiting for him at the designated spot; the red-haired man stood alongside his horse by a fence and chewed on a long piece of grass.

Herc had also learned it was good to be aggressive with White men like Judd Gillman and Junior Dehasset. He called from the trail as he approached, 'How long is it going to take you and your friends to drive out that Black Yank from the old Chatgrove place, Gillman?'

'Rickers?' Gillman chewed on the long piece of grass. 'Don't worry about him, boy.'

Herc tried not to show his irritation at Judd Gillman calling him 'boy'. He said, 'Rickers came up here to see me today.'

'That don't surprise me none.'

'He came up here to make friends. But then he started blabbing about a burning cross being left in his yard.'

Gillman's watery blue eyes became alert. 'You say anything?'

'Say what? What do I know about burning crosses?'

'You're one smart boy. So don't you go worrying none about Rickers. He can't hold onto that land much longer. You'll get it. Just like we promised. You'll get the old Chatgrove place, boy.'

'What about my workers?' Herc demanded. 'When do I get them? I got pens and shacks all built up in the back hills. Nobody will ever find the slave quarters I built, quarters not only for my workers, but a place for you to use for that Rebel Railroad.'

'You'll get your workers. The very first wagonful.'

'You've been promising me that for over six months.'

Gillman explained. 'Things like this take time. Too many Yankee soldiers still hanging around here. It's dangerous. The key man's some important Reb officer. He could still get arrested. Especially if word of this scheme leaks out.'

Herc reminded himself to be aggressive; he ordered, 'Just get me the deed for that land below me. Get me niggers to work. Then I guarantee you the use of High Hill for a stop on your underground railroad.'

Judd Gillman, chewing on the long piece of grass, studied Herc dressed in his fine clothing; he said, 'Let me ask you one question, boy.'

'Go ahead.'

'Don't you – being a nigger yourself – don't you have the slightest little bit of a conscience about helping people back into slavery? You know that's what this Rebel Railroad's all about, don't you? Starting up slavery again. At least for some of them. The shiftless niggers. Slavery for them again. Slavery for the dirt poor niggers.'

'Sheriff Gillman, you're the last man I expected to hear talk about a conscience.'

Herc turned and strode down the wooded path.

Judd Gillman smiled, nodding his head.

*　　　　　*　　　　　*

Judd Gillman rode from High Hill Plantation to one of the new turpentine mills owned by Sy Rowan and was located in a pine forest north of Two Forks Camptown.

The woodland smelled more pungent than most pine forests because the trees had been slashed for gum to drip from the wood. Black women and young girls dressed in drab clothing moved slowly through the trees, cutting streaks across the pine trees, allowing the pine gum to drip into boxes cut into the base of each tree.

Gillman ignored the female workers in the forest and plodded his horse toward a group of low-roofed buildings which included a mill to distill turpentine from pine gum, a boiling shed where the spirits were diluted for bottling, and a packing shed. The reconstruction programs in the South, and the availability of cheap labor, were making Sy Rowan a rich man from his turpentine mills in Louisiana, Georgia, Mississippi, and east Texas.

Judd Gillman had come to visit Sy Rowan's foreman, a Black man who lived in Two Forks Camptown but wanted to buy a small plot of land for his home and was willing to perform extra chores for anyone who would pay him. Judd Gillman was one of his contacts.

162

The subject of their meeting today was Black workers; Gillman asked, 'You talk more to your boss about workers for that new mill he's opening soon across the state line?'

The Black man nodded. 'Mr Rowan's waiting to hear if he can get workers at a good price.'

'You finding people in your camptown willing to go west, to sign up for a few years work?'

'Camptown niggers getting jittery about signing papers, Mr Gillman. Camptown niggers talking a lot about freedom. I'll probably get your folks fresh from the road. You just tell me when you're ready to make the run with them and I'll pull them off the road.'

'What about the wagon?'

The Black man smiled and nodded toward a shed. 'I've been working on the wagon myself, Mr Gillman, sir. I just finished putting shackles and leg irons into the wood bed. I got the wagon right there in that shed.'

'You got the slave wagon *here*? What are you? Dumb or something? Politicians and buyers come snooping around these turp mills.'

'Okay. Okay. Don't you worry Mr Gillman, sir. I'll move that wagon out of here. Don't you worry,' said the Black man named Romer.

'More that slave wagon right away! Tonight!'

'Where shall I move it?'

'How the shit do I know? Just get it away from this mill!'

Gillman looked around him at the trees, at the Black females moving like ghosts through the forest; there was a stillness in the forest and Gillman lowered his voice to say, 'I'll be in contact with you when we're ready to make the first run to Texas. Try to get mostly women workers. Women are easier to control than men. We also can work women as whores for horny settlers out west.'

'You just leave the job of finding workers up to me and Belle, Mr Gillman. Belle's got a good eye for wenches.'

'Belle? Who's Belle?'

'Belle's my wife, Mr Gillman.'

'Oh.' Gillman always forgot how Junior Dehasset was constantly telling him that Black people were beginning to

163

consider themselves equal to White people since the war, that they were wanting to get married in churches and call each other 'husband', 'wife', to adopt the ways of White people.

He grabbed for his crotch, saying, 'You got a gal for me today, boy?'

'Yes, sir. A gal's waiting for you right there in that little shed.'

'She suck good?'

'Supposed to do the best sucking in the state.'

'We'll see about that.'

Gillman strode toward the small shed; he opened the door on its leather hinges, and saw a young girl crouching on the dirt floor; she nervously moved to stand when she saw him.

'Stay down on your haunches, gal,' he ordered. 'I want a good, long suck from you.'

Gillman began unbuttoning his fly; he took out his penis and an odor of uncleanliness filled the small shed; he said, 'Stick out your tongue, honey, and give me a little bath here before you start sucking.' He held out his unwashed penis with one hand and pulled the frightened girl's head toward his crotch with the other hand.

*   *   *

Junior Dehasset had assigned the job of 'running slaves' and securing stops for the Rebel Railroad to Judd Gillman while he himself pursued what he considered to be the more delicate task of trying to win political support in preparation for the unification of all the Southern vigilante groups, The Knights of the Camellia, The Ku Klux Klan, The Brotherhood of Georgia, Liberty Lodge – White men joining in a brotherhood to renew slavery in the thirteen states which had comprised the Confederacy.

Junior Dehasset sat with his father, Senator Dehasset, in the library at Belrose Plantation after supper. Noele Dehasset had long ago disappeared with a book to her pergola. Sabrine had driven to visit neighbors.

Junior sat swirling golden brandy around the inside of a

crystal balloon – the delicate vessel looking alien, out-of-place in his leathery hand – saying, 'It surprises me, Pa, how some men can sit by and let the South go to seed.'

'Men must think more than about the South, Junior. Southerners have to stop being isolationists. We're Americans again.'

'I can't understand that. Take you as a politician, for instance. How can you serve Louisiana voters and still think about the entire country?'

'That's a politician's dilemma.' Senator Dehasset did not tell his son – nor anyone, yet – that he was thinking of stepping down from politics, of letting Louisiana be run by a younger generation of men, men who had fought in the war, men who would fight for a fair Reconstruction Program for the South.

'Pa,' Junior persisted, 'what would happen if a man of your reputation made a stand on a strictly regional platform?'

'Give me an example, son.'

Senator Dehasset had decided to bear no grievances against his son; he believed Junior was too feckless to be dangerous.

'Something popular, Pa. Something spreading through the entire South.' Junior shrugged. 'For instance, vigilante groups.'

Senator Dehasset scowled. 'You know my opinions about hooligans.'

'Just talk for sake of argument, Pa. You're a respected landowner, okay? So a respected landowner like you –'

A loud knocking on the library door disturbed Junior's hypothesis.

Senator Dehasset looked at the panelled door; he called, 'Yes?'

The door opened and the hired man, Clyde Quine, entered the room. He nervously gripped a grimy felt hat in his hands and looked at Junior.

'Mr Dehasset, it's that coon boy. He's escaped and –'

Junior sprang from his chair. 'I told you not to come here.'

'But this be mighty important, Mr Dehasset. That coon boy escaped, I said –'

'Escaped?'

'Who's gone?' asked the Senator, alerted by the gravity of Junior's voice. 'Who escaped from what?'

'You stay here, Pa,' Junior ordered as he moved toward the door.

'No,' Clyde Quine interrupted, 'I think your Pappy better come, too, Mr Dehasset. This involves him now and . . . the missus.'

*　　　　*　　　　*

The enslavement had begun slowly but gone too far, moved too quickly, completely engulfing Noele Dehasset before she realized what was happening to her.

Ken had appeared as usual in the pergola; Noele first noticed the rope when Ken uncinched the cord from the waist of his tow trousers and the trousers did not fall to his ankles as they had done in the past – there was a second rope tied around Ken's waist.

Noele, excited by what she thought was a new game invented for her, reached to uncinch the second rope securing Ken's trousers.

Ken slapped away her hand. 'What do you think you're doing?'

Noele stared into Ken's dark eyes; she felt his hand tighten around her wrist.

She said, 'You're hurting me.'

'You want to be hurt.'

Noele, staring at him, did not reply to the statement; she felt her mouth go dry.

'How much can I trust you?' Ken asked.

Noele did not understand. She said, 'You're the one who's in control.'

Ken slowly shook his head.

'Yes,' she insisted, allowing him to pull her to her knees without a struggle. 'You are in control of me.'

Ken continued shaking his head.

'Please.' She rubbed her face against Ken's baggy trousers, pressing to feel his phallus, his scrotum hanging inside the

166

rough fabric. She insisted, 'You are in control. Completely in control.'

'Completely?'

She reached to take the remaining cord from his trousers, to make his trousers fall to his feet, to prove her devotion.

Holding her wrists, Ken bound them together and whispered, 'I'm really going to get rough with you tonight, woman.'

'I tell you over and over that's what I want.'

'I'm tired of you telling me.'

'I won't talk.' Noele knelt helplessly with her hands tied together.

'I know you won't talk.' Ken pulled a scarf from his pocket. 'I'm going to . . . gag you.'

Noele Dehasset's eyes flared as Ken quickly wrapped the cloth around her mouth.

The first step of Ken's plan was Noele Dehasset; he picked her up from the ground and tossed her over his shoulder. A gold and opal chain fell from her neck to the ground. The chain was not part of Ken's plan. But he stopped, picked up the necklace, stuffed it into his pocket, and stepped out into the night with Noele – gagged and bound – over his shoulder.

Ken had discovered earlier today where Junior Dehasset was keeping Paulie a prisoner on Belrose. He spent the afternoon carefully laying out a scheme, hiding a horse nearby, gathering the necessary food, making all the plans for his and Paulie's escape.

*   *   *

Although it was night Senator Dehasset immediately recognized his wife and moved toward the rusty chain connecting her to the pole planted in the patch of weeds.

Junior raised his hand to hold back his father.

Clyde Quine began to explain. 'I came up to check on the coon, Mr Dehasset, same as always. But –'

'Shut up,' Junior ordered, then slowly approached the post. He untied the gag from his mother's mouth.

Noele lay motionless on her side in the tall weeds.

167

'Who did this?' Junior whispered to her.

Noele's eyes widened; she saw first her son, then her husband.

Junior worked quickly to unbend the wire from the chain slave collar he had made for Paulie but which now encircled his mother's neck.

Senator Dehasset, falling to his knees alongside his wife, demanded, 'Who did this, Noele?'

Noele closed her eyes; a cricket chirruped beyond them in the night.

'Who did this, Noele?'

Tears began streaming down Noele's cheeks. She buried her head in the earth and whispered, 'I feel so . . . soiled. I feel so violated and . . . soiled.'

'Ma, who did this?'

'It's not the jewels,' Noele sobbed. 'Not the necklace. What are material things? It's my pride. My soul. My . . . self-respect.'

'Ma, who did this? Did niggers do this?'

Noele drew her breath; she murmured, 'Yes.'

'Who, Ma? What niggers?'

She began to speak but stopped.

'Don't try to protect them, Ma. Look what they done to you. Who were they?'

'That . . . blacksmith,' she whispered. 'That man called – what is his name? Is it . . . Len? No. Ken.'

Senator Dehasset gasped. 'Ken?'

Noele kept her eyes pressed shut as she reconfirmed, 'Yes, it was that awful man, Ken, and the young colored boy –'

Junior interrupted, 'I think I know who the other one is. And I think I know exactly where those two dirty niggers ran to tonight!'

Junior rose to his feet and ordered Clyde Quine, 'Saddle my horse. There's a full night's work ahead of us.'

Chapter Fifteen

THE CARPETBAGGER

Gemma was enraged by what Warren told her about his visit to High Hill Plantation; she remained furious all day, asking him to repeat every detail he could remember about his brief but unpleasant encounter with Herc. She also managed to glean a few details that evening about Marisse Summers from Sabrine Dehasset while Warren was outside in the barn doing the evening chores.

'Marisse Summers was never a friend of mine,' Sabrine said as she sat by the kitchen table with Gemma; Sabrine had left her father and Junior in the library after supper at Belrose; she had come to the old Chatgrove place ostensibly to see Gemma and Warren, but she knew Cramer Crowley planned to leave tonight for New Orleans and she really wanted to see him; she was anxious, unsettled that Cramer would be away for perhaps another indefinite period of time.

Sabrine tried to answer Gemma's question; she explained, 'The Summers family was always aloof from the rest of the parish. Phillippe Summers studied in France. He returned to Europe every year – Paris, London, Rome, Madrid – and always thought he was better than anybody else in the parish. He even looked down his nose at old Creole families, people like the Deauvilles, the Merrieres, the Lintotts, the Tanets. We all expected Phillippe Summers to bring home a bride from Paris or Rome and were very surprised when he married Marisse Hubbard in Richmond, Virginia.'

'Is she beautiful, this Marisse woman?' Gemma asked.

'Men surround her at parties. Or at least they did at first.'

'At first?'

'When she first came to Longchamp Parish. Before the stories began spreading about the depraved life she and Phillippe led at High Hill. You see, Mrs Rickers, White people do not approve of their women –'

Sabrine hesitated.

Gemma suggested, 'Sharing beds with their slaves?'

Sabrine blushed; she fidgeted with her hands. She admitted, 'Rumors often are cruel.'

Gemma suspected that Sabrine probably was more interested in meeting Cramer Crowley, to talk about her growing interest in him, rather than talk about Marisse Summers. She thought Sabrine was probably even upset about Cramer leaving for New Orleans and his absence from Longchamp Parish. But Cramer still had not arrived at the house and Gemma wanted to seize this opportunity to gather every bit of information she could about High Hill Plantation.

She pressed, 'I do think it's strange that a Black man refused to talk to Warren. Somebody who lives almost right next door. Warren heard stories about this Herc fellow in Kettley. But they were men's stories. Tales about a Negro living with a White woman. Stories that White men like to invent and snigger about.'

'White women also snigger, Mrs Rickers.'

Gemma still tried not to show too much interest in the prurient subject. She said, 'You mentioned a child.'

Sabrine nodded. 'A little boy. Born after Phillippe was killed in the war. The child's seldom seen. He's supposedly not Phillippe's son at all but a half-caste boy.'

'Herc's son?'

'I would guess.'

'Miss Dehasset, it sure does sound to me like an old Bible city up there at High Hill. Husbands and wives sharing lovers -' Gemma shook her head.

'Sodom and Gomorrah? It's been called that. Especially when word spread that Herc kept a harem of Black girls in the big house to humiliate Marisse.'

'A . . . harem?'

Sabrine nodded. 'I don't know how Marisse allows him to do that to her - in her very own house.'

Gemma sat forward in her chair; she said, 'I'm more concerned what Herc does to us, Miss Dehasset. To Warren and me. I don't mean to harp on the subject but I do take it as a very bad sign that he refuses to talk to his neighbors. I get the feeling he doesn't want Warren and me here. It's bad enough when White people don't want us around but when Black people start shunning us too, well, a person begins to worry!'

Sabrine tried to console Gemma. 'I remember Mrs Chatgrove also had some kind of trouble with the people at High Hill. They had their eye on her property.'

'They wanted this . . . land?'

'Oh, yes. Candlewick Plantation would give High Hill direct access to the main parish road. They just have the old back road which leads around Spring Creek to Kettley. That old road is good for supplies. But since the cotton gin opened – and with the lumber and turpentine mills opening now that the war's over and a lot of building is going on – they are very cut off at High Hill.'

Gemma believed Sabrine Dehasset had inadvertently explained the reason why Herc had been so uncivil to Warren.

She said, 'I see. It would be profitable for them to have this place.'

'Oh, in more ways than one! For convenience's sake. For the marketing of their crops. Not to mention the fact that the price of their own land would increase with direct access to a main road. I heard my father himself say that very fact.'

The sound of Cramer Crowley's wagon on the driveway distracted Sabrine's attention; she dashed to the door and excitedly said, 'It's him! It's Cramer in his funny old wagon! He's come!'

'You run meet him.'

Gemma, sitting alone at the kitchen table, thought, 'Herc wants us out of here. That's what he wants. And he's going to get rid of us, get us out of here, if we don't get rid of him first. But how – how, dear Lord – how do we do that?'

*　　　　*　　　　*

Sabrine Dehasset and Cramer Crowley went for a ride in the evening before Cramer left for New Orleans; they chose a back road because Cramer reported seeing Sabrine's brother and another White man galloping their horses to a lather on the road to Bossburg.

Warren returned from the milking barn and found Gemma still sitting at the kitchen table.

'Have the lovers gone to spoon?'

Gemma nodded.

'Is Sabrine very upset about Cramer going away?'

Gemma mumbled, 'He'll be back.'

Warren had lived with Gemma long enough to recognize the distant look in her eyes, her firmly set jaw, the short, clipped answers - signs which betrayed she was laying the groundwork for a plan.

'Okay, gal, what you hatching?'

'I'm thinking about what you told me about High Hill.'

'Is that still bothering you?'

'Of course it is! I'm thinking about us. Our future here. Little Emmaline's future.'

Gemma turned to study Warren. She said, 'Did you ever consider he might have an ulterior motive for not being neighborly?'

'Like what?'

'Ambition . . . greed.'

'Come on, gal, tell me exactly what you're thinking.'

'I was talking to Sabrine about High Hill and the Summers family and -'

Gemma stopped, she blurted, 'That big dandy wants our land, Warren! I know it in my bones! Our land would connect High Hill to the main parish road. That's why Herc wants us out of here.'

'Sabrine tell you that?'

'Not in so many words. But she told me how the Summers family tried to get this land from poor old lady Chatgrove.'

Warren sat down across the table from Gemma. He asked, 'That Summers widow. Herc's mistress, you thinks she's in it?'

'I doubt it. She sounds too spoiled to think much about business ideas. Too concerned about orgies and . . . peckers. That big Black dandy might even be stringing her along, first

172

trying to get control of High Hill for himself, then to get our land.'

Warren considered the possibility. 'He's only got that back road out back of there.'

Gemma said, 'And that old grassy trace connecting them to us.'

'Which could easily be turned into a better road and –'

Gemma finished the sentence, '– and connect them right smack into the main parish road and probably double the price of their land.'

'Honey, what're we going to do?'

'I don't know yet, Mister, but I'm thinking on it.'

Warren was no longer listening; he also was thinking, considering the possibility of Herc having designs on the land he had spent hours, weeks, months, more than a year now, plowing, fencing, harvesting.

He pounded the table. 'God damn it! Things just get worse and worse and worse!'

Gemma knew that Warren often depended on her strong-mindedness and she suspected that this was one of those situations in which she had to show mettle.

She said in a firm voice, 'That's the way life is some times, honey.'

She then sat upright in her chair, saying, 'And that's why we've got to get stronger ourselves so we can fight back.'

'Fight back? Fight how? Fight what? We never know who or what we're fighting, Gemma. Men with sheets over their heads? Black men ordering me off their land? What's that to fight?'

'Hooded riders are one thing. But a Black man who's got him a –'

Gemma stopped; she nodded at the sudden inspiration; she said, 'By jingle, I do think I know how we're going to fight back this time. It's a long shot but –'

'How?'

'It has to do with greed. It has to do with sex. It has to do with greed and sex and White women hoping for big fancy Black men who –'

'Now, honey,' Warren interrupted, 'don't get started on that Black pecker business again.'

Gemma looked sharply at Warren. 'Mister, either you trust me or you don't. Either you have faith in me as your wife or you don't. Now what is it? You and me a team? Or do you and me split the blankets down the middle right now and call it a day?'

Warren took a deep breath. 'I trust you, Coffee Cup. You know I do.'

Gemma rose from the table with full matriarchal authority. She said, 'Then do me a favour, Walnut Man. When Cramer Crowley brings Sabrine Dehasset back from their ride, get her aside. Bring her inside the house. Any place away from Cramer. I want to talk to Cramer alone.'

'What you've got to say to Cramer Crowley you can't say in front of Sabrine Dehasset?'

'I've got a favor to ask him and it isn't exactly ladylike talk. Sabrine and I've been friends for more than a year. But, honey, you know how we still pussyfoot around each other.'

Gemma tilted her head and mimicked, 'Oh, Miss Dehasset, this! Oh, Mrs Rickers, that!'

Shaking her head, Gemma said, 'Sabrine's a delicate gal. Too delicate to hear what I've got to ask Cramer to find for me in New Orleans.'

'What about me? I'm your husband and I'm not delicate.'

'No, you're just downright jealous! Now, you said you trust me, so prove it! Get Sabrine aside when she gets back so I can ask Cramer to do me a favor in New Orleans.'

'And what is this "favor"?'

'No questions.'

'Gemma Mae Rickers, you are one bossy gal.'

'You better believe it, Big Dumpling.'

Warren cautioned Gemma, 'But you watch what you ask that Cramer Crowley to do, you hear, woman? We still don't know too much about Cramer Crowley neither.'

'We've got to start trusting somebody, honey, or we're going to find ourselves living in a camptown with all those poor freed slaves.'

'Bite your tongue, Gemma. Bite your tongue, right now.'

Gemma quickly bit her tongue, a superstitious gesture to keep the words she had spoken light-heartedly from becoming reality.

*   *   *

Ken was too concerned about Paulie's recovery to look closely at the sad condition of Two Forks Camptown. He had wrapped a piece of cloth around Paulie's neck to hide the rawness caused by the chain slave collar and to avoid upsetting Paulie's parents about his mistreatment. Ken coaxed Paulie into a modicum of strength and, with much patience and perseverance, they finally reached the tent where Paulie's family lived on the edge of the smokey camptown. The time was still before midnight.

Stella was pleased with the baskets of food which Paulie and Ken brought with them on the horse from Belrose Plantation, but she judged from their guarded actions that they were running from trouble; she did not ask any questions.

Lou was more talkative than Stella. He told how he had believed Paulie had been the Black boy rumored to have been hanged for raping a White widow near Bossburg.

'I told your Ma it was you.'

'And I said it ain't, that no son of mine pestered White ladies.'

Neither Paulie nor Ken commented on the story. Paulie kept talking about the farm he hoped to buy for them all; he said, 'Ken's all excited for it, too.'

Paulie stood alongside his mother near the bonfire; his father sat next to Ken; the three brothers and two sisters sat on logs in front of the tent. Matthew - wishing he could sneak off to visit Big Spanker - sat whittling a wooden whistle. Mark and Luke played dice in the dirt. Hetty and Willa giggled about Ken being handsome and unmarried, wondering if he could be a possible beau for either of them.

Paulie told his family, 'You don't have long to wait before getting out of this crowded place.'

'Don't worry about us,' Lou said. 'We can take care of ourselves a while longer.'

'Pooh!' Stella chided. 'You don't come back now, Paulie, and that old Pa of yours would've signed us all back into slavery.'

'I would not have!' Lou protested.

'You would've! You would've signed you, me, the boys there, as well as giggly Hetty and Willa here right back into slavery. You'd put your mark on some fool piece of paper and we'd all be in shackles as if Mr Abraham Lincoln had never been born! We'd all be back in slavery!'

'Slavery?' Ken had spoken little since their arrival. But he was jolted by Stella's outburst. 'What do you mean about slavery?'

Lou shrugged his shoulders. 'Just some talk going around camptown. Jobs being offered. Work going across state-line. Work for niggers who put their marks on a piece of paper.'

'Don't put your mark on nothing!' Ken urged vehemently. 'I talked to lots of folks walking the roads. Men and women freed from slavery. They tell me all kinds of tricks White people are using to get Black folks back into the harness. The Civil War freed us. Yeah. But planters and businessmen and bankers in the South ain't giving up all that easy. Black people were the big tool, the big money-makers in the South. How else are the plantations and mills and cotton gins going to run again without our sweat and blood? Pay us the same wages like they pay to White men? No, Lou. The answer is more . . . slavery!'

'That's what I tells him,' Stella blurted. 'Beware of more slavery! And I say don't put your mark on nothing!'

Ken went on. 'Lou, slavery takes on lots of different shapes and disguises. If the White folks don't get us back into shackles one way, then they're going to try some other way. Like share-cropping. But keeping the biggest share of the crops for themselves. Or setting up work camps. Signing up men, women, little girls and boys, for five, ten, even twenty years of their lives. The English done it before. When they first sent people to this country. I read they called it

176

"indentured". I read it in a school book. You sell yourself away. Right on legal paper. Just by one mark.'

'That's what I tells him!' Stella repeated. 'Don't put your mark on nothing.'

'Lou, you and your family hold on here a couple weeks more. Paulie and me got some business to settle. Then we're going to find a little piece of land.'

Lou looked at the burly Black man. He asked, 'Where you get money to buy land?'

Ken avoided the older man's gaze. He had not even told Paulie yet about the necklace which Noele Dehasset had dropped in the pergola, the golden chain which he now carried wrapped in a handkerchief in his trouser pocket.

He answered, 'I have something valuable to sell.'

'You willing to sell it and buy land for us?'

Ken smiled. 'The land won't all be for you, let me tell you that now. Some of the land will be mine, too. But I know Paulie will never be happy until his family's settled nearby him.'

Lou looked up at his son. 'Paulie, this Ken man sure must think the world of you to do all this for you and your kin.'

Paulie shrugged nervously; he did not want his family to suspect he loved another male; he still could not understand it himself.

Stella poked him, demanding, 'What you shuffling your feet for, boy? Don't be shuffling your feet when somebody wants to share life with you! Be proud! Stick out your chest! Stand up straight and shout "Hallelujah"!'

A voice called beyond the tent, from deeper inside the camptown. A Black man was calling to Lou; a shabbily dressed Negress and a White man, carrying a coat, stood behind the Black man.

'Who be them folks, Lou?' Stella asked.

'That's Romer,' Lou answered. 'Romer's the nigger who first told me about jobs being available across stateline. That woman be Belle, his wife, who first talks to me about the new turpentine mills opening in east Texas and jobs going there for the girls.'

Stella asked, 'And who be that White man coming with them toward us?'

Ken interrupted. 'This could be trouble. But don't move. None of you. Not yet.'

The lanky Black man, Romer, moved closer toward Stella's and Lou's blanket tent; he pointed at them and said to the White man, 'That's the bunch you looking for there, Mister.'

The woman, Belle, stepped alongside the White man; she held out her bony hand, saying, 'Now give us the money you promised.'

The White man, ignoring Romer and Belle, raised a gun from under his coat. He pointed at the small group and said, 'Okay, don't none of you move. There's men on horseback out in those trees. They've got guns. You're surrounded.'

Lou called to the Black man, 'Romer, what you and your woman bringing some crazy White man to –'

Romer's wife, Belle, pulled at the White man's sleeve, nagging, 'You promised us money if we showed you where these Belrose niggers lived!'

Stella shouted, 'You betray us for something to Whities, gal?'

'Shut your trouble-making yap!' shrilled the Black woman named Belle.

Stella dashed forward, grabbed Belle by the hair and shrieked, 'You traitor! You Judas bitch . . . traitor!'

Both women fell fighting to the ground.

One, two, three shots were fired at the same moment from the surrounding trees.

Ken dived to pull Paulie to the ground. The girls, Hetty and Willa, screamed. Lou – along with Matthew, Mark, and Luke – dived into the tent.

Men dressed in white robes and peaked hoods galloped from the trees and rode through the camp. Guns pop, pop, popped in the smoky darkness. A burning cross appeared in the middle of frightened people running in all directions. Then sticks of dynamite began to explode with a thundering noise which shook the earth and made dirt fly into the air.

*　　　*　　　*

Cramer Crowley, driving his wagon by the light of the moon along a bumpy road running south from Longchamp Parish, fluctuated between deep sighs and loud laughter, between considering his obsession with Sabrine Dehasset and laughter about what Gemma Rickers had asked him to find in New Orleans and bring back to Longchamp Parish.

Suddenly Cramer noticed that the night's sweet air became acrid, pungent. He reined his horse and stopped the wagon.

Cramer knew he was approaching the encampment of freed slaves called Two Forks Camptown. He sat motionless in the wagon and asked himself, 'What's that smell . . . like dynamite?'

Snapping the horse's brown leather reins, he rattled the old wagon faster along the dirt road.

Cramer Crowley stopped on a bluff overlooking the camptown; he stood on the wooden seat and saw smoke rising above the trees, not the usual smoke from bonfires, but smoke from devastation and destruction, like smoke he had seen in battlefields of the war.

He drove his wagon closer and saw remains of tents, scattered possessions, shambles left by raiders, charred corpses and mutilated bodies – and a cross which had burned itself out to nothing but a charred skeleton of the symbol of Christianity and brotherhood.

Cramer cursed, 'God damn them to hell!'

He jumped down from the wagon and began inspecting the ruins; he found no sign of life, no survivors in the spread of smoldering tents; five thousand freed slaves had once lived here but they had all run into the forest, or lay dead among the scattered debris.

He repeated, 'God damn them to everlasting hell.'

Cramer sifted through rubble; he found a few meagre objects possessed by freed slaves in every camptown in the South – a pot, a fork, tin spoons, a clock, a tin mug, a worn-out leather shoe.

Then he saw the wagon.

'What's that doing here?' Cramer asked himself.

He approached the wagon and recognized it as a slave

wagon, a wagon fitted with chains and shackles and irons.

'What's this wagon doing in a camptown for free slaves? Why wouldn't the people have burned this a long time ago? For firewood?'

Cramer then looked at the fresh tracks left by the wooden wheels; he realized that the wagon had only recently been brought to the camptown, before the raid, but no longer than twenty-four hours earlier.

Cramer Crowley realized in a flash that his mission as a Union Army officer dispatched from Washington to Louisiana was at last bearing fruit. This one slave wagon in a camptown for homeless, out of work Negroes, was the first clue he had found in sixteen months to corroborate the suspicions of the United States Government that there was a movement afoot in the South to revitalize the institution of slavery.

Cramer turned to his swayback horse; he said, 'Come on, big fella. There's work for this old Yankee carpetbagger.'

PART THREE

'STAND UP AND BE COUNTED'

Chapter Sixteen

NEW ORLEANS

Cramer Thomas Patrick Crowley – a commissioned officer holding the rank of second lieutenant in the United States Army, Yankee veteran of the Civil War campaigns at Seven Pines, Chickahominy, Perryville, Vicksburg – reported the casualty of Two Forks Camptown to Captain Frederick Hicks, commanding officer of the Freedmen's Bureau in Concordia Parish, Louisiana.

Lieutenant Crowley did not reveal his identity as an officer, nor that he had been operating as a covert intelligence agent for the U.S. Army since the end of the Civil War. He reported the camptown incident purely as a concerned citizen's observation, as a pedlar travelling through the South in his wagon.

He said, 'I stumbled onto the tragedy about three, four hours after it had happened, Sir. A cross still stood smoldering in the earth. I've heard tell of such crosses, Captain Hicks. I'm told they're planted by groups of Johnny Rebs none too happy with our victory.'

Captain Hicks, a husky, pock-faced man, sat behind his desk. He confirmed, 'These groups are vigilante men. They call themselves The Knights of the Camellia around here. They operate out of a general store at a wide spot in the road called Bossburg. They say their headquarters are a Freedmen's Bureau. But it's more like a crock of shit. They have no Federal authority. Not one bit. They work tooth and nail against every issue in the Reconstruction Program. But we're helpless. President Johnson laid down the law for the Federal Army not to rile nobody, not to risk all the work he's doing, or supposed to be doing, in Washington.'

Hicks began a tirade complaining about President Andrew Johnson's Reconstruction policy, how the terms were less effectual than the policy which Abraham Lincoln had been planning before his assassination.

Taking a deep breath, Hicks rose from behind his desk, shook hands with Cramer, told him to keep his eyes open and to avoid trouble himself in the South.

Cramer intended to report the Two Forks Camptown incident to his own commanding officer in New Orleans. But he continued his charade with Captain Hicks. He thanked him for his time, promised to report any other disturbances he might come across in his travels as a pedlar, bade him farewell and went outside to his wagon to resume his trip South to New Orleans where he would conduct the private business to which he had to attend.

The last week had been an especially tormented time for Cramer Crowley; he had slept little, laying awake at night, deliberating whether he should or should not ask Sabrine Dehasset to marry him. He had already told her he was going to New Orleans on business, but he only planned on making the trip if Sabrine accepted his proposal of marriage – he would then go to New Orleans to buy a wedding ring. Sabrine had instantly accepted his proposal, agreeing on the earliest wedding date possible.

*   *   *

Daylight was fading on Cramer Crowley's second day away from Longchamp Parish when he finally reached New Orleans. He left his horse and wagon at Letour's Stables on Burgundy Street.

Storeowners were already putting up the shutters on their shops, but street vendors – brightly dressed women, bare-footed Negro children, white-haired old men – still roamed the wooden sidewalks, called *banquettes*, selling cakes, flowers, seafood gumbo from tin cups, glasses of fruit punch filled from earthenware pots.

Cramer pushed his way through the foot traffic and went to a rooming house he frequented on Toulouse Street, a clean but inexpensive establishment located among the narrow, iron-trimmed buildings crowding one another in the

184

riverfront section of the city called The French Quarter. Cramer washed away the dust of the road in a bath poured from kettles into a zinc tub. He changed into a fresh suit of civilian clothing but realized it was too late to report to his superior officer. He knew that the jewelry shops would also be closed for the day by now. He decided that the chore most likely to be accomplished at this late hour was the favor which Gemma Rickers had asked him to do for her. He decided that the ideal place to begin it was at a grey wooden house located nearby on Basin Street, a bordello run by a Black woman named Joleen Sykes.

*   *   *

Basin Street, located to the north of The French Quarter, had begun its existence in New Orleans as a gulley lined with tents but had quickly become one of the city's most prosperous - and notorious - tenderloin districts.

Joleen Sykes, as wide as she was tall, with skin the color of a prune, received Cramer Crowley in the small parlor of her four storey bordello.

Joleen sat - was squeezed into - a red velvet loveseat which she filled as if it were an armchair. She asked, 'What girl you want tonight, Irishman?'

'I'm not planning on going upstairs tonight, Miss Joleen.'

Joleen, puckering her small lips, arched one thinly plucked eyebrow and asked, 'You feeling poorly, Irishman?'

'I'm feeling fine, Miss Joleen. Never felt better. But I just got into town -'

Joleen waved her doll-sized hand. 'Irishman, that's more reason than ever to hop straight into bed with one of my big-titted gals. I got some of the loveliest, tastiest, squeeziest morsels on Basin Street.'

'Things are changing for me, Miss Joleen.'

She eyed him. 'You fallen in love, Irishman?'

Cramer grinned.

Joleen readjusted herself in the loveseat; she lifted the corners of her ruffled cream taffeta skirt and said, 'My, my, my. Horny and in love. Poor, poor man!'

'What do you mean? Poor man?'

Shaking her head woefully, Joleen explained, 'Trouble like this often happens to men like you, Irishman. Men who treat women like pin-cushions, poke away like some kind of big old needle. But, then, a nice little buttercup gal comes along and they fall head over heels in love with her, puts Little Buttercup high up on some marble pedestal like some golden angel, keeping her pure and pristine – and tries to turn into angels themselves.'

'My Buttercup is a very special little lady, Miss Joleen.'

'Let me tell you something, Irishman. Don't you keep your special little lady too high up on that pedestal you've carved for her. Ladies don't like heights. Your special little lady's probably got the same human desires as you.'

'I certainly hope you are right!'

'Haven't you been to bed with her yet? Just to sample the pie?'

'Not this one.'

Joleen stared aghast at one of her best customers; she gasped, 'What you fixing to do, Irishman? Wait till you . . . marry her?'

Cramer smiled. 'That's the accepted custom, Miss Joleen.'

'Accepted custom or no accepted custom! That don't mean it's the best! Get your gal in the sack and see if you want to share a bed with her for the rest of your days.'

'Thank you for the advice, Miss Joleen, but I don't think that would work this time. Besides, I shouldn't be boring you with all this talk about my private life.'

'Who you going to talk to? Your horse?' Joleen waved her pudgy hand. 'I tell you what, Irishman. Come back later tonight. You may not want to pester one of my big-titted cuties and I ain't going to force you to. But I'm putting on a little show downstairs in my theatre tonight. You might just enjoy . . . that.'

She winked at him.

Cramer Crowley knew that Joleen Sykes' Basin Street bordello was famous for the shows she presented – dramatic scenes enacted by her Negress prostitutes.

'What time does it start?'

186

'Midnight. But come early. Buy a few drinks. Spread some money around.'

'Will I see you?'

'Have we ever been in the same room together and you *didn't* see me?'

Cramer promised to come back later that night; it was not until he stood outside on the muddy street that he realized he had not mentioned Gemma's request to Joleen. He decided to visit another bordello on Basin Street and, maybe, a few in The French Quarter.

*   *   *

Gemma's request proved to be embarrassing for Cramer Crowley; two madams on Basin Street asked him if he had changed his sexual preferences from women to men and a third madam - a Japanese woman who ran a house on Iberville Street, asked him what was the matter with a Black man, why must he find a White man with a big penis?

Cramer explained, 'There is a rumor that Black men are hung heavier than White men. I want to find a White man to disprove this story, shall we say, in a most colossal way.'

The Japanese madam, Yanura, had come to New Orleans from California, speaking and acting like a White woman hardened by frontier life, but wore a kimono and decorated her bordello with Oriental screens, lanterns, silks.

She said, 'You are about two weeks too late. There was a German here last week with a sausage between his legs, a real big German liverwurst.'

'I'm acting as an agent for a lady. And she is not looking so much for a liverwurst as for a pole,' Cramer explained.

'The German sausage turned into a pole. Poor little Trisha, she's still away recovering from the damage.'

'Yanura, there must be another White man in New Orleans built like that German.'

'Not that I've seen. Not like Heinrich.'

'Don't tell me the Negro legend is true, that Black men *do* have the biggest equipment in the world.'

'Never believe legends, Mr Crowley. They say Oriental

men are built small. Like little boys. I can tell you that legend is a lie. From my own personal experience. And perhaps that's the answer. Why don't you have your lady friend come here and find a man for herself?'

'She's married.'

'So what? It's not unusual for married women to turn a few tricks here. They have a good time. I even let them keep ten per cent!'

'My friend lives in the country. Besides, she's Black –'

'Color's no problem either. Anyway, not in this house. True, there are color restrictions in the White houses in town. Black and White women seldom work together. But Orientals, we have no restrictions. Not in America. But home now, back in the old country, now that is a different matter. But in San Francisco, Chicago, Denver, New Orleans, if it's got a hole and is warm, I can find a mattress for her some place in the house.'

'You still don't understand, Yanura. Or I'm not making myself clear. My friend requires more than big equipment. The man must also be able, talented enough, to tell a few stories.'

The Japanese woman shook her head. 'Then the German, he wouldn't have been any good. Heinrich didn't speak English.'

She tapped her paper fan on Cramer's knee. 'I tell you what. There's a house on Basin Street. Joleen Sykes runs it. She might be able to help you.'

'I'm going to Joleen's tonight. For her show in the cellar.'

'Ah! How I wish I could go with you. I've been to one of her shows and I loved it. But I must stay here and make my own magic . . .'

She then said, 'Hey, you haven't asked about anyone for yourself!'

'I'm getting married. A young lady from Longchamp Parish.'

'Congratulations,' she said, then added, 'you say Longchamp Parish?'

'Near a town called Bossburg.'

'There was trouble up there, wasn't there?'

188

'Trouble?'

'A raid on one of those poor camptowns, those dumps where freed slaves are crowding into these days.'

'Yanura, how do you know about that?'

'A client told me. A man from Montgomery. He heard about the raid when he was here and he became very angry.'

'Was he a Black man?'

'No, a White man. I think he was very important in the Confederate Army. He dashed straight from here to go see about the trouble. I know that for a fact because he sent our handyman, Rufus, to fetch him a horse from the stables.'

Cramer asked, 'His name wasn't Fenton, was it? Colonel Pat Fenton?'

'Why, yes it is. How do you know that? Is he a friend of yours?'

'No, not a friend. But I know who he is.'

Cramer thanked the Japanese woman, went back to have dinner in a small restaurant on St Peter Street and thought about the matter of Pat Fenton being in town and suddenly riding to Longchamp Parish as soon as he had heard about the trouble at the camptown. Cramer told himself there was nothing he could do tonight about Fenton now – an ex-Confederate Colonel also known as Cyclops – and that he best continue the search to find a White man who was sexually endowed as generously as Herc.

Cramer still could not stop smiling about Gemma's adamant wish not only to disprove the so-called Black Myth about Negro men having larger penises than White man, that Negresses were all erotic furnaces, but also to find a White man who could challenge Herc's sexual powers over Marisse Summers at High Hill.

Gemma's grit both amused and impressed Cramer; Gemma had stood with her hands on her hips in the yard of the old Chatgrove place and informed him, 'I know I'm going to have to pay some White stud to travel up here from New Orleans to dazzle that Marisse gal. But I've got money, Cramer Crowley. Don't you think I have planned on getting something for nothing. I've been saving the money I got from selling my upright piano before leaving Philadelphia. I figure there's no better cause to spend that money from my piano than on protecting this land from some greedy neighbor.'

Gemma dug into her apron pocket; but Cramer stopped her, telling her to save the money until he returned from New Orleans – to see if he could find an appropriate White man.

Now, walking along the wooden *banquette* on Basin Street, listening to fiddle music screeching inside saloons, Cramer thought about the pretty little housewife, Gemma Rickers, spending her treasured piano money on a White gigolo to rival a Negro buck, and he smiled at the wonders, the incongruities, the powers of survival in this world.

*   *   *

The sunken stage in the cellar of Joleen Sykes' bordello on Basin Street was lit by tallow candles flickering on a round black iron chandelier hanging by heavy chains from the low ceiling.

A pile of fluffy red feathers lay heaped on golden embroidered cushions; four statuesque, scantily clad Black women passed back and forth on the candle-lit stage carrying wicker baskets of more red feathers, scattering them on the mountain to make it higher, fuller, fluffier.

Cramer took a seat in a chair as a violin began to play in the darkness beyond the sunken stage; the music began in a romantic, lilting cadence, almost waltztime, but became more lively when the male audience filled the chairs surrounding the stage.

Soon, four coal black women, wearing diaphanous pink harem pants and purple jewels glittering on their nipples, appeared from the darkness and carried a litter on their bare shoulders – a chair on which sat a bare-chested, broad-shouldered, mustachioed White man.

A gong sounded in the darkness beyond the stage; the women sat the litter on the floor near the heap of red feathers; the White man arose to his feet; his black satin breechcloth fell to the floor revealing his penis.

Whispers and laughter spread through the audience as the

190

men saw the abnormal size of the performer's large, uncircumcised penis.

The White man stood in front of the mountain of red feathers, planting one bare foot on the feathers as the Negresses began to dance around him, adoring his penis, bending, reaching, twisting to kiss his muscular body, making his penis quickly stiffen, lengthen, become even larger, the foreskin pulling back to reveal a thick crown.

The man bent forward, grabbed a handful of feathers, threw them at the women and they – the feathers and the women – scattered into the surrounding darkness.

The man – his penis jutting straight out from his patch of wiry pubic hair – lowered himself to the mountain of scarlet red feathers as if it were a woman, as if he were going to copulate with the make-believe female, a fantasy in the feather heap.

The men in the audience watched silently as the well-endowed actor began to hump the heap of red feathers, the cheeks of the actor's naked buttocks squeezing together as he quickened, deepened his drives, as he sank his mammoth phallus into the mountain.

Slowly the mountain began to move; the actor pumped faster.

The mountain gradually began to thrust upwards from the floor and suddenly a loud scream filled the theater.

'*Dick me! Dick your big mama good, honey child!*'

Red feathers flew, scattered, swirled from the floor as Joleen Sykes, naked, her prune-black fatness shining in the candlelight, emerged from within the heap of fluffy red feathers. But the White actor kept driving his penis between her enormous black thighs.

The men applauded; cheers filled the subterranean theater; the Black actresses rushed from the darkness to prop cushions behind Joleen Sykes to help her to sit on the stage floor so she could look over the fleshy shelf of her elephantine breasts at the man driving into her.

'Dick your mama good, honey child!' she coaxed. 'Dick your big woman good!'

Louder cries, cheers, applause filled the cellar.

'Hey, now,' she said, spreading her breasts. 'Let's see the child nurse one of big mama's hot titties!'

The actor, still pumping his hips, raised his head, opened his mouth, wrapped his lips around one of Joleen's nipples – a brown nipple as big as a tea cup.

Throwing back her head Joleen screamed, 'You're making your mama feel goooood!'

Cramer Crowley watched the act with amazement. He knew he had found a White man who possessed the sexual endowment which Gemma Rickers required for her scheme.

'I said . . . dick!' Joleen Sykes shrilled. 'I said dick your big mama real goooood!'

Chapter Seventeen

CAJUN LEGEND

Gustave Depardeau - a short, wiry man with a handlebar mustache - wore a green plaid suit and white spats over black patent leather boots when he met Cramer Crowley in the parlor of Joleen Sykes' bordello on the afternoon following the midnight performance in the cellar.

Joleen Sykes sat like a kewpie doll, dressed in a frilly emerald green frock, squeezed into her red velvet loveseat. She listened to Cramer explaining how he was looking for a man to perform a job upcountry in Longchamp Parish, that the task was sexual work, that the assignment could become physically dangerous, that he was offering the work to Gustave Depardeau because of the size of his penis.

Cramer said, 'I came here straightaway yesterday when I arrived in town. I knew I would find somebody at Joleen's to meet the requirements. But, then, we started talking and I forgot to mention what I was looking for.'

Gustave Depardeau sat on the edge of a straight back chair. He held his hands cupped over the silver knob of his walking stick and asked, 'Mr Crowley, do you want me to satisfy a lady? Is that the kind of job you have in mind? To make love to a lonely lady stranded in the backwoods? If so, I can say yes right now. I have satisfied lonely women before. I do not consider such work risky.'

'You may not even have to satisfy the lady,' Cramer said. 'But I suggest you wear tight trousers and tempt her.'

'This lady, she is what's called "cock crazy"?'

'Very.'

'Her lovers, they must be big?'

'Very.'

Depardeau shrugged. 'I disappoint no one. I can match any man.'

193

'You must not match, Monsieur Depardeau. You must excel. Surpass.'

'The only thing I cannot surpass are some donkeys. But, then, I am bigger than many donkeys. But big donkeys, they can be clumsy - or so I am told.'

'I am sure you will perform quite admirably, Monsieur.'

'Performing is my life. My profession. I am an actor. I do not play the stage. I appear in bordellos and bedrooms. They are more profitable.'

'I must repeat, Monsieur Depardeau, this assignment could become dangerous.'

'There is a husband?'

'The husband is dead. But there's a lover. He lives in the house and could become jealous.'

Depardeau shrugged. 'A dead husband. A jealous lover. The story is not new to me.'

'But this story very well could be new. I will explain more details later, how you supposedly knew the wife's deceased husband when you were in the Confederate Army together, how he asked you to deliver a message to his wife. But, for the moment, I emphasize that this is a highly dangerous job and I urge you to consider it carefully.'

'Dangerous? What is dangerous? I have pistols. I shoot. I have sabres. I fence. I even have the *fouet*.'

'*Fouet*?'

'The whip.'

'Why do you mention whips?'

'Whips are the latest fashion in duelling among smart young Creole gentlemen in New Orleans. Since the war, Southern gentlemen have no slaves to flog. They now whip one another in duels. So, I am also a whipmaster, *par excellence*!'

'Then I suggest you bring your whips if you decide to accompany me back to Longchamp Parish. The lover is a freed slave, a Negro who served as overseer during his last years of slavery and is probably quite adept with a whip himself.'

'A Negro?' Depardeau's eyes glistened, his thin lips lifted into a smile. 'The job becomes more attractive. A White lady

194

and a Black lover. My fingers already itch for the butt of my whip. You see, Mr Crowley, I hate Negroes. I loathe and detest them.'

Cramer Crowley looked from Depardeau to Joleen Sykes squeezed into her loveseat.

Gustave Depardeau quickly explained, 'Oh, no! Not all Black people! Not women, children, most men. I hate the Black buck, the Negro peacock, the Black stag who swaggers, swanks, parades himself on the street. Why do they think they are the only men with any meat between their legs? Such arrogance! I want to whip them with my own meat!'

'I hate to feed your hatred, Monsieur, but you sound more and more exactly like the gentleman I am looking for.'

Cramer then studied the dark-complexioned man sitting on the edge of the chair. He asked, 'Tell me about yourself, Monsieur. Are you from France?'

'My family came from France many years ago, but my parents came to Louisiana from Canada. From a settlement called Acadia. We were thrown out by the English. That's how our people got our name. From the settlement called Acadia. The English, they say "Acadians", but the Southerners, they shortened it to "cajun". I am a Cajun, Mr Crowley.'

'Are there many Cajuns living in New Orleans?'

'Cajuns live mostly in the bayous, along the rivers, the lakes, the shorelines, the twisting bodies of water running through Southern Louisiana. Cajuns are fishermen. Sailors. And, of course, lovers famous for their big –'

Gustave Depardeau patted his crotch, saying, 'You just tell me what you want, where you want it and how much you will pay.'

Cramer hesitated; he had dreaded talking about money, to state that the fee could not surpass the price of one second-hand, upright piano – whatever that might have been two years ago in Philadelphia, Pennsylvania.

Joleen spoke for the first time during the afternoon meeting. 'I'm footing this bill. And, God damn it, you better not charge too much, Depardeau!'

195

Cramer Crowley and Gustave Depardeau both looked at Joleen squashed into her loveseat.

She explained, 'Irishman, you told me a little about the couple you're helping up in Longchamp Parish. It sounds like they're having a tough row to hoe up there. I figure there's a time when folks have to help each other in life.'

She looked at Gustave Depardeau, 'You do what you have to do and settle the price with me when you get back to New Orleans.'

He nodded his agreement.

Joleen looked at Cramer. 'Is that okay with you, Irishman?'

'I never thought I'd see an angel dressed in a frilly green dress!'

*   *   *

Cramer Crowley still had not bought a gold wedding band for Sabrine. But before he went shopping, he visited the United States Army Headquarters in a new section developing north of Canal Street, a neighborhood referred to by the local residents as The American Sector.

Cramer delivered his report to his commanding officer, General Theophilus Bacchus, on the vigilante activity in northern Louisiana, his observations on the Knights of the Camellia, the catastrophe at Two Forks Camptown. He learned from General Bacchus that the U.S. Army was aware of ex-Confederate Colonel Pat Fenton's presence in New Orleans, and that Fenton had departed hurriedly last night for Longchamp Parish.

General Bacchus sat under a framed portrait of President Andrew Johnson in the sparsely furnished office. He said, 'Fenton arrived in New Orleans last week. He attended a concert the first night at the Opera House down on Toulouse Street. A performance of some Italian chamber orchestra, I believe.'

'Colonel Fenton started out as an actor, am I correct, Sir?'

'Fenton studied together with John Wilkes Booth! There's some proof on them being involved in the Lincoln con-

196

spiracy. But one thing we know for a fact is that they're both making their reputation *off* the stage.'

Cramer thought how the world still buzzed with the name of Abraham Lincoln's assassin. He said, "Booth at least made his bid for fame inside a theater.'

'We'll know more about Fenton after he leaves Longchamp Parish. He's obviously hurrying there to meet that Dehasset fellow.'

Shaking his head, Bacchus then said, 'That poor old Senator Dehasset. His career on the decline. And then being saddled with a worthless son like that.'

'I'll get a report back to you as soon as I can, Sir.'

'When do you go back there, Lieutenant?'

'Today. Tonight. As soon as I buy a wedding ring.'

'A wedding ring? You're finally getting married?'

'Let's hope so. I found the right little lady.'

'Congratulations,' Bacchus said, reaching across his desk to shake Cramer's hand. 'When's the date?'

'Soon as I get back.'

'What's her name?'

Cramer had anticipated this question; he did not want to reveal his fiancee's identity - divulge that she was the sister of Junior Dehasset, the ringleader of the Knights of the White Camellia - and worry his commanding officer about compromising his interests.

He replied, 'If you don't mind, Sir, I will tell you that once I get the ring on her finger. I don't want to jinx it. I don't want to jinx anything.'

'Still selling Firefly water?' The general's eyes twinkled.

Cramer nodded. 'Still playing the fool. Still being a wee bit of the actor myself, Sir.'

*   *   *

The news about the calamity at Two Forks Camptown spread through Longchamp Parish; many White families who suffered financially from the loss of slaves nevertheless agreed that it was criminal and immoral for the freed Negroes to be killed, injured, or driven from their hovels by a band of vigilante riders; the true identity of the masked riders remained unproven but respectable Longchamp Parish families, such as the Merrieres, the Tanets, the Lintotts, had their suspicions, and sympathy rose in the neighborhood for Black people. Despite the news about Two Forks Camptown, though, the important subject of discussion at Belrose Plantation was Sabrine Dehasset's unexpecte announcement to her family that she was going to be married.

The news devastated Noele Dehasset. 'Married, Sabrine? You are getting married . . . next Saturday?'

'Not *next* Saturday, Mother. This Saturday.'

'Impossible!' Noele said, sinking back in the apricot silk covered *fauteuil*. 'Absolutely impossible, insane – and in terribly bad taste.'

'Mother, I don't think anybody at Belrose should be talking about bad taste. Not after what's been happening around here.'

'What's been happening here?' Noele challenged. She glanced across the sitting-room at her husband reading the New Orleans *Times Picayune*. 'What have you been telling this child?'

Before her father had time to reply Sabrine protested, 'Mother, I am not a child. And don't interrogate Papa as if this were The Spanish Inquisition. He didn't tell me a thing. I am an adult. I know about adult weaknesses. I also know – or I am beginning to realize – how patient Papa has been with you all these years.'

Senator Dehasset had tried to rationalize, tried to assimilate certain realizations he had made about his wife in the last few days; he pleaded, 'Sabrine, please.'

'Papa, excuse me, but it is far past the time to discuss many important matters happening at Belrose. I am not deaf. Everybody who works, who steps foot in this house, is talking, gossiping about hideous, absolutely hideous incidents.'

'Gossiping? Who's gossiping?' Noele demanded. 'I'll get rid of them straightaway. How dare they gossip!'

'Mother, you and Junior are perhaps a little too good at getting rid of people. That's half of our problem right there.'

198

'There you go again, Sabrine. Deriding your brother. Just because Junior chose not to go to a military academy when he was a boy, you still call him a lunkhead, a dullard, a redneck –'

'Mama, Junior has progressed beyond – or below – lunkhead and dullard.'

'What has he done to you now?'

Sabrine looked directly into her mother's grey eyes; she asked, 'Why, Mother? Why, on the night that the camptown was destroyed – when all those poor homeless Black people were burned out or driven from their sad little hovels by men wearing white hoods – why did I see my very own brother and his friends from Bossburg riding in the direction of that camptown?'

Noele said, 'Probably to help. You know you do not have the monopoly on being nice to colored people, dear.'

Sabrine ignored her mother's remark; she elaborated, 'Riding to the camptown *before* the catastrophe happened, Mother?'

Senator Dehasset again spoke from his corner of the sitting-room; he advised, 'Sabrine, do not dig in ground where you may find skeletons. And I mean that quite literally, dear girl.'

'I don't know what is happening here, Papa, but I can tell by your manner recently, your voice, your aloofness, that you probably know what's afoot and don't like it very much at all.'

Noele Dehasset interrupted. 'Sabrine, you were announcing your intention to get married this coming Saturday. Do continue to explain that folly. And, resume, dear, by telling us who is the . . . lucky man?'

'A pedlar.'

'Oh, a pedlar. I see. I see.'

'His name is Cramer Crowley.'

'Cramer Crowley. That sounds distinctly . . . Irish.'

'He is Irish, Mother. First generation. He's from the North.'

'When you slum, dear, you really slum.'

'Could it be hereditary, Mother?'

Noele ignored the jibe; she asked, 'And are you inviting guests? People like your colored friends from the house you never moved into?'

'The Rickers family? Yes, I am inviting the Rickers family, Mother. I thought it was long past time for them to be guests at Belrose. They are coming. As well as our other friends. The Deauvilles, the Merrieres, the Lintotts, the Tanets.'

'You invited all those people to come to a wedding reception in . . . three days time?'

Noele Dehasset leaned back her head and, laughing at the idea, said, 'Of course, Sabrine, you realize that none of them will show up, don't you? There's no time to prepare.'

'Do you mean, Mother, there's no time to buy gifts?'

'That, too.'

'That's precisely one of the reasons I want to be married at such short notice. To save people the expense of buying gifts. The war left many families penniless. They have little money to spend on gifts. I want their good wishes. I do not want to embarrass them into spending money they don't have. Cramer and I decided to give tradition a holiday.'

Noele unsnapped her fan. 'Oh, to be young and idealistic and . . . poetic! How refreshing!'

'If you're worried about the lack of gifts, Mother, have hope. I'm also inviting those awful Rowan twins, those red-haired monsters whose father owns those nasty turpentine mills. They will probably bring a whole set of silver!'

Noele Dehasset slowly fanned herself as she arched one eyebrow. 'Sabrine, tell me one thing. And do not be ashamed to answer.'

'Yes, Mother?'

'Sabrine, how many months pregnant are you with this . . . Irishman's child?'

'Mother, if my father weren't in the room I would slap your face. But I don't want Papa to think there's not a lady left in the Dehasset family.'

Sabrine rose from her chair. Her skirts crackled as she walked across the Aubusson carpet toward the double French doors; she opened one door and stepped out into the hallway. She quietly shut the door behind her.

Chapter Eighteen

THE REBEL RAILROAD

Broody Hen and Big Spanker, overhearing Francey Dasher telling her imaginary lady friends that she might have to marry Mr Hiram if her husband did not return home soon from the war, decided they could not wait for Gemma Rickers to receive a reply to the letter she had sent to a friend in Philadelphia to find a home for the girl.

Broody Hen told Big Spanker to take Miss Francey for a walk while she took a stick and chased away the shaggy old dog named Mr Hiram from the farm, the dog which Miss Francey believed was the only person who could save her make-believe baby from being born a bastard child.

Big Spanker, determined not to make Francey Dasher suspicious that they were getting rid of the dog, strolled leisurely along the dusty parish road in the afternoon sun; she tried to discuss with Francey the precautions which a pregnant woman must take with her health.

Francey Dasher nervously brushed at her sandy-coloured hair. She irritably replied, 'Don't be nice to me, big nigger woman! Don't sweet-talk me just so Broody Hen can midwife my baby!'

'Broody Hen? Midwife the baby you expecting? I'd never dream of pushing that idea into your head, Miss Francey, Mam.'

'Just don't try it.'

'But I'd never dream of it, Miss Francey, Mam. Fact is, why do you think I never get knocked-up myself? Do you think I want that crazy old woman midwifing my baby?'

'Hmmph! There's no comparison between us. It's as easy as pie for you colored women to birth babies.'

Spanker tried to be patient. 'Sure it's easy for us colored gals to birth babies, Miss Francey. Easy as cows to calf. We ain't delicate like you refined White ladies. We colored gals built hefty for birthing. But I still wouldn't let Broody Hen do no midwifing on my baby.'

Francey airily announced, 'Besides, my husband is taking me North where his family lives. My husband wrote to say we're leaving any day now.'

'Yep, I hear folks talking about you moving North, Miss Francey. I do envy you. Getting a fine new home and all. I do envy you.'

Francey Dasher, spotting a cloud of dust rising farther down the parish road, said, 'Look! That's probably my husband coming back for me now! He's jealous and bound to have heard about other menfolk hereabouts trying to win my attentions.'

Big Spanker knew that the only men to ride the parish road these days in numbers were the White men who congregated at the general store in Bossburg. She grabbed Francey's arm and said, 'No, it's too early for your husband to be coming to get you. Why don't we stop here in the woods? Why don't we pick some berries so you can bake your husband a nice deep dish berry pie? There's a nice berry patch right here in these woods.'

Francey brushed away Spanker's grip. 'You pick your own stupid berries. I want to see if it's my husband coming home from the war to get me!'

'Your husband's arriving tomorrow on the paddle-wheeler Miss Francey. I remember you telling me that distinctly.'

She grabbed again to pull the girl into the woods.

Francey broke away from Spanker's hand again; she raced down the dirt road, running toward the horses galloping nearer.

The riders reined their horses to avoid running over Francey Dasher; a cloud of yellow dust surrounded them. Whoops of laughter arose from the riders when they saw the identity of the girl for whom they had stopped. The White men were emboldened by the success - the notoriety - of their mission as masked vigilante riders at Two Forks Camptown.

One man was Judd Gillman. He said, 'Lookee who we have here!'

Dave Cooper shouted from his horse, 'Howdy do, Miss Dasher. Ain't seen you socializing for a long time.'

Dwight Pine leered at the nervous young lady. 'Looking for some company, little miss?'

Big Spanker stood motionless in the trees watching the White men surrounding Francey on their hoses; Spanker knew that Francey's mental instability was common knowledge in Longchamp Parish.

Judd Gillman, leaning from his saddle, patted Francey's hair, saying, 'You sure look right pretty today, Miss Francey.'

She slapped at his dirty hand. 'Don't touch me!'

'Oh, ho!' laughed Billy Collins. 'Little loco gal's got some spunk to her!'

Dwight Pine leaned from his saddle to pinch Francey's buttocks. 'Let's see if crazy gal's got any flesh on her bones.'

Francey, pulling away from him, shrieked, 'Don't touch me, you White . . . trash!'

A silence followed her words.

Billy Collins said, 'That was a mean thing for a crazy girl to say, Miss Francey.'

'Mean and ornery,' Judd Gillman said. 'You've done gone and spoiled all our playfullness.'

Big Spanker, seeing Gillman pull a rope from his saddle, hurriedly emerged from the pine trees. She politely called, 'Excuse Miss Francey and me, gentlemen. We best be going on our way.'

'Why, look who else is here!' laughed Billy Collins' brother, Sammy, as he looked at the cotton dress straining against Big Spanker's Amazonian body.

'Hey! The little White loony's got a nigger mammy with her out on a walk.'

'It's that big nigger gal from the Dasher place,' said Dwight Pine. 'I always wanted to try a piece of that nice big nigger stuff. Hey, look at those hams!'

Spanker ignored the men's remarks; she called, 'Miss Francey! You be coming home with me now, you hear, gal?'

203

Sammy Collins said, 'This little lady's going nowhere, big poontang.'

'And neither is you, giant gal.'

Judd Gillman threw his rope. It landed around Francey Dasher's thin shoulders. Spanker ran forward but Dave Cooper tossed his rope too, and the noose landed around Spanker's arms.

Spanker struggled to free herself; she shouted, 'You let that girl be, you hear me? That girl, she ain't well!'

'I'm pregnant!' Francey screamed. 'I'm pregnant and don't you White trash dare touch a pregnant lady, you hear!'

'Pregnant?' hooted Dwight Pine.

'If she ain't pregnant, she sure in hell's going to be when we get through with her.' Judd Gillman pulled the rope toward him, reeling Francey closer to his horse.

'I'm pregnant,' insisted Francey, tugging on the rope. 'My husband will kill you.'

Gillman pulled his pistol with the other hand; he ordered in a sterner voice, 'Leave off with the lip, loony.'

Spanker shouted, 'Don't you hurt that girl, you hear me?'

'You shut up too, nigger.'

Francey began tugging on the rope; she ran in frustration toward Judd Gillman, for his pistol.

Gillman pressed the trigger. The pistol fired. A circle of blood appeared on the front of Francey's faded cotton shift; she gasped, her eyes went blank. The red circle grew larger, spilled down the skirt. Francey slumped to the dirt.

Spanker, summoning up all her strength, hurled herself onto the ropes holding Francey to the ground, trying to protect the girl's body from further abuse.

Sammy Collins tossed another rope around Spanker; he and Dwight Pine tightened their ropes to pull Spanker away from Francey who was sprawled in a pool of deep red blood.

'Hold the bitch tight!' called Dwight Pine.

'Rein her like a son-of-a-bitching bronco!'

Sammy Collins and Dwight Pine held Spanker between them by their ropes; she tugged, fought, pulled at the ropes like a wild animal. She heaved her head back and forth; she kicked and cursed.

Billy Collins jumped from his horse; he snatched his rifle from its leather saddle holster and raised the butt to strike Spanker on the head; she kept kicking, twisting, fighting the ropes.

He finally struck her with a loud thud.

Spanker reeled backwards; she caught herself and lunged forward again with the ropes still tied around her, lowering her head to butt Collins in the chest.

'I'll be shitted!' Collins laughed, side-stepping her move. 'This nigger's a tough one!'

Collins brought his gun down again on her neck. Cooper and Pine again tightened their ropes for Collins to hit her a third time.

Spanker, taking deep breaths, crossed her arms and suddenly gripped each rope. She used all her strength to tumble both men from their horses.

'Shit me to hell!' shouted Collins.

Judd Gillman jumped from his horse; he joined the Collins brothers in beating Spanker into submission.

Spanker finally lay motionless on the ground.

Dwight Pine hopped down from his horse. 'Ever seen such a mean cow?'

'Strong as an ox,' said Cooper. 'Go steady. She might be playing possum. See, she's still got wind in her. Quick! Tie her hands and feet.'

Hurrying to get more ropes, Sammy Collins said, 'She's going to be some good screw.'

His brother added, 'If we ever get her tied down good to the ground.'

The White men hurriedly knotted ropes around Spanker's wrists and ankles; they pegged her to the ground, alongside the parish road, where they had dumped Francey Dasher's corpse beside a mossy log.

Dave Cooper, Billy and Sammy Collins, Judd Gillman, Dwight Pine. The White men satisfied themselves with Spanker's large brown body, then poked twigs, pine cones, the barrels of their guns, their rifles, deep into her vagina, amusing themselves with her womanhood long after there was life left in her body.

205

They left her alongside Francey Dasher; both women covered with dried blood, smeared with sweat, dirt, pine needles.

*   *   *

Broody Hen creaked back and forth in a hickory rocking chair on the front porch of the log cabin sitting in the weed field at the Dasher place. The sun hung low and orange in the evening sky as Broody Hen still considered the bad news about the deaths of Big Spanker and Miss Francey Dasher.

Gemma and Warren Rickers stood solemnly in front of the sagging porch. Gemma held their baby daughter, Emmaline, in her arms. She and Warren tried to convince Broody Hen to accept consolation, condolences, some kind of help, a temporary room at their house.

Broody finally stopped rocking; she broke her stubborn silence. She said, 'No need for you two to stick around here all night, is there?'

Gemma knew the old midwife did not want pity.

She said, 'We hate to leave you alone, Miss Broody.'

'I've been alone before.'

'Why don't you come and stay with us? At least a few days.'

'Leave this place? Let squatters take over? Think I'm crazy, gal? This is the only place I've ever known.'

Warren said, 'You can't stay here all alone.'

'Why not? Think the bogey man might come get me?' She cackled and began rocking again - creak and back, creak and back.

Warren offered, 'What about if we find somebody to help you out here? It ain't hard to find somebody to help. Not these days.'

'Some stranger will want to take me over.'

Gemma tried. 'Have you got enough food?'

Broody asked, 'You need some?'

Seeing that Broody Hen was not going to accept help, food, consolation, Gemma finally said, 'Fine, we'll leave you alone. But if you need any help, you know where we are.'

206

'Three o'clock.'

'That's right. And you're welcome to come day or night, you hear?'

Warren drove the buggy across the weed field toward the parish road; Gemma sat alongside him, cradling Emmaline to her breast; Broody Hen continued rocking on the rickety porch of the old cabin.

*   *   *

Gemma sat in the buggy, patting Emmaline into a lull, saying, 'It wasn't too long ago, Warren, when we first saw the Dasher place. Remember that morning when we got here? How we dragged ourselves across this very same field? How loaded down we both were with suitcases and carpet-bags and the-Lord-only-knows-what?'

Warren clearly remembered the morning. 'We were tired. And scared from witnessing that hanging the night before. And remember – you were all ready to scrap with old Broody for calling us "niggers"?'

'And Broody told us how to get to our place – by a clock face?'

'I thought she was crazy. Crazy as a bedbug.' Warren shook his head. 'She turned out to be a right tough old gal.'

Gemma nodded, then said, 'We first saw Francey Dasher that morning. She was wearing that raggedy old bridal veil and jabbering away like a bluejay to the big old dog.'

Gemma patted Emmaline, saying, 'I sure wish we'd heard from Dorothy Bliss. I wonder if she ever got my letter at all?'

'It's not easy to find a place for a crazy gal to live.'

'Well, her problems are all over now.'

The horse continued at a smart canter down the parish road; Gemma and Warren rode in silence, both remembering the good times, the bad times, the many changes which had happened to them since they had arrived in Longchamp Parish; suddenly, the horse shied and jolted the buggy.

Warren tightened the reins, coaxing, 'Whoa! Steady, fella!'

'What made him do that?' Gemma asked. 'What happened?'

'I don't know,' Warren said, steadying the horse. 'He acted like somebody pitched a stone at him.'

Warren looked in the fading evening light toward the trees lining the side of the road; he saw the shape of a man, a Black man emerging from the shadows; he then saw another man leaning on the first man's shoulder.

But it was Gemma who recognised them.

'Paulie!'

*   *   *

Junior Dehasset decided again that evening not to ride into Bossburg or Kettley; he still worried about his name being linked to the Two Forks Camptown trouble and, then, when Judd Gillman told him about leaving Big Spanker and Francey Dasher dead alongside the parish road, Junior Dehasset believed he definitely would be wise to spend the evening at Belrose Plantation. He arose irritable the next morning, annoyed by his sister's preparation for marrying a Yankee stranger. His mother refused to talk about the wedding as well as pretending as if the incident with Ken had never happened. Junior did not blame her for wanting to forget about the incident but his father's conduct confused him. He sensed his father was having difficulty in speaking to him, that the gulf of dislike, distrust was widening between them. And, then, at late morning, a housegirl knocked on Junior's door and announced that a White visitor was waiting to see him downstairs. The housegirl gave Junior a small white calling card on which was printed 'Patrick Fenton'. She said, 'The gentleman told me tell you he doesn't have much time. That he's seeing with only one eye. I don't know what he's talking about. One eye? I seen two eyes in his head!' But Junior understood the cryptic message. The man Cyclops was waiting downstairs to see him.

*   *   *

208

Junior Dehasset took his late morning visitor immediately into the privacy of the library, closed the door and said, 'You must excuse all the activity around here, Colonel Fenton. My kid sister's getting married. It's not usually this unsettled at Belrose.'

Colonel Pat Fenton was a tall, hawk-nosed man with a deep, theatrically-trained voice; he was not interested in apologies or weddings; he thundered, 'I want to know what happened at Two Forks Camptown. What was that slave wagon doing there?'

'How do you know about that?'

'I stopped there, that's how! I stopped there on the way here and that slave wagon's still there. I had to drive it over a cliff myself.'

Junior Dehasset tried not to perspire, tried not to let the Confederate officer see his sudden nervousness; he explained, 'Some of my boys got a little overly excited.'

'There's no time, no place in our organization for excitement, Mr Dehasset. Now tell me why you rode on that camptown at all?'

Junior Dehasset felt his mouth go dry. He spoke slowly, saying, 'It was sparked by personal reasons. Local people trying to keep a local situation from getting out of hand.'

'Personal reasons play no part in our movement, Mr Dehasset. Local reasons do not figure in the large scheme of our ambition. You have stirred up so much suspicion, Mr Dehasset, worked up so much sympathy for the freed slaves, that I would not be surprised if your entire state starts calling for some action to assist them.'

Junior began shaking his head. 'Oh, no. No, no. I don't think that could ever happen.'

'Let's just hope not. But they certainly are focussing on this tragedy, wondering who perpetrated it.'

'People mentioning any names? Names of a . . . group?'

'Of course they are! You left a cross!'

'Maybe that's in our favor. That might spread our name around. Strike some fear in more niggers.'

'There's that benefit to consider, yes,' Colonel Fenton admitted. 'But I suggest you leave this part of the state for a while, Mr Dehasset. And I mean for longer than a few weeks.'

'But, Colonel Fenton, I can't just disappear.'

'Neither can you stay around here and risk being arrested if the Army conducts a full scale investigation. And I tell you, the Yankees are going to come snooping around here, if they aren't already doing so.'

'We would have heard about that by now, wouldn't we?'

'We can never be too sure, Mr Dehasset. Those carpet-baggers are wily devils. But, here, I'm giving you introductions to some men in Tennessee. You go there.'

Junior took an envelope from Colonel Fenton. He asked, 'Tennessee? Do you mean Klan members?'

'It doesn't matter to you at this point who they are, what they call themselves, Mr Dehasset. The important fact is that we keep unified with other men who have our same interests.'

'When should I leave?'

'Immediately.'

'Where exactly do I go in Tennessee?'

'There's a point on our railroad near a town called Brownsville.'

'You're finally getting The Rebel Railroad organized? All though the South?'

'Slowly. But I never suspected we'd have to use it to run our own men out of trouble.'

'What do I do about my men here?'

'Tell them to lay low and not mention the word "slavery". And not to say one word about the railroad. Just to go about their own private work.'

'But what about the club? The Knights? Its future?'

'Between you and me, there's no future for the Knights of the Camellia. There will soon be a consolidation of lodges and clans all through the South. A reform which will emerge as chapters and one strong group. I have plans for an important part for you to play in the organization of the new group.'

'What will it be called?'

'You ask too many questions, Mr Dehasset. Just leave

210

Longchamp Parish. Your family connections make you an easy target in this vicinity. Go away and let the smoke settle.'

'Shall I contact you in Montgomery when I get to Brownsville?'

'Definitely not. I had to break cover by coming here. Your group has done enough harm to our plans. And I do not exaggerate facts when I say that every wrong move affects the ambitions, the hopes, and millions of precious dollars laid down to reestablish our plantations, our mills, our industry, the entire colored work force in the South.'

Colonel Fenton raised one finger; he spoke as if he were now delivering a sermon, or reciting a soliloquy by Shakespeare on the stage at Stratford-upon-Avon, declaiming, 'Slavery is a phenomenon of mankind. Not the work of animals. Not the work of the devil. But the machinations of human beings. Slavery is not only needed. Slavery is not only required. Slavery is *demanded* by all people. People throughout history. There are those who are of the master hierarchy, and those who are slaves. Never forget this fact, Mr Dehasset, and you will always help grease the tracks for the Rebel Railroad. Now let us depart one another's company in the Lord's name.'

*　　　　*　　　　*

Colonel Pat Fenton, bidding Junior Dehasset goodbye, opened the library door and stared straight into the face of a tall, broad-shouldered Black man.

'Herc!' Junior blurted from behind the Confederate Colonel. 'What in hell are you doing here?'

'Some private business.' Herc spoke but stared into the Colonel's cold blue eyes.

Colonel Fenton asked, 'A colleague of yours, Mr Dehasset?'

Before Junior could reply, Fenton walked across the foyer, passed through the front door and untied his horse from the iron hitching post.

*　　　　*　　　　*

Herc asked, 'Who was that guy?'

'Never mind who he is,' Junior irritably answered. 'What are you doing here?'

'I saw somebody you might be interested in.'

'Who?'

'The boy. Paulie. I saw him with another buck from here. That blacksmith.'

'Ken? Where?'

'Going into the old Chatgrove place.'

'Going back there? Those Yankee coons taking Paulie back?'

Herc nodded, then asked, 'You going to help me now? Get me that land?'

Junior held out his hand for Herc to enter the library. 'You damn right I am.'

*   *   *

Senator Dehasset saw the tall White man ride down the sloping driveway from the big house at Belrose Plantation. He had also seen the Black man arriving; he knew the Black man was named Herc, the ex-slave who shared a bed with the widow, Marisse Summers.

Senator Dehasset did not know why Herc had come to see his son. But he suspected why the earlier visitor had come to Belrose Plantation. Senator Dehasset remembered briefly meeting Colonel Fenton in Richmond, Virginia at the outset of the Civil War. He had subsequently heard rumors how Fenton had been involved in the John Wilkes Booth plot to assassinate President Lincoln, that Colonel Fenton - driven by a perverted loyalty to the South - planned a scheme by which the enslavement of Negroes would be revived in former Confederate states.

Senator Dehasset turned from his bedroom window overlooking the driveway and opened the top drawer in his walnut bureau.

He withdrew a small pepperbox pistol, a handgun given to him by his own father, the gun he would use to prevent his

212

own son from further besmirching the Dehasset family name. Senator Dehasset's only regret for the action he planned was that a murder would inevitably darken the wedding of his beloved daughter, Sabrine.

Chapter Nineteen

MAN, MAN, WOMAN

Gustave Depardeau parted company with Cramer Crowley in Longchamp Parish near a fork in the road known
as The Kettley Turn. Cramer wished the Cajun actor good
luck and said he would meet him here at the same spot this
evening for his report.

Gustave Depardeau galloped toward High Hill Plantation,
readjusting his beige gabardine jacket, tightening the white
linen stock around his neck, finally slowing to a canter when
he saw a large redbrick house fronted with graceful white
wooden pillars.

Dismounting, Depardeau tied his horse to a hitching post,
flipped the tails of his jacket and crossed the bricked
forecourt to the front door.

A Black girl, wearing a loose-fitting smock, answered the
door. Her casual apparel surprised Depardeau. He presented
his calling card, saying, 'Madame Summers, please.'

The girl looked at the engraved card; it was apparent to
Depardeau she could not read.

He explained, 'I'm a friend of Captain Phillippe Summers.'

The girl raised her eyes. 'Oh, Master Phillippe! He got
killed in the war.'

Depardeau gallantly bowed. 'That is why I am here.'

A woman's voice called from the foyer. 'Who is it, Sari?'

The Black girl kept her eyes on Gustave Depardeau. She
answered, 'A gentleman, Miss Marisse. A White stranger
asking for the dead master.'

'If he's a bill collector, Sari –'

Marisse Summers moved behind Sari. She stopped when
she saw Gustave Depardeau standing in the doorway; she
surveyed his trim body, his fashionable city clothing, the
obvious bulge in his white riding breeches.

Depardeau stepped across the threshold; he appraised the

curving balustrade winding for three stories above the foyer and topped by the stained glass skylight.

He said, admiringly, 'No wonder Phillippe talked so much about High Hill.'

'You knew . . . Phillippe?'

'Are you his wife?'

'Yes.'

'I knew your husband very well, Madame. Phillippe and I often spoke of you. Especially in the evenings. Phillippe always spoke very warmly, so lovingly about you to me.'

Gustave Depardeau saw that Marisse Summers looked tired, but that nonetheless she was a beautiful woman. He also noticed that she was dressed in the careless manner of a recluse, a woman who no longer went out into society. But her body was still shapely, her eyes had a defiance flickering in them. He was not disappointed that he had agreed to accept this job at High Hill.

Marisse Summers turned to the Black girl. 'Sari, go to the kitchen and tell Rosa to bring tea to the parlor.'

'But Master Herc, Mam –' Sari paused to glance quickly at Gustave Depardeau, to stare at his crotch, ' – Master Herc said he would be back soon from Belrose Plantation and want his dinner.'

'I don't care what Herc said! Do what I say.'

Depardeau interrupted. 'If I am disturbing your day, Madame Summers, forgive me. I only bring a few messages from the past. They are not pressing. I can return some other time in the future or can forget all about the little, personal stories I have to share.'

'Personal . . . stories?'

Depardeau smiled. 'Very personal stories. About your husband. About me. And, of course, about . . . you.'

Marisse opened one of the double doors leading into the sitting-room. She said, 'Come inside. We shall talk in privacy.'

Gustave Depardeau and Marisse Summers soon sat side by side on a sofa; Depardeau confided, 'Your husband loved you very much, Madame. I did not come here today to talk of his death. I want to tell you about his life. His love. His wishes. His admiration and obsession with you. His hope for all of us to spend time together.'

'Together? Us?'

Depardeau nodded. 'Phillippe and I often lay -' pausing, he corrected himself, ' - spent the evening hours talking about you.'

Marisse's eyes became alert like a cat.

Depardeau continued. 'Phillippe invited me many times to come home with him.'

'He did not write me about you.'

'Of course not. My visit was meant to be a surprise. He also did not write for another reason. There was a man in your house, a free man of color, whom Phillippe feared that my presence might have - shall we say - upset?'

'Phillippe told you about Herc?'

'Is this Herc a man of color?'

'He's a Negro. He was one of our slaves but Phillippe gave him his manumission. Before the end of the war.'

'He spent time in the big house?'

'Yes.'

'Then Phillippe spoke to me about Herc. I did not know what Phillippe meant when he said I could teach this Herc man a few lessons, but then, later, when I learned what Phillippe enjoyed, how Phillippe enjoyed pleasure, liked stories, liked hearing stories, liked telling stories, liked talking about himself, talking about you, telling me what he wanted to share with you . . .'

Marisse was becoming increasingly nervous; she fidgeted with her hands, played with her ringlets, finally confessing, 'This talk about Phillippe, these stories, all these memories are making me excited.'

Depardeau remembered the few details about Herc and Marisse Summers which Cramer Crowley had told him. But he decided now to proceed on intuition, his own knowledge of women, married couples, exotic twists within relationships.

He asked, 'Upset? Is that bad? This excitement that . . . upsets you?'

'No. But . . . Herc is still here at High Hill.'

'Do not apologize for a man in your employ.'

216

'I do not know how to say this, Monsieur. But Herc is more than an employee. He has become more powerful in the household since my husband's death. I have even become more dependent on him.'

'But you are a lady!' Depardeau exclaimed. 'Ladies are allowed to be dependent on men. Do not apologize.'

'You are very kind, very considerate.'

'I am merely honest. Never apologize for being devoted. Some men need devotion. I know. Phillippe was devoted to me. He wanted to share that devotion with you.'

Marisse sat stiffly on the edge of the sofa. 'I have not felt this light-hearted for years.'

'Is it uncomfortable?'

'No. It is . . . exciting.'

'Do I speak too honestly?'

'Very honestly. But it is like . . . fire.'

'A fire you enjoy?'

She nodded. 'An enjoyment I need.'

'Then I only wish I had made this visit before, Madame. That business had not kept me in New Orleans. I only wish I would have rushed to High Hill to begin sharing stories with you long, long ago.'

Depardeau reached for Marisse's hand; he held it on his knee, near his crotch; he slowly raised her hand toward his lips, lightly kissed it, then lowered it back to his crotch where his penis had begun to swell into an erection.

He laughed. 'I am afraid I must stand,' he apologized, 'or else leave the room.'

She gripped his hand tighter. 'Do not leave.'

'I don't want to leave, Madam. I want to tell you stories about your husband. About our times together. Perhaps even to fulfill some of his fantasies for me.'

'Phillippe loved me participating in fantasies,' she whispered.

Depardeau's enlargening penis made it too difficult for him to sit on the sofa; he arose, allowing his penis to spread down his leg.

He said, standing above Marisse, 'I know many of your fantasies.'

217

'Phillippe told you?' she asked, staring at the penis outlined in his breeches. 'You knew him that well?'

'I knew him very well. We spent many hours together.'

'Just the two of you?'

'He wanted it to be three. A man, a man, a woman.'

'And he served you?'

'He often pretended he was you serving me.'

'Like a woman? He served you like I would. Like a . . . woman?'

'Except for your clothing. But he wanted you to send him some of your intimate clothing. Your husband wanted to wear your under clothing in bed with me.'

Marisse was breathing heavily, staring at the phallus.

'Does that bother you to hear? Hurt you?'

'Hurt can be pleasure.'

'Stand,' he ordered.

'Stand?'

'In front of me.'

She obeyed, but asked quizzically, 'Like this?'

Depardeau extended one hand toward her thigh; he curled his fingers and rubbed them between her legs; he smiled, saying, 'You are excited. I can feel through your clothing you are . . . wet. My stories about your husband excite you.'

Marisse took a deep breath as Depardeau's hand rubbed harder, more firmly between her legs; she groaned as he felt his hand grabbing her, clutching her more strongly, working, prodding, probing through the thin fabric of her robe to excite her.

He stared into her eyes, smiling at her, finally saying, 'If I make you this wet when you are dressed, think of the flood I will have when you are without clothes.'

'May I touch your . . . beautiful cock?'

'Not yet.'

'Why? I want to touch it.'

He worked his hands, his fingers clenching harder between her legs; he said, 'No. I want to see you tremble for me. I want to know that I am the only man you want. I want to know you will devote yourself only to me, to worship me, to dedicate yourself to me.'

218

'It must be beautiful. Your cock must be so beautiful. I could see the head through your breeches. I imagined me rubbing the tip of my tongue all the way around it.'

He nodded. 'You will do that. And more.'

'What will I do? What do you want me to do? I want to adore you, to devote myself only to you. So you must tell me what you want.'

'You must be prepared for pain. You must bring me whips, paddles, canes - any and everything I can use to punish you with to keep you devoted to me. The more that I punish you, hurt you, chastise you and make you -'

Gustave stopped; he saw the mask of hypnotic pleasure disappear from Marisse's face; she stared at the door.

'Herc!'

*   *   *

Herc closed the door behind him; he demanded, 'Marisse, who is this man?'

Marisse moved to stand between him and Depardeau.

She answered, 'A friend of Phillippe's. From the Army.'

'What's he doing here?'

Gustave Depardeau assured him, 'There's no need to be jealous.'

Herc's eyes lowered down from Depardeau's face to the bulge in his crotch. He muttered, 'Get out of here!'

'You order me?'

'Damned right I order you!'

'But I came to see Madame Summers.'

'You saw her. Now leave.'

'Do you challenge me?'

'I more than challenge you -' Herc lunged forward, pulling back his fist to strike Depardeau.

But Depardeau side-stepped the jab; he cut the edge of his own hand down on the back of Herc's neck. He said, 'Perhaps we should go outside, Monsieur?'

Herc, clinging to the edge of the table, muttered, 'I'll send you to . . . hell!'

Gustave Depardeau was still not sorry he had accepted the

offer of posing as a friend of Phillippe Summers; the smell of Marisse's womanhood still clung to his fingers; he wanted to tear away her gown and clench the nakedness of her furry cleft, to prepare her to take not only his phallus but the increased pressure of his hand. Depardeau had also seen that the woman's nipples were pierced. He was pleased. He imagined how he would hang small weights from the golden rings, enlargening the nipples. He believed he had found not only a rich woman but an obedient love slave. Yes, he was pleased he had come to High Hill Plantation.

*   *   *

Marisse Summers anxiously, excitedly listened to Gustave Depardeau offer Herc the choice of pistols, sabres, even whips to defend himself. She thrilled at Depardeau scoffing at Herc's attempt to have a fist fight.

Depardeau said, 'We are men, not animals! At least be brave enough to defend your cowardly self like a man or else go crawling off into the trees like some slimy snake!'

The two men, stripped to the waist, stood facing one another in the yard fronting the redbrick house. Marisse had ordered the Black girls to stay inside, telling Sari to keep the four year old boy, Alain, upstairs. But the first crack of the whip brought the girls to the windows. Marisse ignored them now though as she stood alongside a pillar, admiring Depardeau's tight muscular body as he unfurled his black leather whip.

Herc, still angry from his visit a few hours earlier with Junior Dehasset at Belrose Plantation, felt fury rising inside him as he worked his bullwhip back and forth, back and forth next to his black knee-high leather boots.

Depardeau acted as the aggressor; he snapped his whip on the ground dancing toward Herc, then retreating, then darting forward again, trying to goad Herc into a rash fury.

Herc struck; Depardeau dipped to one side; Herc struck again; he landed the second strike across Depardeau's naked shoulder.

Instead of flinching, of screaming with pain, Depardeau

220

laughed – laughter filled the yard as he suddenly struck back, snapping the tip of his oily whip a second and a third time, all three strikes catching Herc's brown skin.

Herc charged forward; Depardeau met him chest to chest; they stood facing one another, crossing the butts of their whips, pressing to topple the other one backwards. Herc's strength was greater and he pushed Depardeau to the ground.

Depardeau, falling, lifted both legs and caught Herc on the stomach with the soles of his feet; he flipped him over his head.

Then, jumping to his feet, Depardeau pulled back his whip, casting to strike Herc sprawled on the ground.

But Herc rolled sideways; he pulled a knife from his boot and hurled it at Depardeau.

The blade momentarily flashed in the sunlight and struck Depardeau's chest.

At that same moment a gun shot fired.

Herc staggered; he grabbed for his pectoral muscle; blood covered his hand.

Depardeau lay on the dirt; he tried to pull Herc's knife from his chest but blood was trickling from the side of his mouth, his hands were becoming weak, his fingers unable to grasp the knife's ebony handle.

Herc, weaving unsteadily above Depardeau, saw Marisse standing alongside a white pillar and using both hands to shoot him again with a pistol.

'You dirty White . . .'

Marisse pulled the trigger; the second bullet ripped the side of Herc's face.

Toppling, Herc fell over the body of Gustave Depardeau.

Marisse, holding the pistol in her hand, moved alongside Herc and said in an expressionless voice, 'You killed him. You killed the man who came for me.'

Herc, holding one hand to his bloody face and flinching under the pain cutting through his chest, muttered, 'You faithless . . . slut . . .'

'Faithless? What are you to me? What were you ever to me?'

221

'I believed . . . your words . . . all these . . . years . . .'

Marisse smiled at his pain. 'More the fool you.'

'The boy . . . You gave me a son . . .'

'Don't mention Alain!' She looked down at Herc staring up at her through fingers spread across his bleeding face. 'To Alain you are already dead . . . *Dead!*'

Herc continued staring at her through his spread fingers.

Marisse smiled. 'Dead! And I don't shed one tear. You killed the man Phillippe sent for me. A real man. A White man! Not some field slave trumped up to be a gentleman . . . master!'

She glanced at the penis limp inside his trousers now soiled with dirt, blood, a spreading stain of urine; she spat at it.

Herc's eyes did not close. He slumped lifelessly across the corpse beneath him on the ground.

The pistol dropped from Marisse's hand; she muttered, 'Scum!'; she turned toward the red brick house fronted by white columns.

*   *   *

Dusk was fading into night; Gemma and Warren sat on the kitchen steps listening to the lazy chirrup of crickets in the balmy air. Emmaline lay asleep in the cradle alongside the wooden steps; Gemma still postponed the job of waking up Emmaline, giving her an evening bath on the kitchen table and putting her to bed upstairs in the room they now called the nursery – Gemma wanted to spend just a few more minutes talking to Warren.

She had bought out a plate of the fresh sheet cake she had baked with the shredded coconut which her brother, Jay, had included in a big parcel he had sent to them from his travels. They nibbled at the chewy cake and discussed the sudden reappearance of Ken and Paulie, how Ken and Paulie had left a few hours ago for the Dasher place to find a temporary home there, and about tomorrow's wedding at Belrose Plantation.

Warren said, 'Paulie and Ken would've been back here

by now if old Broody Hen chased them off her place.'

'Oh, I don't think Miss Broody's going to do that. She knows Paulie from that stormy night he brought her here in the buggy, the night little Em was born.'

'If she does let them stay I bet she finds a couple of wide-hipped gals to mate up with them.'

'Something tells me Miss Broody won't have much luck mating those two – except maybe with each other.'

Warren smiled understandingly; he said, 'I wouldn't have minded them staying on here. Paulie, he lost his Pa and little brother, Matthew, in that camptown disaster. We couldn't invite Ken and Paulie without inviting the rest of Paulie's family to come, too. But I know this land can't support his Ma, two sisters, other two brothers. Not yet at least. His family's best staying in that new camptown till Paulie finds a place for them all to move.'

'Don't worry about that, Warren. Paulie's devoted to his family. And I bet Ken helps find them someplace to live as much as Paulie.'

'Too bad about Ken losing that piece of jewelry he told us about.'

'I don't think it's too bad,' Gemma disagreed, handing Warren another slice of coconut sheet cake. 'Ken wasn't too clear how he got that necklace and no Black man can sell something valuable without arousing some suspicion from somebody. I say good riddance.'

'There's no doubt they'd work hard on the old Dasher place, if Sabrine's brother just lets them alone.'

'Talking about Sabrine, when do you think Cramer's coming back from New Orleans?'

'Should be back already. Start getting ready, all spruced up for tomorrow.'

Warren then reminded Gemma, 'Honey, you still got to press your dress and maybe give that suit of mine another brushing.'

Gemma glanced down at the cradle made from the bureau drawer. 'At least little Emmaline's dress is ready to go. That sure was thoughtful of brother Jay sending us that big parcel. Outfitting us all.'

223

'Some brother you got, Coffee Cup. What I like best of all about the things he sent us was that tin box, that rainbow painted on the side. Little Jay, he said he's send us a piece of the old rainbow.'

Gemma corrected, 'Jay told you, honey, the rainbow was right here, that the rainbow ends here and we just might not know it.'

Breaking off a morsel of coconut cake for herself, Gemma continued, 'Talking of presents, do you think Sabrine and Cramer's going to like the candlesticks we made them?'

'We can't afford to buy nothing and there was barely enough time to finish carving and painting what we did make.'

'Well, I think they're pretty.'

'Gemma, you don't think we'll look out of place with all their fancy guests tomorrow? Us? Our handpainted present? Our homemade clothes?'

'Will it bother you if we do?'

'No. But I –'

Warren lifted his head; he listened. He asked, 'You hear something coming?'

Gemma nodded; she heard a galloping. She said, 'Maybe it's Cramer, bringing somebody from New Orleans. I do worry if I was plumb crazy to ask him to find a White man who –'

Gemma stopped; she saw the smudges of light, the torches approaching from the darkness of the end of the driveway; she and Warren simultaneously jumped to their feet; they saw the white shapes of men galloping toward the house.

Gemma grabbed Emmaline from the cradle and Warren cried, 'The creek! Head toward the creek!'

They ran across the field as more than a dozen riders – dressed in white robes, carrying blazing pitch torches – swarmed into the yard, setting fire to the house, to the hay in the barn, throwing kerosene, and – with a loud clap – making the earth burst into fire.

Chapter Twenty

'DEARLY BELOVED . . .'

'*Dearly Beloved, we are gathered here in the sight of God and in the face of this congregation, to join together this man and this woman in Holy Matrimony . . .*'

Noele Dehasset, sitting in an armchair placed in the front row of the wedding guests seated on the lawn facing the big house at Belrose Plantation, listened to Reverend Perry from Kettley begin the rites of matrimony between her daughter, Sabrine, and the Yankee stranger, Cramer Crowley.

Noele held the simple nosegay of pink and white daisies which Sabrine had given her before the ceremony. Noele also held the letter which Junior had left her last night in her bedroom, a quickly scribbled farewell saying that he unexpectedly had to leave home, asking her to explain the sudden disappearance to his father with the excuse that he could not bear seeing his sister ruin her life by marrying a Yankee.

Noele Dehasset clasped both the letter and the nosegay in her lap; she felt strangely as if the two objects were keys to a new stage in her life. The last meeting with Ken in the pergola had brought her sexual life to a dramatic end and then brutally concluded it. She saw that her daughter had undeniably grown up, had become a woman in her own right. Sabrine was not only threatening to dethrone her as mistress of Belrose but was also challenging her credibility as a lady.

Noele wondered if a new breed of woman, outspoken, worldly females would soon replace the graceful, protected, genteel Creole womanhood once called 'The Flowers of the Confederacy'. She felt as if she had already begun to wilt.

*   *   *

'*It was ordained for the procreation of children; to be*
225

brought up in the fear and nurture of the Lord and to the praise of His holy name . . .'

Senator Dehasset sat soberly alongside his wife in the front row of guests gathered on the lawn at Belrose; tears brimmed in his pale aging eyes as he watched Sabrine, his pride and joy, standing alongside a stranger, soon to be his son-in-law.

Senator Dehasset had always envisioned Sabrine marrying a local young man, the Chatgrove son, that she would live nearby on Candlewick Plantation. But then the Civil War exploded; life drastically changed. Traditions were shaken by cannons and dreams collapsed under gunfire.

The Civil War had been like sudden adulthood cast upon the Southern states; their frivolous, lighthearted, infantile years disappeared overnight. The Confederacy found itself facing pain, dire problems, crises of maturity.

Senator Dehasset regretted that he was not a young man, that he could not help solve the new problems facing the South; but he was a wise man; he knew he must leave such work to a younger generation, to people like Sabrine, to this young Northerner named Cramer Crowley.

Senator Dehasset had put the pepperbox pistol back into his bureau drawer last night; he had decided not to shoot his son; he had decided to do something much more drastic – to disinherit him.

Senator Dehasset had spoken to his attorney this morning, had said that he must trust his daughter's choice of a husband, to have faith in his new son-in-law's character, integrity, honor; the deed of Belrose Plantation was to be Sabrine's and Cramer's wedding gift.

*   *   *

'. . . if either of you know any impediments, why ye may not be lawfully joined together in matrimony, ye do now confess it . . .'

Cramer Crowley listened to Reverend Perry's rambling words read from The Book of Common Prayer and thought how he would not be marrying Sabrine if the Civil War had

226

not been waged between the North and the South, that some young Southerner would probably be standing in his place.

Cramer had not yet told Sabrine about his true identity, that he was not – had never been – a pedlar, but, instead, was a covert military agent in the Reconstruction Program.

He wondered whether he should tell her tonight, on their wedding night. Or was that not the proper time to divulge such an important fact? If so, when was the right time? Had he waited too long? He appreciated Sabrine always being blatantly truthful with him. She had confided this morning that her brother had disappeared from Belrose last night. Cramer was not surprised. He had seen Colonel Fenton yesterday afternoon on the parish road and suspected where the Confederate officer had been going and why Junior Dehasset had suddenly, mysteriously disappeared from home shortly afterwards.

Cramer suspected that Junior Dehasset would not return to Longchamp Parish for a very long time. Cramer also had learned from his friend at High Hill – his ex-lover, Sari, who had showed up at The Kettley Turn last night instead of Gustave Depardeau – about the duel between Gustave Depardeau and Herc. About the two men's deaths, how Herc had killed Depardeau, that Marisse Summers had shot Herc, had ordered both of the men's corpses to be buried in a pit of lye and then locked herself and her small son in the house.

Cramer felt responsible for Depardeau's death yet relieved that Herc was no longer a threat to Gemma and Warren. But, then, had they been delivered too late? The sky had blazed red last night – men had put torches to the Rickers' house, their barn, the out-buildings, the old slave quarters. Cramer knew that the fire was arson, that the wilful destruction had been wrought by Junior Dehasset as his farewell gesture to Longchamp Parish. Was it involved with Herc? Connected to the Black man's desire to gain control of the old Chatgrove place? Cramer Crowley suspected he would never know the true story.

*   *   *

Sabrine Dehasset marked the first major change in her life with the arrival of Gemma and Warren Rickers in Longchamp Parish. Their love for one another, their laughter, their sense of humor, their struggles, everything about their lives made Sabrine see that people could get what they wanted in life if they worked for it.

She knew the bravest thing she had done to date was to accept Cramer Crowley's proposal of marriage. She did not know what he did for a living. She did not know how - or where - they would live once they were married. She turned a blind eye to all the basic facts of life, of survival, which she had been raised to respect. She merely followed her instincts: she knew Cramer loved, respected her, shared the same interests, compassion, dreams.

Sabrine had invited Gemma and Warren to the wedding but was not expecting them to come. She had heard this morning about the fire; she also had heard that her brother had mysteriously disappeared - she intuitively knew that the two incidents must be related.

And Sabrine was still planning what she could do for Gemma, for Warren, for their daughter, Emmaline, when she heard Reverend Perry repeat the words, '*Sabrine Claire, wilt thou have this man to thy wedded husband, to live together after God's ordinance in the holy estate of matrimony?*'

*   *   *

Sabrine did not reply to the matrimonial question. She instead turned from Reverend Perry and faced the guests sitting on the lawn.

She began, 'I know Cramer and I broke a few rules by inviting you here today at such short notice. So, please be good friends and allow me to break just one more rule. I must speak honestly.

'Today is one of the saddest days of my life.

'Oh, I'm very lucky to be marrying the only man I have ever loved. But a great tragedy happened in Longchamp Parish last night. I just heard about it this morning.

'Some of you may have seen the fire. Or heard about it yourselves. It happened at the old Chatgrove place.

'The war made life hard for all of us. But we still live so isolated, so separated from each other. There are even some people in our parish – people with different colored skin – who are kept from enjoying the many privileges we do. And this is still happening after we fought a . . . war.

'The late Mrs Chatgrove willed her land to a young colored couple from the North. They moved here to be part of our community. But last night their house was burned completely to the ground. There's a young mother, a father and a little baby girl. Fortunately they were not harmed. But today they don't have a roof over their heads. They don't have blankets. A bed. A table. Chairs. Nothing. Absolutely nothing.

'Cramer and I specifically requested that you bring no presents to our wedding. But do not be offended if I now make one more request.'

*　　　*　　　*

Gemma Rickers, the hem of her long skirt tucked into her leather belt, stepped through the smoky debris, poking a stick into the ashes, the charred timbers, the remains of her house, looking for something she might save.

'Save?' Warren had shaken his head when Gemma had stubbornly announced her intention. 'Save for what? To cart back to Philadelphia?'

Warren was determined to move back North.

But Gemma argued, 'Nobody can drive me off this land! Nobody! I don't care how many times they come back! I don't care how many torches or burning crosses they bring! What they wear! This is our home!'

'Home? What home? Show me a home?'

Warren had taken Emmaline down to the creek; he had built a small lean-to out of the one blanket they had managed to save. The temporary shelter was not even as good as the tents built by freed slaves in their camptowns.

Gemma stopped in the ash field; an object had caught her

229

eye; she bent down and picked up a piece of wood. She saw that it was one of the candlesticks Warren had carved, the gift-to-be which she herself had painted for Sabrine and Cramer's wedding day.

Gemma dropped the candlestick back into the ashes; she continued making her way through the ankle-deep mess, stirring more smoke as she moved.

Stopping again, Gemma next saw the tin box which her brother, Jay, had sent them. The tin box had been painted with a rainbow, but now the rainbow was blistered by the heat.

'Some rainbow's end!'

She flipped the tin box with her stick and kept moving through the ashes.

Next Gemma stood in the section of the house which once had been the dining-room, the room which they had used for their first bedroom, where Broody Hen had helped her give birth to her child.

Thinking of Broody Hen, Gemma remembered Big Spanker, the White girl, Francey Dasher, how they had been brutally murdered, and she asked herself, 'Why do people get so . . . mean?'

She stopped; she looked around her in the smoking remains; she wondered, 'Is Warren really right? Should we move back North? Am I just being bull-headed? What am I trying to prove? That they can kill me, too? And Warren? And baby?'

Gemma wiped the soot from her forehead, wondering, 'And who'd take care of Emmaline if something happened to Warren and me –'

She heard a noise; she stood alert like a doe, motionless among the wisps of smoke rising around her from the ash grey ground.

Hearing the galloping of horses, she screamed, 'Warren!'

Gemma did not turn to look at the driveway; she took long steps, running toward the creek, smoke rising from her footsteps as she kept screaming.

'Warren . . . Warren, they're coming back! Warren, they're coming back!'

Gemma then saw Warren emerging from the poplars which lined the creek bed. He stood holding Emmaline in one arm and waving the other arm.

'He's gone crazy,' she thought. 'He's gone plumb crazy.'

The galloping grew louder behind her.

Warren began running toward Gemma, with Emmaline in his arms.

'*Warren!*' she hysterically screamed.

But he was smiling, laughing as he pointed down the driveway. Gemma turned. She saw wagons – a long line of wagons and buggies and people on horseback – stretching down the driveway.

The first wagon carried Sabrine and Cramer. They were followed by men, women, White people, Black people, friendly people, neighborly people, people bringing wagonfuls of lumber, nail kegs, wooden boxes, chairs, tables, a brass bedstead, a pig squealing in the back of a wagon, two cows pulled behind another wagon, a crateful of cackling chickens in the next, a hutch of rabbits, a crate of geese.

Cramer slowed his old horse. Sabrine – wearing her wedding dress – stood up and called, 'Do you mind a few visitors, Mrs Rickers?'

Gemma, clinging onto Warren's arm, answered, 'No . . . not at all . . . Miss Dehasset.'

'It's Mrs Crowley now!' Sabrine corrected, holding out a gold band encircling her finger. 'Mrs Cramer Thomas Crowley, Mrs Rickers!'

Wagons kept arriving, surrounding Gemma and Warren, buggies full of women bringing food, linen; men and boys anxious to join in the house-raising, setting to work with lumber and hammers and nails and window sills and shingles and bricks and mortar, ready to build a new house, barn, sheds.

Gemma let her tears flow freely; she lay her head against Warren's arm and gulped, 'We never liked . . . that old house much . . . anyway . . . did we . . . Mr Walnut Man?'

'Wasn't ours in the first place, Coffee Cup. Not like this one's going to be.'

231

'So I guess . . . I guess the rainbow does, really does stop here after all.'

Warren, holding his baby daughter in one arm and hugging Gemma to his chest with the other, agreed, 'Yep, pudding face. The rainbow ends right here sharp at three o'clock.'